Silently, **S0-CAJ-167**
the door and crept out.

She made the trip to the Great Hall easily, now
being familiar with the stairs and passages, but
she had to summon her courage to cross the cavernous room. She made her way to the door that
Edgemont had pointed out as the entrance to the
library and stepped inside.

There above the mantel hung a case with a
glass front. It was dark inside, but the flickering
firelight caught tiny gleams of gold. The settings! The tangible proof that her rubies really
existed! She drew closer, holding her candle
high to light the case—and screamed as something moved in the huge winged chair before
the hearth.

Not the ghost but a man! He rose and turned
toward her, the failing candle lighting his face
from below and giving him the features of a
satyr. He swayed and caught at the back of the
chair to steady himself.

Mary stifled another scream. She stood face-
to-face with the notorious Rake Halliburton.
And he was very, very drunk . . .

❁

THE
RUSHMORELAND RUBIES

THE RUSHMORELAND RUBIES

Wynne Smith

PAGEANT BOOKS

PAGEANT BOOKS
225 Park Avenue South
New York, New York 10003

Cover artwork by Bob Berran

Printed in the U.S.A.

First Pageant Books printing: September, 1988

10 9 8 7 6 5 4 3 2 1

For Russell

THE
RUSHMORELAND
RUBIES

Chapter One

With an incredulous snort, Clarence Henry Augustus John Danforth, the should-have-been tenth Earl of Rushmore, threw his *London Times* down on the low table before him and bounced from his seat on the faded brocade library sofa.

His daughter, the would-have-been Lady Mary Beatrix Charlotte Elizabeth, looked up at him suspiciously, detecting a gleam of unholy triumph lighting his bright hazel eyes. If ever a cat had upset the cream-pot!

She tucked a stray wisp of dark hair back into her muslin mobcap and dropped the cloth with which she had been polishing a hopelessly out-of-fashion Queen Anne desk. The current finances of the Danforths did not merit the services of a housemaid. Clarence, who supported

1

them both by gaming, had been plagued by an unusual run of ill luck at cards, and even the dice had been devilish against him.

Mary sat back on her heels and considered her erratic parent. "Whatever are you so pleased about?"

"Hah!" Clarence retrieved the paper, slapping his knee with it. "Harborough! He's dead! Struck down by Mohocks on his way home from his club. And only last week he signed to jump off the dock with the Bellemont female and set up his nursery, putting us even further from the succession."

"Father," she reminded him firmly with a regretful shake of her head, "we were never in line for that title. We'll never regain Rushmoreland and you know it."

Clarence dismissed this blasphemous thought with a casual wave of his hand. Rushmoreland Castle, the hereditary seat of the Earls of Rushmore, would have been theirs had not his grandfather lost title and estates, confiscated by the king for merely dabbling a bit too deeply in the affairs of Charles Edward Stuart, the Young Pretender. Most unfairly, to Clarence's mind, Rushmoreland had been bestowed on the Halliburtons, a family of loyal upstarts newly created the Earls of Harborough. The only freehold to pass to Clarence was the London town house in which he and Mary lived, inherited from his grandmother who had been given it by her father after the execution of her Jacobite husband.

Mary applied the rag with vigor to a padded wooden foot. A sudden thought struck her, and she turned back to her father. "Who will succeed him? Are there any Halliburtons left?"

Clarence subjected this to some thought. "Oh, well, there's the Rake, of course, but he doesn't count. Bound to be more of them, tucked away somewhere."

Mary returned to her polishing. It didn't really matter, but she could not help but wonder who would be living in what should have been their home.

Clarence glanced down at her and hurriedly looked away, hunching an annoyed shoulder. "Really, my love, it is no pleasant sight for me to see my daughter engaged in such a menial task. Can that not wait until we can once more employ a domestic?"

While we watch what little furniture we still have fall apart, Mary thought, but diplomatically held her tongue. "Then why do you not go along to one of your clubs as you usually do? This must be done to preserve the wood and I don't mind doing it in the least."

Clarence shuffled his feet guiltily on the worn rug. "Well, of course, if you don't mind—perhaps I'll saunter out to learn what gossip holds of this event." Keeping his eyes averted from the faded and patched stuff gown Mary wore while doing her chores, and leaving the various sheets of the *London Times* scattered about the floor for her to pick up, he beat a strategic but dignified retreat.

Mary turned to bid him farewell but saw only the long tails of his elegant coat of olive green superfine and the heels of his polished Hessians

as he disappeared out the door. The coat had
been bespoken from the masterful hands of
Weston after a particularly successful evening at
a discreet gaming hell in Pall Mall. He would
probably head to White's or Boodle's now,
where stakes were lower. Experience had taught
her not to expect to see him before breakfast the
following morning.

For once she was wrong. The mantel clock in
the drawing room directly below her bedchamber had barely chimed five when heavy footsteps came bounding up the creaking stairs. A
moment later her door burst open, and Clarence's portly figure made its way into her dark-
ened room. He tripped over an unseen low stool,
swore as it connected with his shin, staggered a
bit, and came to rest with a thump on the foot
of her bed.

"You're home early," Mary commented.

"Ah, you're awake, my love." He peered at
her through the shadowy grayness, blithely un-
aware of the fact that his arrival, which in many
ways resembled that of a myopic mastiff, would
have wakened the dead. The throbbing just below his knee momentarily replaced the importance of his news. "Why you keep these odd
pieces of furniture standing about where one
must needs fall over them all the time, is quite
beyond comprehension!" he complained.

Mary prudently refrained from trying to ex-
onerate herself, recognizing the futility of any
such attempt. "What brings you home so
early?" she asked instead.

"Hah! Only listen! You'll never guess who inherits Rushmoreland now!"

Mary eyed her father with patience born of long experience. "Not until you tell me."

"None other than Rake Halliburton, that's who!" Clarence, in high gig, beamed at his daughter. "Earl of Harborough, hah! Imagine it! The Rake! There's one in the eye for those blasted usurpers! A real loose screw! I hear he dropped five thousand of the best at White's last week. He'll sell up Rushmoreland and waste the whole in six months." This last damped his spirits somewhat. He gave a lusty sigh. "And there will go the noble estate of Rushmoreland. If only those damned rubies had been found! We might have bought it back, regained our own."

"Well, we don't have them," Mary remarked with a practicality that masked her own regrets. "And if you're right, the Halliburtons will soon lose their chance to search for them, too." She pulled her coverlet up to her chin. "I don't have to get up quite yet," she pointed out. Clarence, taking a hint for once, headed off in search of his own couch.

Mary snuggled back into her bed, a prey to unhappy reflections. The inability of the late Lady Beatrix, ex-Countess of Rushmore, to locate her husband's cache had, for seventy years, been a canker on the souls of the successive and poverty-stricken Danforths. They might have been living in luxury on the monies from that fabulous collection instead of existing in near poverty. The jewels were pried from their settings by the Jacobite ex-earl to further the cause of Bonnie Prince Charlie. According to legend, the Jacobite had secreted the rubies somewhere on the vast estate while arranging for their safe delivery. But then the Pretender's campaign ended, the Jacobite was arrested, and the rubies remained hidden, no one knew where. The usurping Halliburtons searched in vain.

Mary pounded on her pillow. Somewhere, within the bounds of Rushmoreland Castle and its surrounding park land, lay a fortune in rubies that belonged to her. The thought was frustrating, to put it no stronger. Mary abandoned her attempts to recapture sleep, donned her old stuff dress, and made her way down to the kitchens to prepare breakfast.

It was well into the afternoon when Clarence, wrapped in a magnificent dressing gown of burgundy satin, wandered into the drawing room where Mary once more engaged in waxing the old Queen Anne desk. He settled himself on the sofa and rattled open the pages of the *Morning Post* he carried.

Mary, recognizing the signs, sighed. She dearly loved her devil-may-care father, but there were times when she wished he were less improvident. "How did it go last night?" she asked at last.

"Oh, toll-loll." He waved a hand airily.

Mary threw him a piercing glance.

Clarence fiddled with the newspaper for a moment, then cast it aside. "Time I was getting dressed," he declared. With studied nonchalance, he strolled from the room.

Mary watched him go, her heart sinking. It would seem her father's streak of ill luck had not let up. If it continued, they would lose their last anchor. Their home would be sold up to settle their monstrous debts. She resumed her polishing, attacking a strip of carving set into a panel on the desk and rubbing in the mixture of beeswax and lemon oil with more force than might be considered prudent. She squeaked in dismay as a tiny fragment of the carving tore loose and twisted sideways.

And then more separated. In a straight line. And not merely the carving but a segment of the panel itself came away, revealing a small, rectangular drawer.

Mary stared at it, then slowly pulled it out. Within, tied with a faded pink ribbon, lay a thin packet of yellowed papers.

She sat down on the floor by the desk, untied the fraying ribbon, and unfolded one of the sheets. It was a letter, addressed to Lady Beatrix. She glanced down at the signature—from the Jacobite and written from his prison cell! Rapidly, Mary sorted through the rest. Beatrix had kept them in order, carefully preserving these mementos from her beloved husband.

The last bore the date of the day before his execution. Mary opened it and scanned the lines through misty eyes. Then she read it again, puzzled by the cryptic words of the message. It hardly seemed the sort of letter one would write to one's wife on such an occasion.

"My dearest beloved," she read,

> I must beg you to do me a great favor. I find I
> have left behind my copy of Pope's translation of the
> Iliad and I am having difficulty ascertaining the
> meaning of several lines in my Greek version. Make
> all haste, my heart, and discover for me the true
> content of the following references:
> Book XXIII line 383, Book XXIV line 662,
> Book III line 208, Book V line 371,
> Book XIII line 106, Book III line 312,
> Book XXII line 484, Book XII line 283,
> Book III line 357.

And here it ended. He had not even been able to
sign his name. Mary blinked back sympathetic
tears. Poor Lady Beatrix. As a child, she had
wept over the story of her great-grandmother,
and this new discovery brought back all her
heartfelt feelings for that romantic lady.

The door opened behind her as she mused
over the missives, and Clarence poked in his
head. "Just off, my dear," he announced.

"Father, only see." She held out the slim
packet. "Their last letters! I found them in a hidden drawer in the desk."

Clarence came into the room, resplendent in a
coat of gentian blue and inexpressibles of the
most fashionable shade of pale yellow. A paste
jewel glinted in his Mathematical neckcloth and
an array of fobs and seals dangled across his
bulging waistcoat. He cast a casual glance over
the faded pages Mary held out for his inspec-
tion. "Whose letters?"

"Great-grandmother Beatrix and her Jacobite husband. It is so sad, Father." Mary dabbed at an eye with the corner of her apron. "She must have received this last one too late, when there was no longer any reason to look up the wanted translations. But is it not an odd request for him to make at such a time?"

She pored over the pages in her hand again, and her puzzlement grew. "Why are the references not listed in order, by book? He jumps back and forth so strangely! Almost as if he wished them looked up in that order. I wonder . . ."

She broke off, suddenly thoughtful. "Have we a Pope translation of the *Iliad?*" Other than her own well-worn works of Shakespeare, she feared their library was rather thin of classics.

Clarence glanced over her shoulder at the yellowed papers. "The *Iliad?* I hardly think so. My grandfather would have left his at Rushmoreland. I doubt there would be one here, unless Lady Beatrix's father went in for the classics." He wrinkled his patrician nose, dismissing such a questionable taste as unlikely. "Not an avid scholar myself, but I fancy I remember a little from my expensive schooling." He brought forward with pride the few lines that had caught his boyish fancy many years before and intoned them with appropriate drama.

" 'The day shall come, the great avenging day —which Troy's proud glories in the dust shall lay!' "

"That is not much help," Mary informed him.

"We need the edition used by the Jacobite to decipher his message."

" 'Tis not a volume easily obtainable in these days, I should think." Clarence shrugged. "Daresay it was published nigh on a hundred years ago!"

"Hardly that, Father. It must have been at the height of popularity during my great-grandfather's day. And surely it has been reprinted since."

"Well, it's not a form of reading I'd relish," Clarence declared, losing interest in anything that smacked so distressingly of the scholarly. "Put those letters back in the desk, girl. All behind us now, and best forgotten."

Mary ignored him. "But why did he ask her to send him translations when he knew he would die on the morrow?" She tapped the letter with a finger, her brow creased in thought; then her eyes opened wide. "Father, what a nodcock I've been! He must have been trying to tell her something—something he dared not say openly—and this is a cipher!" She bounded to her feet. "Only think! This may be what we have searched for all these years! The clues to the hiding place of the Rushmoreland rubies!"

She took a hasty turn about the room, her eyes blazing with excitement. "I am going to decipher my great-grandfather's clues! Oh, if only I could be at Rushmoreland right now, I'd soon find our rubies! Only think what it would mean for us! An end to all our debts—a life of comfort and ease with never a dunning tradesman at our door!" She stopped suddenly, still as a statue, as a momentous idea formed in her head.

"No, here now!" Clarence remonstrated uneasily, recognizing the signs with dismay.

"What?" Mary looked up and noticed that her father was eyeing her with no little concern. Not wishing to upset him—or arouse his curiosity—she assumed an expression of such careless innocence that he panicked.

"See here, Mary, you're not to go kicking up any high jinks. You can't go haring off to Rushmoreland if that is in your mind. They'd never let you into the castle—why, the Danforths and the Halliburtons haven't spoken for three generations!"

Mary smiled sweetly. "Yes, Father."

"Just what do you mean by that? Look here, my girl, there's no earthly use hunting for those rubies. You can take my word for it, someone dug them up and sold them off on the sly years ago. Why, those damned Halliburtons must have scoured every inch of our land!" A thought struck him. "Hah. Wonder if any of them stumbled across the entrance to the secret passage my father used to tell tales of."

"A secret passage?" The look of one peeping through the door of Paradise transfigured Mary's mobile face.

Clarence, who was gazing out the window, unwisely waxed reminiscent. "My father lived at Rushmoreland as a very small boy—before the debacle, that was—and the Jacobite used to tell him ghost stories to keep him from hunting for the passage."

"Oh, tell me!" Mary begged. "Tell me about it."

"Well, I daresay it is all fustian, but as my old governor related the details to me, pirates dug a tunnel from the cove at the base of the cliff. It led up somewhere into the interior of the castle. Rumor held the hemp-bait were in the employ of the renegade first Earl of Rushmore. He amassed the family fortune by—ah—trading on the high seas."

Pleased with her reception of his story, he added a further embellishment. "After a particularly successful run, the earl decided to retire. An argument over the loot ensued, and he is supposed to have slain the pirate captain in the passage and left his body where it lay as a warning to trespassers. My father's grandfather told him the skeleton still remained and that as a child he had personally seen the bones of 'Captain Hideless' before the tunnel was sealed and the secret lost forever."

"It is sealed?" Mary's face fell comically, for her hopes of a real adventure had been running rampant.

"Oh, yes," he assured her. "My great-grandfather considered it an open invitation to sneak thieves and cutthroats. He had the entrance closed up and hidden before my grandfather was born. He used to tell him the ghost stories to frighten him out of searching for the entrance inside the castle. My favorite," Clarence rambled on dreamily, "was the one that told of the skeleton of Captain Hideless guarding the tunnel. He said that the dry bones would rattle and come together when anyone came near. Then the skeleton would spring to its feet and cut the unwary intruder down with one blow of his rusty sword. Not true, of course." He smiled at Mary, whose eyes were wide. "A Canterbury tale to scare any of the family children who might feel like exploring."

"Well, it doesn't scare me. I would have found that passage had I been there." She paced restlessly about the room once more, clasping and unclasping her hands, as an idea grew in her mind. They needed those rubies. Their creditors were becoming unpleasant and of late, Clarence's well-meaning attempts to restore their finances had only led them deeper into Dun territory. "Father," she said slowly, "has no one found that passage? Can you be sure? Your grandfather must have known where it was. Did he never say?"

"No, he disremembered." Clarence watched her, growing a bit anxious. "If you're thinking of the rubies, you're fair and far off. That tunnel was sealed before he was born; he couldn't have put them in there."

Mary sank down into a chair and picked up the Jacobite's letter. She was silent for so long that Clarence's nerves began to quiver.

"Mary—" he began.

She held up the letter. "You and I are the last of the Danforth family. I feel we were fated to find these clues. Those stones belong to us. If this isn't the guide to the passage entrance, I'll— I'll eat it. He must have found the way in and placed his treasure there for Captain Hideless to guard. Oh, Father, if only I were a man!" She sprang up again. "I wager we'd soon have our rubies." She headed for the door, a purposeful swing to her stride.

"Look here, Mary—I say, where are you going?"

She threw a saucy smile over her shoulder. "Only to put on my last year's chapeau, Father. And my old brown pelisse. I believe it may be about to rain again."

"Yes, and then where are you off to?" Clarence snapped open an ornate snuffbox, his recourse in times of crisis. "You've always had an odd kick in your gallop, my girl. I don't trust you an inch when you get the bit between your teeth. You keep away from Rushmoreland. Demme if you're not just like me at your age— always ripe for a lark! Not at all the thing for a lady of your quality."

Mary looked at him and tightened her lips. Quality be—dashed! Of what good was her quality to her? Did it help with the cooking? Or make up the beds?

"I'm merely going out to a bookshop," she replied, her voice bland. "To see if I can't find a Pope translation."

"Oh, well, if that's the case. Wouldn't mind knowing the meaning of that skimble-skamble myself. Go ahead, I can't stop you when you've a bee in your bonnet, but mind you take care, walking alone." He took too large a pinch of his special sort and sneezed violently.

Before he could wipe his streaming eyes, Mary slipped quietly out of the room. She had spoken the truth, she told herself, feeling self-righteous. After all, she had to find the book first. While she was out anyway, what harm could there be in taking care of another matter?

So full of plans was she that the lack of a Pope translation in the bookstore seemed a small annoyance, a lack she could soon remedy. She walked briskly down Park Lane, the bee continuing to buzz within her unfashionable bonnet. Her destination lay across Hyde Park and she paused, looking in at the gates, somewhat like a child at the window of a forbidden candy shop.

It was the height of the Season and the hour of the promenade. All society walked or drove sedately along the paths between the flowering hedges and green-leaved trees. Would the notorious Rake Halliburton be among them? Perhaps in his curricle, driving the famous team of matched grays that Clarence would have given his eyeteeth for—had he not already lost both of them long ago. How she'd love to see that equipage sweep along Rotten Row, putting all others in the shade! Her injudicious father had dropped enough hints about the Rake's regrettable career to make her wild to see him in person.

It would do no harm to take a shortcut. Mary did not often venture into the park, having no abigail to accompany her and her father not often willing to waste his valuable time taking her about. But I am all of two and twenty! she assured herself. I am no longer a green girl in need of a chaperone but a spinster quite left on the shelf. Surely I can walk alone in the park, very discreetly, of course, and watch the ton pass by.

As she headed down the nearest path, she followed with wistful eyes the dilatory progress of a pair of elegant ladies who were accompanied by an Exquisite in yellow pantaloons, a short-tailed lavender coat and a beehive hat. From his vacuous expression, Mary was sure no bee ever buzzed inside his ridiculous head gear. She smiled, but it went awry.

It would have been all that was wonderful to have had a come-out in style, to have been accepted by the lofty patronesses of Almack's and paraded in the marriage mart that Almack's had become. She might have gone off in her first season. Mary was not vain, but she had a mirror and couldn't help knowing that although she was not an accredited beauty, she was quite well enough. Stylish gowns and fancy furbelows were all she'd need to hold her own in any gathering.

A hat like the one on the lady on the right, for instance—only in smoky blue to match her eyes and lined with silk in the lovely shade of apricot worn by the other lady. How it would set off her dusky curls! And a new walking dress of merino with two—no, three—flounces on the narrow skirt and long tight sleeves puffed at the shoulder and stitched with bands of ribbon . . .

Oh, do wake up, you ninnyhammer, she scolded herself. Be thankful for the roof over your head and that you've not more hair than wit under your dowdy hat!

She had paused, deep in her thoughts, standing by an empty bench as though waiting for someone. Coming to with a start, she realized that a veritable coxcomb ogled her through his quizzing glass from across the path. She accidentally caught his eye. He smiled knowingly and started toward her.

Suddenly alone and vulnerable, she looked about anxiously for some acquaintance from whom she could claim escort. The only familiar figure in sight was one of her father's more raffish cronies, on the strut in all the glory of a Bond Street Beau. But Clarence had warned her to have nothing to do with Sir Archibald Andover and always sent her up to her room when he was to be among the evening's company. She knew him to be far too loose in the haft where females of a certain order were concerned, not at all the sort of gentleman with whom a young lady should be seen walking. She could not ask his aid and worse, should he recognize her as Clarence's daughter and accost her, the coxcomb who now approached would consider her fair game.

Blushing furiously with mortification at having looked at him and seemingly invited his audacity, she turned abruptly and hurried out through the park gate.

Crossing the street, she sought the safety of Miss Tibbet's Domestic Employment Agency only a few doors away. This establishment, operated by a prim ex-governess, was Mary's original destination. Miss Amelia Tibbet had come to mind instantly when entry to Rushmoreland

Castle had become of prime importance. Mary knew she could count on Tibbie, the beloved companion of her schoolgirl days before Clarence had run through his meager inheritance. Tibbie would back her in any scheme to regain the lost fortunes of Rushmore. In Mary, the repressed governess had recognized the adventurous spirit stifled from her own youth and she had aided and abetted her harum-scarum charge in many innocent escapades that would have been frowned on by a father more straitlaced than Clarence.

The odious man from the park followed Mary right to the entrance of Miss Tibbet's Domestic Emporium, and she panted for breath as she shut the door behind her and raced up the two flights of stairs. Luckily, the lady was not engaged and Mary flew into her motherly arms.

"Oh, Tibbie, I am having the most exciting day!" she gasped, stepping back and collapsing into the chair by the desk. "You'll never guess!"

Miss Tibbet beamed fondly at her favorite former pupil and patted her hand. "My, how you do take me back." She laughed, a cheery sort of chortle. "You look just like you did ten years ago when your father chased Henry the pot-boy clear out of the mews for breaking his tobacco jar and a porcelain vase. And all the time it was you who coaxed young Henry into rolling them down the front stair for a race."

"Poor Henry." Mary giggled. "He forgave me, you know, for not admitting it was my fault. Father never knew and Henry could run much faster than he. It had all blown over by next morning."

"Well now, Miss Mary, I sense that something of that ilk is in the air right now. You are the very picture of mischief. What have you broken today?"

"Only my word to Father. I told him I was going to the bookshop—which I did, so I haven't actually broken my word—only really I was coming here. I must remember to stop at another on my way home. Seriously though, Tibbie, I need your help. The most excruciatingly fantastic thing has happened!"

In a tumble of words, she told Miss Tibbet of finding Lady Beatrix's letters. Coming to the possible cipher contained in the last, she was rewarded by an answering sparkle in the ex-governess's eyes.

"Well, I never!" that lady exclaimed. "The rubies is it, at last?" She plumped down in the chair behind the desk. "And what do you want of me? You intend to find them yourself, I wager."

"Of course, Tibbie, and I thought of you at once. You told me, not a month ago, that Rushmoreland always applied to you for housemaids. I remember you said you had sent at least three to the castle in the last year. Tibbie, the next maid you send there will be me!"

Chapter Two

At first shocked by the idea of his daughter becoming a servant, Clarence soon decided, since it was in his own interest, that she would come to no harm in the castle.

"Indeed," he declared, "I believe the experience may do you a deal of good. Settle your inquisitive spirits."

"And only think—if I should find the rubies!"

"Well," Clarence said, as he stroked his clean-shaven chin, "that's as may be. Not much chance of it. But"—he waved his arms expansively—"above all, it will enable you to at last set sight upon the seat of your ancestors. You will view the glory that should be ours!"

Mary brushed his dramatics aside. "I cannot, of course, go as the daughter of the should-have-been Earl of Rushmore. I must have a suitable pseudonym. Something very housemaidish and yet one I shan't forget to answer to. I think my own first name. Mary . . . and perhaps Brown. Yes, I shall be Mary Brown."

Clarence raised scandalized eyebrows. "Brown!" he exclaimed. "What a paltry cognomen! Let's have a little imagination, if you please. We must choose something more suitable to your rank."

"Such as Barnstable?"

"Good Lord, no! Ramsbottom, perhaps, or Bolingbroke? Oh, I have it—Appledore! Or perhaps you would prefer Melkinthorpe?"

Mary shook her head. "Who ever heard of housemaids with such names? Brown it is."

"Mary, my girl, you are as stubborn as I am." He shook his head and sighed. "You inherited that from your mother, rest her soul. How she would frown to hear her daughter addressed by such a common appellation!"

"Come now, Father. If this is to succeed, we must be practical. If I may not be a Brown, then Jones or Robertson—or perhaps Hayfield."

"Hah, I have a solution!" Ever the gamester, Clarence put forward a typical suggestion. "We shall leave it to fate. Put all the names into my hat and you may draw one."

Mary eyed him with distrust. "Equal representation," she decreed. "I put in as many names as you."

This agreed to, reluctantly by Clarence, Mary tore a sheet of writing paper into small strips, and for several minutes silence filled the room except for the scratching of pens as they wrote their selections. Clarence grinned as he scribbled and once he laughed outright. Mary laid down her pen and he looked up, all innocence.

"Fate," he reminded her mildly, and she grimaced.

Their nominations completed, Clarence went up to his dressing room and selected an ancient *chapeau de bras* as being the only headgear suitably grand for this momentous occasion. All the names went into it and Mary, closing her eyes, reached in. After stirring the papers about while Clarence urged her to get on with it, she finally selected one, unfolded it, and read.

"Father! Wherever did you come up with such an outrageous name? Migglesworth!"

"The very thing!" He beamed with satisfaction. "My favorite. That's it, then. Mary Migglesworth you are. I knew we'd come up with something worthy."

"Migglesworthy?" Mary gurgled. "I couldn't. They'd laugh me out of the castle!"

Clarence shrugged his eloquent shoulders. "It was fate. Either you go as Migglesworth or I put my foot down and you don't go at all."

Mary felt about in the hat. All of Clarence's slips bore the same name. About to remonstrate, her sense of the ridiculous got the better of her and she succumbed to a fit of the giggles. "W–why not? I will use it—only every time I hear it spoken, I shall break up!"

"Well, you won't hear it much," Clarence prophesied. "As a housemaid, plain Mary will be your lot."

"Oh, but I'll have Migglesworth in the back of my mind to sustain me. Whenever anyone orders me about by my given name, I shall think 'Miss Migglesworth to you, ducks!' "

She selected a fresh sheet of notepaper and laid it before her smug parent. "And now I must have a glowing letter of reference from the head of the Danforth family, telling them that I am indispensable."

Her father looked at her, suddenly serious. "That you are, my dear. You take care. I'm not saying the Rake ain't a good man to have along on a cheery evening. In fact, I hear he is demmed good company," he admitted, "but I

know only too well how he is with females of a
certain type and I know where he'd class a
housemaid in his own establishment. Mind you,
keep out of his way. The man's not to be
trusted. Don't let him catch you under the stairs
or in a dark hall. Or," he amended, "even in a
well-lighted one."

Mary shivered, remembering the odious man
who had followed her from the park. "He'll
never know I am there, you may be sure of that
—for whatever would he do if he learned I was
after the rubies?"

"Make sure he don't learn it."

"He won't. Now, Father, my reference. Write
that Mary Migglesworth—" She paused to giggle, and then resumed with a straightened face.
"Mary Migglesworth has been in our service for
many years—no, best to give an actual length of
time. We must be quite honest, Father. For how
long? When did Tibbie leave us?"

Clarence scratched the end of his nose
thoughtfully. "It was the year Mansfield's horse
failed to win the second Ascot Gold Cup. That
would be 1808."

Mary calculated rapidly on her fingers, using
both hands. "Seven years. That sounds as
though I've given satisfaction. You must say I'm
leaving only due to your current pecuniary difficulties. And add that you shall be pleased to
take me back."

"Now that they'll doubt within a week."

"Write it, Father; then, in the unlikely event
that I find nothing, I shall be able to leave gracefully."

Clarence sharpened the nib of his quill pen with care, and dipped it into the ink pot. The tip of his tongue protruded as he attacked the unaccustomed task of composing an epistle. Mary watched his labors over his shoulder.

"Say that I am honest, hardworking, and—and my character is above reproach," she dictated. "Tell them I am reliable and steady."

Clarence put down his pen and made a face at her. "How am I to write all that rubbish when you are planning to pull the most tremendous larks about the place? Poking around, snooping, sounding the walls—just don't you get caught! Mind my reputation!"

She giggled again. "They'll believe your words in spite of it."

A message came from Tibbie within two days and, trembling with excitement and anticipation, Mary packed her few garments into a small trunk. Armed with the recommendation from Miss Tibbet's Domestic Employment Agency, Clarence's letter of reference, and with a copy of the Jacobite's last instructions to his Beatrix tucked into the bosom of her brown merino traveling gown, Mary prepared to leave for the village of Market Rushmore.

Clarence, with many admonitions for his tongue-valiant daughter to watch her tendency to give as good as she got, accompanied her to Golden Cross Inn where she boarded a "yellow bone shaker," on her way to restore their fortunes at last.

Rushmore Castle lay at no great distance from London, and Mary endured a new and thankfully short experience seated in the hot, crowded stage. She found herself jammed between a farmer who apparently raised pigs and a fat housewife who munched garlic cheese and brown bread rolls from a cloth-covered basket. Mary soon wished the woman would offer her some for she had heard that if you consumed onions or garlic, you could not smell them on another's breath. On the seat opposite, a boy sat between his parents sucking sticky sweets, and she could only be grateful that his small size gave her room for her knees.

After what seemed an interminable hour, she was set down before a small public house at the crossroads of the London turnpike and Market Rushmore High Street. She drew a few deep breaths of fresh air while the coachman unstrapped her trunk from the back of the carriage.

Market Rushmore, other than the tavern, seemed to consist of a dozen cottages, some with shop-fronts, lining one cobblestoned road that ended in a tiny green facing a gray stone Norman church with a four-square tower. Other than a few hangers-on holding up the wall of the public house, there was no one else in sight.

Mary looked about, feeling a bit anxious. Somehow she had expected to see the castle immediately. Where could it be—and how was she to get there?

Her small trunk hit the dusty road with a

thud; the coachman clambered up to his seat and chirruped to his team. The stage lumbered off and she was alone. She had been nervous before, wondering a bit about her reception at the castle; now suddenly she was terrified. Never had she been alone, miles and miles from home, deserted and vulnerable.

Suppose a drunken man came out of the tavern—suppose no one from the castle came to meet her—suppose they had no idea she was coming? But surely Tibbie must have written, announcing her arrival. Then, just as unusual tears threatened and a lump had begun to form in her throat, she heard the clop of a horse's hooves on the dry bed of the lane on the far side of the tavern. She forced her shaking knees to support her and crossed to the narrow road. To her great relief, an open cart, drawn by a fat cob, pulled up beside her.

A short burly man climbed laboriously down from the cart and approached, while the cob, swinging his head so he could see past his blinders, eyed her in a friendly manner. With a tumultuous return of her buoyant spirits, Mary noted that the long-faced man resembled his horse in more than one way. He, too, looked friendly.

"Yew the new maid fer the castle?"

"Yes. Oh, I'm glad to see you!"

The man sniffed. "That's as may be." He picked up her trunk as though it were empty and tossed it into the cart. Hitching his buckskin breeches a notch higher, he slowly looked her over, and spat on the ground. "Don't reckon you'll last any longer than the last one." He turned and hoisted himself into the cart, leaving her standing in the roadway. "Well, come along then."

Since he obviously felt no need to give her a hand, Mary caught up her skirts and scrambled onto the seat beside him. The cob started off at once.

"Why shouldn't I last?" she asked, curious.

The man shook with a burst of silent laughter. "That's fer me to know and yew to find out, but yew won't catch me sleeping inside that old pile."

Mary's interest was piqued. "Why not?" she demanded.

The man just shook his head. Still consumed with that aggravating silent laughter, he clucked to the horse, who showed signs of wanting to stop and grab a mouthful of leaves from the hedge bordering the path. He changed the subject. "What's tha' name, lass?"

For a frantic second, she couldn't remember and then couldn't bring herself to say Migglesworth. "Mary," she compromised.

"That all?" His shoulders shook again. "Won't take up much space on a tombstone. O'course, they might not be no body to bury come the funeral."

"Why not?" she asked, startled, wondering what she had gotten herself into. "Tell me what you mean."

He looked at her sideways. "Na then, they up at the castle will tell yew it be all nonsense but I say, see that yew ain't never alone by night."

After this pronouncement, he refused to speak again and they continued along the narrow winding lane in silence for a while.

He was gammoning her. And she had risen to his fly! Mary set her lips firmly, refusing to believe a word he had said—but a small niggling doubt remained. All at once she remembered Tibbie sitting in her little office and remarking on the rapid turnover in maids at the castle.

Mary felt a mounting excitement—or could it be fear? Surely the infamous Rake was not yet in residence; Clarence said that he was journeying back from a shooting trip in Scotland. That would take days. If not the Rake, what could be the danger? And why might there be no body? Oh, the man was bamming! He probably enjoyed frightening gullible housemaids. Well, she was not a simple girl to be taken in by such tactics. She restrained an urge to cling to the edge of the seat in the jolting cart and folded her hands primly in her lap.

After what seemed miles of a meandering lane passing lush fields, orchards, and scattered thatch-covered cottages, they emerged from a thick grove of trees to face a massive wrought-iron gate.

Into the ornamental arch above it, a great letter *R* had been worked into the pattern and Mary felt a surprising thrill deep within her. She hadn't realized that seeing her lost heritage would strike such a chord. The cart turned in at the open gate and traveled along a smoothly raked gravel drive between pollarded trees and tall rhododendrons. Then, so suddenly that she

gasped, they rounded a corner and Rushmoreland Castle loomed before them across acres of
shaved lawns.

The castle's imposing size came as a shock.
Wide-eyed and openmouthed, she stared up at
it. Such splendor lay beyond the dreams of city-
bred Mary, to whom a large establishment
meant a London town house. Rushmoreland
seemed to stretch as far as she could see, a great
wall of ivy-covered gray stone, broken at inter-
vals by tall crenelated towers. On the right there
were orchards in the distance, a small lake, rose
gardens, and shrubberies. The left wing abutted
a cliff where the ground fell away perhaps
twenty yards to the estuary below. The basic
structure she thought to be Norman, with a new
Georgian addition.

As she gazed at the castle, her heart pounded
with a warm rush of emotion. This was her
rightful home, the abode of her ancestors. Here
lay her roots. And it belonged to a usurper—a
rake! A smoldering anger filled her as the cart
rumbled past undulating terraces, past the great
oak-and-iron double doors that must have
opened to royalty, to throngs of elegant visitors,
all welcomed to resplendent balls. But not to a
Mary Migglesworth.

Apparently long familiar with the route, the
horse turned off on a cobblestoned drive that
circled around the castle and passed under an
archway. Mary peered eagerly at rows of multipaned windows, at French doors and stained
glass. Which would be the library? How would
she ever find her way through the maze of

rooms in this mountain of ivy-covered stone? No wonder the rubies still lay hidden—but, she thought as she hugged herself, she had the clues! She touched her bosom, reassured by the crinkle of paper. She would find her rubies, and hopefully before Clarence's gaming brought them to *point non plus*.

Moving ever along the massive walls of the older portion, cartwheels sunk in deep-worn ruts, they drew up at the rear of the castle, where a huge door stood open. Her driver climbed down, scooped out her trunk, and disappeared inside with it. Mary sat where she was, gazing after him helplessly.

A small scullery maid popped out of the door and stared up at her.

"Ain't you coming in?" she asked.

"Oh—oh, yes." Mary slid from her seat. "Only I don't know where to go."

The little maid gave her a brisk nod. "You go with me. I'm to take you to Mrs. Greenfield. She's our housekeeper," she added confidentially. "And a rare tartar she is. Come on now, she's awaiting. The cob'll stand till old Harry comes back."

Mary followed the girl through the door and along a dark stone-flagged passage. Somewhere in its far reaches must be the kitchens. Enticing odors of fresh-baked bread and cooking meats awoke vivid pangs of hunger, for Mary had not eaten since breakfast. She wondered when housemaids were allowed to eat—after the noble family and guests? Would it be hours yet?

She bumped into the little maid who had stopped before a closed door.

The girl tapped briefly, and stuck in her head. "The new maid, Mrs. Greenfield, ma'am," she announced, and scuttled away, leaving Mary alone and suddenly scared.

Tentatively, she pushed the door the rest of the way open and stepped into a large room. At least she supposed it must be a large room, for it managed to hold the woman who faced her and blocked her view. Mrs. Greenfield was quite the most dignified female Mary had ever seen. Garbed all in black, her gray hair pulled into a tight bun, she seemed a terrifying ogre—and then she smiled. The flood of relief caused Mary's knees to sag.

"Welcome to Rushmoreland Castle, my dear." Mrs. Greenfield held out her hand—not to be shaken, Mary realized just in time. "I believe you bear a reference from your last post."

"Yes, ma'am." Mary struggled with the drawstring to her reticule and managed to extract Clarence's letter of reference and Tibbie's recommendation.

The housekeeper gestured to a chair beside the fire that crackled in a wide stone hearth. "Sit down—Mary, is it?—I'll be with you in a moment."

Mary collapsed into the chair, remembered her position, and sat up straight, folding her hands in her lap. The room was even larger than she had thought, for a long table, set for a number of places, took up one side, and here by the fire was a cozy area with two rocking chairs and a settee. The table drew her. Food! she thought. At last.

Mrs. Greenfield folded away the letters and placed them in a desk that was far newer than Mary's outmoded Queen Anne.

"Most satisfactory," she said. "I believe you may do very well here. Miss Sarah Clintock is head housemaid; she will tell you your duties and show you to your room. You will be sharing with Holly, another of our girls." She hesitated, an inquisitive spark in her eyes. "You were employed by the Danforths for quite some time. You must know of that family's former ownership of our castle."

Mary thought rapidly. Here was an excuse for her to explore a bit. "Yes, ma'am. That was my reason for applying for this post. I was wishful to see the place the master should have owned."

Mrs. Greenfield sniffed. "That's as may be. I see you left his service due to his financial difficulties." Mary could see the housekeeper was striving to disguise her curiosity. "I understand he is sadly improvident. Quite run off his legs in fact, is he not?"

This last was said with a condescending air of sympathy that Mary was hard put to swallow. In spite of herself, she rushed to her father's defense. "Oh, no, ma'am, at most times we—he— his situation is very comfortable. He is a gamester, you must know, and though he does have losses, very often his affairs are in plump currant." She stopped, aware that Mrs. Greenfield eyed her strangely.

"Your speech is not that of a housemaid." The

lady spoke sharply. "Where did you learn to speak the King's English with such ease?"

Mary felt herself pale. Why couldn't she mind her unruly tongue? She would give herself away before she even started! In her confusion, she uttered the first words that came to her. "From my mistress—I—served as her lady's maid."

The housekeeper's eyebrows rose. "Your mistress? I understood Danforth to have been a widower of a great many years. I had thought— oh." Apparently she had thought. "I see. No doubt you served a great many mistresses."

Now Mary's face flamed for sure. She could not spring to Clarence's aid and had to bite her tongue to refrain from a blazing answer.

Mrs. Greenfield nodded understandingly, obviously misinterpreting Mary's embarrassment. "Well, my dear, we shall say no more of that. And here is Sarah Clintock ready to initiate you in your duties. You will report directly to her. After she takes you to your room, you will come to the Servants' Hall for supper. In twenty minutes. Please do not be late."

Mary rose quickly to her feet, remembered to bob a brief curtsy, and turned to follow the austere young woman in a neat gray uniform who had appeared at the door.

"Mary, is it?" the woman asked. "I am Sarah. Come along, you haven't much time and Mrs. Beecham don't care for tardiness at her meals."

Mary trotted to keep up. "Mrs. Beecham? I thought—Mrs. Greenfield—"

"She is the housekeeper. Mrs. Beecham is

head cook." Sarah looked back and smiled. "You'll get to know us all soon enough. But you won't dine with Mrs. Greenfield and Mr. Wesson, who is our butler. They eat in the Housekeeper's Room with the upper domestics. The footmen and the rest of us take our meals in the Servants' Hall. Hurry now."

Brisk and efficient, Sarah led her down the long stone-flagged corridor, up two narrow flights of stairs, and stopped at a cell-like room on the third landing.

"Holly will be your bedfellow. She has much the same duties, so you will go around with her in the morning and she will show you how to go on."

She threw open the door and a girl who had been washing her face at a stand in the corner screamed and threw a towel at them.

"Really, Holly!" Sarah picked it up, annoyed. "Do stop being so silly! Do you think to rout a ghost with a wet towel?"

"Oh, I'm sorry, Sarah, but I was that startled!" She saw Mary standing in the doorway and gave another shriek, this time one of delight.

"This is Mary, Holly. She will work with you and be your roommate. Come inside, Mary. I see your trunk has been brought up, but you've no time to change. You must come down as you are. Perhaps Holly will allow you to use the towel and basin to freshen up, but no more than five minutes now."

Holly caught Mary's hands in a fervent squeeze. "I'm that glad you've come, you can't believe! I'd not stay the night alone in this room for ever so much. Last night I slept with Amanda and Jane, three in their bed, and complain! They won't have me back!"

Sarah frowned. "You're being foolish beyond permission, Holly. Belinda was a nonsensical, fanciful girl with far too much imagination and you shouldn't have paid any attention to her. She listened to the gossip of the scullery maids, who no doubt manufactured the whole story from tales told by the stable hands to frighten stupid girls."

Abashed, Holly closed her mouth, but she gave Mary a very speaking glance.

Sarah left them alone and Holly helped Mary out of her pelisse and bonnet, hovering over her like a hen who'd recovered a lost chick. The room contained one bed, two chairs, a table, and the washstand. There was no wardrobe, and Holly's garments hung along one wall on a row of hooks, half of which were bare.

"Those are for you," she explained, adding the pelisse to the row. "I'll help you unpack after supper. There isn't time now." Holly chattered happily, tossing Mary's best bonnet on the table. "We can do that tonight. Lord, ducks, but I'm that glad you're here. We got to run."

"I've been running ever since I arrived!" Mary tried to smooth her rumpled curls as she followed Holly out the door. "Are we to be always so rushed?"

"Oh, no. You've just come at a most exciting time. The new master, you see. He comes tomorrow and all is at sixes and sevens and Mrs. Greenfield that jumpy! She's very nice, really.

So is Sarah. It's just that everything is upset what with the late master dying so sudden. We were all in mourning with black bands on our sleeves and now Mr. Wesson tells us we're to celebrate."

They reached the foot of the stairs and at last headed toward the delicious smells. Mary's stomach growled in anticipation.

The Servants' Hall lay next beyond the Housekeeper's Room and the door stood open. Conversation stopped as they entered, all eyes on Mary. She knew a moment's qualm facing so many strange people, but Holly steered her to the two empty seats, next to Sarah.

"This is Mary," Sarah announced to the company in general. She called off names that fled instantly from Mary's mind and talk broke out once more, although she detected covert glances in her direction. Why? she wondered. *Am I a curiosity?*

A hall boy served her with an excellent fricassee of mutton with caper sauce, far better than she would have consumed at home. Even he looked her over with uncalled-for interest.

She soon learned the answer. Mrs. Beecham, the motherly looking cook who presided over the table, voiced the topic on all their minds.

Turning to Mary with a kindly smile that failed to hide an eager curiosity, she asked about Mary's previous position. "Come from old Danforth, are you? And he having to let you go! We have heard he is quite monstrous in the wind."

The whole room stared at Mary, waiting. Conversation stilled and she saw they were agog for tidbits of London gossip. She had never given her father's way of life much thought before, but now all at once she realized how it must look to those whose lives ran on steady, sober lines. The sooner she found the rubies and established their credit, the better!

Meanwhile, she attempted a casual manner, toying with her fork and adopting phrases from Clarence's vocabulary. "Oh, no. He is not fatally scorched. Merely a trifle cucumberish. He will come about, the way he always does, and then I shall go back into his service."

This drew astonished gasps.

"What? Leave the castle?" Holly grabbed her arm, causing a bite of mutton to fly onto the tablecloth. "You cannot!"

"There now," Mrs. Beecham remarked pacifically. "She has but just come. We must let her get to know us."

The door from the hall opened and there entered an Adonis. His footman's livery fitted him like raiment for a prince's personal equerry. His curling hair, dark and shining, was brushed and pomaded à la Brutus, his liquid brown eyes set beneath a noble brow. A patrician nose, cleft chin, and mobile mouth were assembled in a manner to incite the admiration of females from eight to eighty.

He posed just over the threshold. " 'Masters, spread yourselves,' " he declaimed.

The footman called James eyed him sourly. "Listen to the man. Acts like he thinks he's the host."

The handsome newcomer ignored the remark,

having discovered Mary seated between her counterparts. "What have we here?" he cried, sweeping down upon her, his every action larger than life. " 'Her beauty makes this vault a feasting presence full of light.' "

Mary smiled. "Sir, I am afraid I am no Juliet."

He stepped back, flinging his arms wide. "What ho! A housemaid conversant with the Bard!"

Mrs. Beecham rapped on the table with the handle of her knife, calling the children to order like a nanny. "That will do, Edgemont. Stop your showing off for the new girl," she ordered. "Now only see, you've put the poor thing to the blush!"

Sarah made the introduction. "Edgemont Darracombe, Mary. Our second footman."

"But not forever, dear lady." He bent and kissed Mary's hand with a courtly bow before removing to his place.

James, from the other side of the table, gave a low growl. "If you've got your eye on my job, cocky, you can forget it."

"Never fear. 'I'll note you in my book of memories,' " murmured the irrepressible Edgemont, reaching for his spoon.

"None of your lip!" James half rose in his seat. "I know you're after my job. And if you think you're getting Wesson's when he retires, you've got rats in your cockloft! I'm first footman, your superior, I'll have you remember! Ten years I been here to your one!"

Edgemont winked across the table at Mary,

and smiled sweetly at James. " 'Nay, an thou'lt mouth, I'll rant as well as thou.' "

James turned purple. "Listen at the man! He's mocking me using words I don't understand! Just because he's an actor from the London stage don't make him material for a butler!"

Mrs. Beecham spoke placidly from the head of the table. "Give off, Edgemont, now do. Stop teasing James."

Edgemont had the grace to look sheepish. "Sorry, James. Believe me, I do not aspire to become a butler. I shall return to the boards one of these days, soon as I find me a company doing Shakespeare as he should be done."

Somewhat mollified, James sank back down, though he kept a suspicious eye on Edgemont. Mary, too, had her suspicions, but of a different nature. Why was such a man—an actor with his looks—working as a footman? Could he, too, be here under false pretensions like herself? Perhaps after her rubies? A cold hand seemed to touch her heart. How many people knew of their existence? A great many, she was sure. But she had the clues. She clung to that knowledge and felt it warm her again. She and she alone held the key to the mystery, only she must find the Jacobite's copy of Pope's translation. She pressed a hand to her breast, listening for the reassuring crackle of paper.

". . . tomorrow," Mrs. Beecham was saying, and the word caught Mary's attention. "It will be mighty strange," the cook went on, "a new master—and such a one! Mind you girls keep out of his way. Just because Rake Halliburton has finagled himself the title, don't turn him into a gentleman overnight! Leopards don't change their spots." She shook a warning finger. "To a man like him, housemaids are fair game and don't you girls forget it!"

"It will seem strange for sure," Sarah said, nervously picking at her mutton. "Us all so quiet and respectable. What kind of a house will this be now? I've half a mind to leave."

"So say we all of us." Mrs. Beecham nodded wisely. "It is all so very odd. I cannot believe what has happened. I come all over queer just at the thought! One day the master is here, the next gone! And both his heirs before him, taken away so strange. Almost as though fate wanted us to have this libertine in the house!" She sat back, flapping her ruddy face with her napkin.

This was the first Mary had heard of other heirs. She plucked up her courage to speak. "What happened to them?"

"A hunting accident," said Sarah.

"Ah, and if that were all." Mrs. Beecham shifted her heavy bulk in her chair, and her tone lent an eerie quality to her words. "Only two weeks ago it was, at their shooting box in Leicestershire. Both the uncle and the nephew found dead of gunshot! Stray bullets, they said, but I know better and so do we all. Then the master!

"They do say as it was footpads done him in, but I have me doubts. Mr. Wesson only the other night said to me that the master was that excited at dinner, babbling to another man about them rubies everyone is on about. Like as though he had an idea where they might be. And that very night on his way home from his club, he dies in the road!"

The girl Holly, seated on Mary's other side, shivered, her eyes round with fear.

"Mrs. Beecham, ma'am," she exclaimed, "he won't walk here, too!"

"Who's to say," broke in James. Determined to wrest center stage from Edgemont, he lowered his voice in a sepulchral moan. "Violent death chains a ghost to the earth. And why not walk here, his home?"

"By all means." Edgemont grinned at him. " 'Let's talk of graves, of worms, of epitaphs!' "

Holly squealed and Mrs. Beecham reproved him. "Do be quiet now, Edgemont. I declare it's enough to give us all a fit of the vapors what with so many deaths. We don't need another ghost!"

Another ghost? This was all that was needed to make her adventure complete! Mary's excitement grew. Not only her rubies, but a secret passage guarded by a skeleton, and now a ghost who walked her ancestral halls!

First from the man with the cart, now here in the castle, she heard fascinating hints of the supernatural.

"Oh, please tell me," she begged. "You said another ghost. Who walks here already? I didn't know the castle was haunted."

"Here now," said Mrs. Beecham. "Don't you listen to James and his fancies. It's all a pack of nonsense!"

"That it is not!" James exclaimed, annoyed. "I

have it from Mr. Wesson himself. He says the girl told him she saw our ghost!"

Holly pressed Mary's hand. "She did!" she whispered. "Belinda told me all about it! That scared she was, she ran screaming back to our room! She packed her things and left next morning."

"Who is it?" Mary asked. "Who did she see?"

James turned to her, his eyes fanatic. "It's God's truth. The Jacobite who hid them rubies! He walks the Long Gallery where her portrait hangs, looking for his wife to tell her where he put them."

Mary gazed at him, her eyes wide. Truly, she thought, I must meet this ghost!

Chapter Three

Mary let her eyes wander around the crowded table as she ate. She felt unnaturally shy, surrounded by so many strangers. Never would she remember their names! She tried to fix a few in her memory: Mrs. Beecham the cook, Sarah and Holly, the gorgeous Edgemont and the other footman, James; and there were two more housemaids she should have been able to place. Whatever would she call them when they worked together in the morning? Housemaid A and Housemaid B, she decided. The rest she gave up on. A coachman, perhaps, three others and four striplings. Pages? Hall-boys?

She laid down her fork, and Sarah spoke to her at once.

"You have yet to unpack, Mary. I suggest you go up now. You shall not be needed this evening."

Grateful, Mary thanked her and slipped from her seat. The whole evening—now that she was here, she could not bear to waste a minute. If she could just find her way to the library . . .

Outside in the stone passage, she paused, confused. Ahead on one side lay the kitchens; she could hear the rattle of pans and crockery and the high-pitched laughter of scullery maids whose cook was safely out of sight. The other way must lead toward the front of the castle. Somewhere there should be a baize door leading to the exalted premises of the upper classes. She walked firmly away from the Servants' Hall.

Before she had gone four steps, the door behind her swung open and Edgemont Darracombe strode up beside her. He would know the way to the library. She turned to face him and he pinned her to the passage wall, one hand pressed against it on each side of her waist.

"Whither goest thou, fair one? Your room lies back in the other direction." His head bent toward her and she jerked her face away before he could complete the kiss. She shoved at his chest with both hands.

"What do you think you're doing? Let me go!"

"What am I doing? Surely you know," he admonished. " 'She's beautiful and therefore to be wooed. She is a woman, therefore to be won.' "

Mary shoved harder. "You're not winning this one." She tried to duck under his arm and he laughed.

" 'Ah, was ever woman in this humour wooed? Was ever woman in this humour won?' "

Mary stopped struggling, and drew herself up. "You are confusing your kings," she said. "First it's Henry IV and now Richard III."

"A bluestocking, by all the gods!" he exclaimed. "Who'd have thought to find a mind capable of intelligent communication in this beehive of ignorance!"

"Do you always speak in quotations?" she wondered. "Can you not think of words of your own?"

" 'A hit, a very palpable hit!' " He sighed. "Alas, fair lady, it has become a habit. You are right. No longer can I think in other terms."

"Then the sooner you go back on the boards the better."

"Aye, my own conviction, I'm afraid." He dropped his stage manner, and also his hands, letting Mary step free. "But, do tell me, where were you going?"

Mary thought quickly. He could guide her to the library if only she could think of an excuse—of course, the settings for the rubies were rumored to be there. "I wanted to see the golden bracelets and things that once held the Rushmoreland rubies. Is that legend true? Are they really there for all to see?"

"Oh, yes. In a glass case over the mantel in the library. I've gazed at 'em many times myself and tried to imagine all the stones in place."

"Where is the library?" she asked, trying to still the eagerness in her voice. "Can you take me there?"

"Not I!" He shook his handsome head. "When old Wesson catches me out of place, he kicks up the devil of a dust. He's a stiff-rumped knaggy old gager, always nabbing the rust. He don't like me above half and it's James who is on call in the Great Hall evenings."

"Oh." This was a facer. If the butler should be there, how could she search the shelves? But why should he be in the library? She had only a hazy idea of a butler's duties but . . . "Won't he be serving dinner now? Or dining himself?"

Edgemont hesitated. "Come on, then. We'll have a quick look."

He led her down the corridor, past the still rooms and another narrow flight of stairs. Mary noted its position. She might need an exit at this end of the hall, and just ahead were the double green baize doors.

"Those are old Wesson's private stairs back there." Edgemont pointed at the narrow steps. "You keep off them. He sleeps just by the landing so's he can get down quick when his bell is rung. These here doors give directly on the Great Hall."

Pushing one side open tentatively, he peered through. "All clear."

They stepped into a huge, gloomy chamber, the oldest part of the castle. The floor was stone, as were the walls—what could be seen of them, for they were covered with ancient banners, shields, paintings, and tapestries. The few long, narrow windows at the front were draped in heavy velvet. When thrown open, the oaken double doors at the entrance could accommodate a horse-drawn carriage.

They were barred now, for the night, and bolted with iron. Curiously carved chairs with embroidered seats lined the walls along with great dark tables and chests. At the back, near where Mary and Edgemont stood, a wide stairway split at its base like an upside-down Y, and sheltered a fireplace a full ten feet high and twenty wide. Suits of armor stood guard on either side. A shadowed gallery circled the hall above the drapes; the high ceiling was out of sight in the darkness. Overwhelmed, Mary clung to Edgemont's arm.

"Over there," he whispered. "The third door down. That's the library."

Mary left him and started to cross the stone-paved floor, stepping from faded Chinese carpet to moth-eaten Indian rug. She was almost to the center when a door opened on the other side of the hall. She looked back—and Edgemont was gone. The green baize doors swung slightly on their hinges. Deserted, she stared up at an imposing figure that for a moment struck terror to her heart.

Butlers, Mary knew, were a breed unto themselves, their majesty exceeding that of kings.

Rigid of back, impressive of bearing, and cold of eye, they could grind better persons than mere housemaids to dust with a look. This butler looked, but Mary was no mere housemaid. She stood her ground.

There seemed to be an impasse. Mr. Wesson's bulging eyes could protrude no further. "Who are You?" he asked in a richly rolling tone that resembled the pouring of old brandy made audible. Years of the good life had increased his girth and mellowed his vocal chords, but his gaze had the warmth of a halibut's on a marble slab.

Miss Migglesworth, Mary told herself firmly. Miss Migglesworth to you, ducks. It worked.

She curtsied. It seemed a good idea, but it didn't go over very well.

"Sir, I meant no harm, I'm new here. They told me the tale of the rubies and said if I was to look in the library, I would see the actual gold they once was in."

The great man unbent slightly. "You are the new housemaid sent to us by Miss Tibbet." It was a statement, not a query.

Mary nodded. "Yes, sir."

"I," he informed her, "am Mr. Wesson."

Not sure what to say, Mary ventured a timid "How do you do?"

"Housemaids," he continued pontifically, "are Permitted in the Front of the Castle only when their Services are required." He spoke with capital letters and had a trick of widening his eyes to emphasize every capitalization. Mary watched him, fascinated. "May I Suggest you repair at Once to Miss Clintock for Instruction in your

Duties." He turned his back and trod with stately pace back the way he had come.

Mary, relieved to find she had not been slain, stuck out her tongue at his retreating figure.

When she returned to the servants' wing, the craven Edgemont had vanished. " 'A plague on all cowards, I say,' " she muttered, and made her way to the flight of stairs that led to her room. At least she now knew which door led to the library, and the volume she sought was sure to be there. The only problem was how to get to it. A roommate complicated matters quite dreadfully unless the girl proved to be a heavy sleeper. A midnight raid seemed her only chance.

After trying several doors on the third floor and surprising two scullery maids and the hall-boys, she peeked carefully into one across the hall and, to her relief, discovered Holly sitting on the rope bed peeling an apple with a murderous-looking kitchen knife.

"Where you been?" the girl demanded. "I'm right nervous up here by myself now it's dark!"

"Sorry," Mary came in meekly. "Edgemont waylaid me in the passage."

Holly sniffed. "Oh, him. He's a one, he is. Given us all the rush, one time or another. Belinda, the girl who left, was that keen on him you wouldn't believe. Went for his looks. Not me, mind you." She spoke so airily that Mary gave her a sharp look. And then looked again, for Holly was acting most strangely.

She had finished working on her apple, peeling it in one long continuous strip, and now stood up. With her eyes shut, she held the peel by one end and swung it once, twice, three times around her head before dropping it over her left shoulder. Then without touching it, she began to circle about the floor studying the peel from every angle.

"What on earth are you doing?" Mary bent to look also.

"See can you make out a letter," ordered Holly, circling once more. "I'm trying ever so hard for an E. M's and G's are easy, but I've never had no E." She sighed. "I do begin to think he's not for me, either. Belinda got a E once, but that don't count now, her being gone."

"Is this some form of divination?"

"Oh, no, nothing church-like. You see, if you do it right, you get the initial of your intended."

"I see." Mary sat down on the bed. "Edgemont?"

Holly's face flamed. "Well, I got as good a chance as any, no matter what that Belinda said. Fat lot of good it done her, making her sneak out at night to meet him. If she'd stayed put she'd never have got caught by that ghost!" Holly shuddered. "Nothing don't get me out that door after dark!" As she spoke, she turned the key in the lock and dragged over a chair to jam under the knob. "And there it stays till morning."

She pulled a chunk of dry bread from her apron pocket and broke it in two, offering half to Mary. "Here you go. Happy dreams."

"I'm not really hungry." Mary eyed the chunk she had accepted dubiously.

Holly gave a hoot of laughter. "Don't you

know anything? You must eat a dry crust before you go to bed, then your dreams will come true!"

"No, thanks." Mary handed it back. "There's no telling what I might dream after tonight."

Holly shrugged. "Suit yourself. It ain't never worked for me yet, but I'm still going to try." The deep pink flooded her cheeks once more. "Usually I dream the same thing."

Mary grinned and began to unpack her trunk, hanging her few gowns on the empty hooks while Holly donned her nightdress and crawled into the creaking rope bed. It seemed far too early to retire, but Holly reminded her that their day began at five A.M.

"And Sarah will be that crabby if we're late! Ain't it going to be exciting, though, seeing the new earl come driving up? I've heard such tales of his goings-on, I declare I'm quite afraid of him."

She chattered on until Mary joined her and blew out the candle. The ropes that held up their thin mattress creaked and groaned with every movement and Mary's heart sank. However would she sneak away?

It seemed an hour before she could make a move, though actually Holly, accustomed to going early to bed and arising before dawn, fell asleep almost instantly. Mary eased herself to the floor as silently as she could, but the creaking of the rope springs roused the other girl.

"Pot's under the bed," Holly muttered groggily, and began to snore.

Mary let out a long breath and donned her

thin cotton wrapper. So far so good, but she
dared not light the candle and stumbled her way
in the dark to the chair under the doorknob. She
managed to get it free quietly. The key
squeaked in the lock and for a moment she
froze. Holly snored on, no doubt feeling secure
for the first time since Belinda's precipitous departure.

Cautiously, Mary opened the door and
slipped out into the corridor. The dank air
reeked of last night's mutton, and the chill of
the uncarpeted floor bit into the soles of her
bare feet. The door scraped shut behind her, the
sound magnified in the echoing hall. Where
there had been faint light in her room from a
tiny, high-up window, here she stood in the
stygian blackness of a tunnel to the underworld.

She felt her way to the head of a staircase—
and stopped. In no way could she force her feet
to carry her down into that yawning pit to the
vast caverns below, now devoid of life. And devoid of nonlife, she hoped. Mary was not fanciful. She told herself so, firmly, but what could
one expect of a Migglesworth filled with stories
of ghostly apparitions roaming the halls? This
would never do, but she was not going down
into the empty kitchen area. At least here in the
servants' corridor, the reassuring sounds of muffled snores filtered from closed doors. She was
not alone.

Mr. Wesson's staircase lay comfortably close
to the green baize doors and she began to creep
along the wall toward it. She traveled forever.
Several times she wondered if she had lost her

way and several times reminded herself how much longer any journey took when one couldn't see where one was going.

She reached her objective at last and paused at the head of Wesson's stairwell. From his closed door came the sonorous, rolling sounds of a basso profundo in the arms of Morpheus. She let out a breath she had unconsciously been holding and, clinging to the banister rail attached to the wall, she inched her way down two long flights to the stone-flagged floor below. A few steps more and she reached the baize doors. There was no latch—they swung easily at her touch—and she stepped out of the blackness of the servants' passage into the Great Hall.

The dim glow from dying embers in the huge hearth made the cavernous chamber seem almost light after the darkness she'd been through. From somewhere, a draft of cold air moved the hanging banners as though a ghostly presence floated by. Mary swallowed. For some reason her tongue had the consistency of a woolen stocking and her heart hammered in her chest.

That was what she heard, her own heart beating—only it raced and the thuds that came faintly to her ears were slow and even. She listened, hard. The sounds came again, unmistakably measured footfalls passing along the open gallery over her head. She looked up, and a faint wavering glow flitted along above the ancient banners. All at once, as never before, she missed Clarence. She was a fool to undertake such a mission alone! She did not believe in ghosts—

and even if she did, suddenly she no longer wished to meet this one, ancestor or not! She'd find the rubies without his help!

As she stood trembling, a hazy cloud took shape in the glow before the hearth, like a wraith drifting upward. She knew it was only a puff of smoke from the dying fire, propelled by the same draft that swayed the banners hanging from the gallery, but somehow it didn't help. She backed through the baize doors, missed Mr. Wesson's stairs, and fled the length of the rough stone passage, pursued by who knew what demons until she found a staircase leading up. She gained her own room, recognizing it because she had not shut the door tightly. She hadn't tried the knob, fearing to wake Holly. She had no such fear now. Her legs had turned to wavering ribbons, her hands shook so she could hardly turn the key after herself, and she replaced the chair with so much noise that Holly raised up sleepily.

"On—only me," Mary reassured her, fighting to keep her voice level. "I—I couldn't find the chamber pot."

"Under the bed," Holly repeated, apparently under the impression that no time had passed. "And mind, it's you as empties it in the morning!"

Mary crawled into the bed, considerably curling her frozen toes away from the other girl's warm body. Now, in comparative safety, she felt shamed by her cowardice and forgave Edgemont for his. It could happen to anyone in that ghostly Great Hall—but it wouldn't happen tomorrow night. She would try again, and this time remain until whoever walked along the gallery had returned to bed. The ghost of the Jacobite? No. Here, tucked into bed, she almost believed it impossible. Or, at any rate, she decided, worthy of further investigation.

She could have sworn she hadn't shut her eyes when she was aroused by a banging on their door and Edgemont's voice shouting without.

" 'Hark! hark! the lark at heaven's gate sings,' " he caroled. " 'My lady sweet, arise.' "

Holly groaned. "How can he be beastly cheerful so early in the morning? I declare, I'm ever so glad I didn't get no E!"

The room was dark and incredibly cold— Mary snuggled down under their quilt while Holly found the tinderbox and lit their one candle. The flickering light brought no sense of warmth.

"Get a move on, ducks, or we'll be all behind like a cow's tail."

Mary sat up, suddenly aware of that odd tingle of excitement that heralds an important event. Her first day at Rushmoreland Castle, yes —but also her first sight of the infamous Rake Halliburton of whom she had heard so much. No, not Halliburton; she must remember he was now Lord Harborough, the earl who owned her castle. But not for long, she told herself grimly. He'd soon waste his fortune and once the rubies were found, she and Clarence could buy back their ancestral home and old Wesson would work for her. The errant thought made her smile. Was that now the height of her ambitions? To lord it over that august personage?

Holly swung her feet to the floor and Mary followed suit, feeling about for her carpet slippers. They chilled her feet and the water in the pitcher on the washstand fairly froze her fingers.

Holly already sat on the edge of the bed pulling on a pair of long black cotton stockings.

"There's Belinda's uniform on the back hook, better put it on. Things being all at sixes and sevens today, no one will think to fit you out."

The uniform turned out to be a somewhat shapeless affair of dove gray cotton, designed to fit a variety of housemaids. However, it could be shaped to Mary's trim figure with the tight strings of the crisply ironed bibbed apron. She splashed her face with cold water in the basin, toweled it dry, and tugged a comb through her dark curls before a tiny scrap of cracked mirror. Once into the uniform and with most of her hair tucked into a ruffled white mobcap, she stood back for Holly's approval.

The girl's eyes opened with surprise. "Coo, you're right pretty in that getup. Much better than that old brown merino you had on last night. It didn't do a thing for your color. You better keep out of our Edgemont's way for sure!"

Mary flushed with pleasure. It had been a long time since she'd received an unsought and honest compliment.

"Do I really look all right? As a housemaid should? I've never worked in a castle before," she confessed. "I don't know how to go on!"

"Same as a house," Holly assured her. "Only bigger and there's more of us to do the work. Not half bad long as there's no guests. The last earl was a quiet man, but I wager there'll be no end of excitement now. We'll see the other side o' life for sure."

She gave her apron a last pat and began to lay out some seeds on the table. "For when we go downstairs," she explained. "These is oats. You put nine grains in your mouth and walk without saying a word until someone speaks the name of a man, and that will be the name of your intended." She sighed. "I never can keep from swallowing some on the steps, so's I don't know if it works, but I keep trying."

"Would you like me to say 'Edgemont' as you walk out the door?" Mary offered.

Holly turned, horrified. "Oh, no, that would never count! It has to be just natural! And there's others here besides him. Oh"—she clapped her hands—"we're going to need a bigger staff if the new earl holds parties! Mr. Wesson will need an under butler and old James will get his big chance. And then there's maids." She ticked them off on her fingers. "Only four of us and Sarah, two in the still room and six in the laundry. And Cook will want more help. Mrs. Greenfield will be wild, she'll have to send to London at once."

"Miss Tibbet—" Mary had begun a recommendation when the door flew open and Sarah bustled in.

"Good, you are up and ready. This will be a very busy day, Holly, for his lordship is due in the afternoon. Take Mary with you and show her what to do. She will be under housemaid and clean the grates in the bedrooms that he might wish to use. Then lay the fires ready, and change the linen on the beds. Mrs. Greenfield will tell you which rooms. Then both of you brush and dust the drawing rooms and the morning room. Amanda and Jane will do the front parlors and the library." She stopped and looked Mary over. "Yes. Thank goodness that flighty Belinda left her uniforms. They will do you very well. Now hop it, girls. Breakfast will be in only two hours and you have a great deal to do."

She hurried out and Mary stared after her openmouthed. "All that before breakfast?"

Holly grinned. "You'll get used to it. Come on, then." She popped the oat grains into her mouth and led the way to the stairs. Halfway down, she chewed up her seeds in disgust as they heard James shouting for the hall-boy.

The day passed in a veritable tornado of work, leaving Mary, as she sank into her seat at the tea table, with a mountain of respect for housemaids. The castle, or at least the portions in current use, stood in readiness down to the last gleaming chamber pot. Mary had begun to think her life centered around chamber pots. These being a duty of the under housemaid, she had washed and polished forty-three, one for every bedroom in the current wing.

The conversation that bandied back and forth was concerned entirely with the notorious Rake Halliburton, his past peccadilloes, athletic tri-

umphs, and his prowess with the ladies. Edgemont proclaimed him a real out-and-outer.

"He's a bang-up fellow," he told the company. "A regular top-of-the-trees. Wait till you
see! He drives his high-perch phaeton random-
tandem."

"What?" Holly set down her cup with a little
splash. "What does that mean?"

Edgemont waved a hand impatiently. "Uni-
corn, you know. A team of three, a pair, and a
leader in front."

"Lord love us," exclaimed Mrs. Beecham, the
cook. "Won't that be a sight! Finish up now, all
of you, for Mr. Wesson wants us every one in
the Great Hall for orders."

"For rehearsal." Holly nodded wisely to
Mary. "We're all to stand in rows and curtsy to
the new earl."

"Aye," murmured Edgemont. " '. . . bear welcome in your eye, your hand, your tongue . . .
but be the serpent under't.' "

They assembled as ordered in the Great Hall,
and Mary took the opportunity to study the
area carefully. The long threadbare banners
moved in the ever-present draft and gusts of
smoke, as like as could be to hazy ghostly forms,
puffed from the huge fireplace. All right, now
she knew what to expect. Tonight's foray would
be successful; no specter would frighten her
away. Any footsteps she heard would be hu-
man. Now, in the bright light of day, it was easy
to ridicule her fears of the night before.

Mr. Wesson entered the hall with his measured tread, his aspect forbidding. He raised a hand for silence.

"I have just," he intoned, "received Distressing News that will affect us all. We have been, I am sure, an Exemplary household up to this point. I sincerely regret to inform you that this will no longer be the case. A Great Change has come upon us." He continued in this vein for some time.

Several people in his audience began to stir and whisper. Immediately behind her, Mary heard Edgemont, sotto voce, for her alone.

" 'He draweth out the thread of his verbosity finer than the staple of his argument.' Why can't he get on with it?"

She glanced at him and met a warm look that brooked no mistake. Apparently he had picked her for his next conquest. Nay, sir! she thought. Mary Migglesworth is not rising to your bait. She has other fish to fry!

Mr. Wesson had reached the meat of his discourse, his emotion bringing him perilously close to apoplexy. "His lordship's First Orders, I am sorry to say, relayed to me by his man of business, were to Remove both the Funeral Hatchment from the entrance and the Black Crepe that tied up the Knocker. His next were to have the Countess's Suite prepared for a—a Guest."

He paused for effect. "His lordship brings with him," he announced in trembling tones, "A Female. I do not say a lady, but one with whom he has Cohabited!"

Mrs. Greenfield squealed in horror and Mr.

Wesson condescended to give her a look of approval.

"An Actress," he went on. "I believe well known on the London stage. She Calls herself Rowena La Fleur." Had he not his dignity to maintain, Mary felt sure he might have spat on the floor.

Edgemont failed to stifle a tiny choke of laughter. "Good for the Rake! 'All hell shall stir for this!' " Fortunately, his words were drowned in the general hubbub.

Mr. Wesson signaled again for silence. "In view of this, I do not intend to call upon my staff to present a Formal Welcome to his lordship. You will all of you remain below stairs or in the Servants' Hall. I alone shall open the door. In this way, we will Demonstrate our Disapproval in a dignified manner. You may be dismissed."

Excited conversation broke out on all sides as the company dispersed. Mary found Edgemont holding her elbow. Mysteriously, he signaled her to drop back beneath the stairs.

" 'A hollow welcome' indeed," he chortled. "I for one do not mean to lie in hiding. Do you want to see the show? I know a point of vantage from which we may view it all."

Mary hesitated and her mischievous spirit got the better of her. Nothing, no nothing at the moment, could be more entertaining than watching Wesson's face as he welcomed the infamous Rake and his equally infamous demimondaine.

Edgemont pointed upward. "Do you see the

place where the upper gallery joins the staircase? Where those heavy drapes meet at the landing? As soon as the hall is empty, slip up there. I'll be waiting."

It smacked of a clandestine rendezvous, but the stakes were too high to resist. This scene she must witness. She nodded her agreement.

Less than an hour later, Mary heard hooves clang and a carriage creak as it bounced on the cobblestones by the entrance. Wesson, supported by James as his second in command, stood peering from one of the front windows awaiting the moment to throw open the great front doors. Their backs were turned, and Mary scurried up one side of the double staircase and joined Edgemont behind the drapes.

As she choked from the dust of the velvet drapes while fending off Edgemont's advances, the great door knocker banged and a bell echoed through the hall. With a stately, pigeon-toed march, Mr. Wesson made his slow way to the entrance. He threw wide the doors and stepped aside. Mary nearly fell onto the landing in her effort to see and Edgemont caught her about the waist. As she disentangled herself, Rake Halliburton—no, she must remember, the Earl of Harborough—walked into the hall.

Her heart pounding, she peered down at him. He came as a shock. Somehow, she had expected to be disappointed, that he would be thin and weedy or perhaps short, but he was neither. He was tall, at least as tall as Mr. Wesson, whom she had considered a giant.

As the new earl handed his butler a driving

coat bearing at least fifteen capes, Mary saw he had a commanding breadth of shoulder. His tailcoat was olive green. He wore tight fawn inexpressibles, and a blue Birds-eye Wipe for a neckcloth. He removed his Bit-of-Blood hat, revealing dark, pomaded curls.

As he looked up and around the Great Hall, Mary had a clear view of his face; he was not at all what she thought of as a ladies' man. She considered Edgemont far handsomer, but the Rake's features were arresting. Heavy black brows over half-lidded eyes that may have been blue, though she couldn't be sure. A beak of a nose, square jaw, and a wide mouth, now drawn downward in an expression of restless boredom. She found him somehow disturbing. Very sensitive to the intrinsic moods of others, she felt in him a kinship with a caged wolf she had once seen in the wild animal exhibit at the Tower of London.

She shivered, recognizing the fatal fascination of a gazetted rake for delicately nurtured females. More than just curiosity, for such a man brought with him a sense of exciting danger best viewed from a distance, safely behind the protective fence of gentility. Mary had no such fence now.

Beside her, Edgemont sighed ecstatically. "Ain't he a sight?" he whispered, squeezing her hand.

A moment later, he forgot Mary's existence, for the Rake turned back, holding out his arm. It was taken, and he led a vision into Wesson's apoplectic presence.

Her beauty was undeniable, despite a garishly painted face and impossible orange hair piled high with orchid ostrich plumes waving in her curls as she moved. Mulberry satin clothed her voluptuous figure, the skirt triple-flounced, her décolletage positively indecent. Coquilicot roses and knots of silver ribbon decked her gown, an emerald green shawl of the finest cashmere looped over her elbows, and long lavender gloves covered half her arms.

"Good God!" Mary gasped.

Edgemont for once was bereft of speech. And not from shock, Mary was amazed to perceive. He gazed at the actress with the stunned expression of one hypnotized. He licked his lips and finally found words.

"She might be the Empress of Rooshia!"

The woman sailed into the hall, acting the part of a great lady, but her first remark shattered the spell.

"A-aow! What a plaice! A genuine palace!"

The Rake let out a burst of laughter. "Well, of course it is. What did you expect?" Amusement transformed his sardonic face. That wide mouth was made for laughter and his shadowed eyes lit up with genuine humor. All at once, Mary saw what made him so attractive to the female sex.

Rowena La Fleur turned to Wesson, once more the grande dame, and made an enemy for life.

"Hey, you—cully! Bring up me trunks. To the countess's sweet, *if* you please."

They headed up the stairs, directly past Mary and the infatuated Edgemont. Mary shrank back into the shadows, but Edgemont remained where he stood, visible to the oncoming pair. The Rake went by unseeing, but Rowena La Fleur had sharp eyes for a handsome man. Her full red lips curved and she lowered one eye in a broad, inviting wink. Mary felt Edgemont tremble beside her as he watched her retreating figure.

"Gawd," he breathed. "Did you ever?"

"No," Mary agreed. "I certainly never did."

Mary and Edgemont weren't the only surreptitious watchers. When they reached the lower halls, the story of Rowena, and Wesson's reactions to her, spread rapidly once the butler was out of earshot. James had been sent for the trunks and, Edgemont not being handy, he had to call the hall-boy, odd-job man, and the coachman to help carry them in. He was somewhat bitter about Edgemont's absence, but it was nothing compared to Edgemont's chagrin on learning that James had been in her boudoir and received a gold crown for his labors.

It was well after two in the morning when Holly quieted down, and she fell asleep before Mary climbed into bed. And why should she climb in? Holly snored gently and Mary recognized her opportunity. Pulling on her cotton wrapper and slipping her feet into her carpet slippers, she blew out the candle and pocketed the tinderbox. Silently, she opened the door and crept out. If she were caught, she'd say she couldn't sleep and had come down for a book.

She made the trip to the Great Hall easily, now being familiar with the stairs and passages, but she had to summon her courage to cross the cavernous room. She made her way to the door that Edgemont had pointed out as the entrance to the library. She stepped inside to meet a dim glow of light.

A single candle guttered in a candelabrum on a table near the dying fire. Had Mr. Wesson forgotten to extinguish it? Or was that the duty of one of the housemaids—Jane or Amanda—who might get in trouble? She had best snuff it before she left.

But now—there above the mantel hung a case with a glass front. It was dark inside, but the flickering firelight caught tiny gleams of gold. The settings! The tangible proof that her rubies really existed! She drew closer, holding her candle high to light the case—and screamed as something moved in the huge winged chair before the hearth.

Not the ghost but a man! He rose and turned toward her, the failing candle lighting his face from below and giving him the features of a satyr. He swayed and caught at the back of the chair to steady himself.

Mary stifled another scream. She stood face-to-face with the notorious Rake Halliburton. And he was very, very drunk.

Chapter Four

Mary shrank back, the lurid tales she had heard of the Rake's corruption scattering her very wits. She was at his mercy! What would he do to her? Alone in the wee hours of the night, with a reprobate—and she belonged to him! She'd have no recourse—she a lowly housemaid in his establishment, and he her lord and master . . . She backed toward the door.

Lord Harborough sank down on the arm of his chair. His half-lidded eyes took in her uniform and mobcap. "A housemaid—at this hour? Are you sent to clear up after your drunken master?"

Mary shook her head, struck dumb with fear, and reached for the door handle behind her.

"Come here." His voice was soft, gentle, only slightly blurred by the brandy from the decanter by his side.

Mary hesitated. Could he catch her if she ran? Should she hit him with the candelabrum? No! That would extinguish the candle, the only light.

He grinned, wickedly, and his deep-set eyes crinkled with the humor she had noticed before. He raised a hand, pointing a wavering finger. "You," he pronounced his words with care, "are afraid of me."

"Y–yes, my lord."

"You needn't be. I am a gentleman now, haven't you heard? Everyone keeps telling me so. Mustn't chase housemaids. Mustn't visit the dressing rooms at the Opera House. Mustn't—mustn't—I've forgotten the rest. But I showed them. I brought Rowena with me." He chuckled. "Have you seen Rowena?"

"Yes, my lord."

He chuckled again, and fell backward into the seat of the chair. "Come here, my pretty little housemaid. Sit with me awhile. Come and talk to me."

"No—I'd rather not, my lord. I—I have to go."

For a moment his expression turned ugly. "No, you don't. You're my housemaid. You do as I say. Sit in that chair. Right here by me." Suddenly his mischievous grin reappeared, daring her. "I'm harmless tonight."

Mary moved toward the seat, her courage returning. He was far too foxed to run after her and she felt sure she could be out the door before he was out of the deep chair.

"I just want to talk," he went on, a wistful note in his deep voice. "I want to talk to somebody—somebody who doesn't matter. I want to be just me. Sit. Please."

She sat.

"That's the barber." He regarded her through sleepy eyes. "I like looking at you. You look nice. Do you know, I don't believe I know any nice females. You are nice, are you not?"

Surprised into speech, she answered firmly, "Yes, my lord."

"My lord!" He sneered. "I'm a great lord now, am I not? Harborough. Hah. Do you know what my beloved family used to call me?" He opened his eyes wide, owlishly, and shook his head. "Not fit for a female's ears."

There seemed nothing to say to him but, "Yes, my lord." Really, she felt in a conversational rut —and not a little nervous. How long would he keep her here?

"Don't call me 'my lord,' " he ordered. "My friends call me Rake. Be my friend."

Mary objected to this. "It's hardly a word for a lady to use, my lord."

"Oh, but it's all right for a housemaid. And you are a housemaid. My housemaid."

"Yes, my lord."

He glowered. "I said to call me Rake or we shall come to cuffs!"

"Yes, my—Rake."

"That's better." He leaned back and closed his eyes. Mary glanced at the door. "Rake," he repeated. "Much better. You call me Rake—at least when we're alone. It's not a nickname to make one proud, but it's what I've become accustomed to—and no one now will use it."

"It—it is hardly proper for the Earl of Harborough."

"It is proper for me." He opened his eyes and they were suspiciously bright in the dim light from the fading candle. "I miss it—I miss the freedom it stands for. Can you understand that, my little housemaid? Can you not see how I feel? 'Cabin'd, cribb'd, confined!' "

Mary stared at him, startled to hear him quote Edgemont's favorite playwright.

He waved a sweeping arm. "It makes me want

to break out and do something truly outrageous
—only with my reputation, nothing I do will
shock a soul. My hands are bound. I am one
'. . . so incensed that I am reckless what I do to
spite the world!' "

"Good God, my lord—I mean, Rake—have
you already been associating with Edgemont?"

"Who?"

"That was Macbeth, was it not? You will have
to make the acquaintance of your second footman. I perceive you have similar tastes."

He seemed to have already forgotten the subject and was pouring himself another glass of
brandy. To Mary, the whole scene began to take
on a fairy-tale quality, but his next words
brought her back down to earth.

"I'll show them." He gestured with the glass.
"Do you know what we're doing, little housemaid? We're sitting on a treasure. Rubies! A
king's ransom, and I'm going to find them. What
do you think of that?"

Mary thought quite a bit of it, but he didn't
wait for her to speak.

"And do you know what I'm going to do
when I find them, my pretty little housemaid?
I'll hang them all on Rowena and see how my
damned family likes that!"

He slumped down in his chair and Mary, silently vowing he'd do no such thing, jumped up
and caught the tipping glass from his hand.

"My lord—"

He roused briefly. "Rake."

"Yes, my lord—Rake. You've had enough. You
should be in bed, my lord, and so should I."

He ogled her. "With me?"

"No, my lord."

He nodded. "Just as well. Only spoil a beautiful friendship. You are my friend, aren't you? My only friend in this devilish castle. Do you know where my bed is? I seem to have forgotten."

Mary knew, having changed his sheets and washed the chamber pot. She lit her candle from the one guttering out in the candelabrum.

"Come along, my lord—Rake. I'll show you where you sleep."

She helped him from the chair and partially supported him out of the library and up the stairs, managing to spill hot wax on most of the treads as she went. When they reached his room, he fell over the bed, facedown. Exasperated, she put down her candle and struggled with his booted legs until she managed to get most of him up onto the mattress. There was no way she could loosen his coat or remove his boots.

She left him and made her way, taking only a few wrong turns, back to her room and the sleeping Holly. It was nearly time for the servants to be up and she had a lot to think about. She didn't have the Jacobite's book, but it could wait until the morrow, she told herself, and crawled into the creaking bed.

She awoke barely two hours later, startled out of a dream. The Jacobite and his Beatrix were leading her to the rubies and just as she reached for them, Edgemont banged on their door with a cheery shout of "Bring out your dead!"

She barely heard Holly's chatter as she
dragged on her uniform for another long day.
The events of the night before kept churning in
her mind. Uppermost for some odd reason was
the fact that Lord Harborough's eyes were blue
—and he'd asked her to be his friend. The man
was drunk as a wheelbarrow, to borrow a phrase
from Clarence's colorful vocabulary. He hadn't
meant a word of it, of course, but what a different view she now held of the dangerous Rake
Halliburton!

She shook off such thoughts. He was after her
rubies and therefore an enemy—and one to be
reckoned with. After all, he owned Rushmoreland and he no doubt believed he owned the
rubies also. The sooner she found the Jacobite's
copy of the *Iliad,* secured the stones, and escaped
with them, the better. It never entered her mind
that she might fail—or if it did, she buried the
thought.

Her dream returned to her, vividly, when she
tried to remember it, except that the faces of the
Jacobite and Beatrix were now vague blurs, although she had recognized them in her dream at
once.

James said the Jacobite walked in the Long
Gallery because the portrait of his wife was
there. Mary's heart thumped suddenly. Beatrix
—her great-grandmother. She had to see her! All
her life she had known the sad story and as a
child she'd woven daydreams with happier end-
ings for the bereaved woman who had lost husband, home, and heritage at one blow of the
executioner's ax. And now she *could* see her!

As soon as she could escape her duties, she sneaked away and ran up to the third floor, only to encounter Mr. Wesson at his most formidable. Edgemont stood before him, looking innocent. The butler broke off in mid-expostulation when he saw her coming down the passage.

"Ah, Mary, is it not? Yes." He nodded as she bobbed a nervous curtsy. "I hear from Sarah that you are Doing Well. I hope," he intoned heavily, "that you Intend to Stay with us. Very Few maids remain here long. They listen to Foolish Tales from the villagers until soon their Overactive Imaginations create Specters in every dark Shadow."

Edgemont, who had been mimicking Mr. Wesson's facial expressions behind his back, declaimed in an eerie voice, "We are '. . . haunted by the ghosts they have depos'd.' "

Mr. Wesson so far forgot himself as to tell Edgemont to button his trap. Remembering his dignity, he drew himself up and stalked off in a huff.

"Coo!" said Mary, playing her part as a housemaid. "Ain't you afraid of being fired off?"

Edgemont flicked a speck of dust from his livery sleeve. "Not me. Old Wesson don't like me, but he knows I can put up a front as elegant as ever he can, and he thinks I add a touch of class to his hall. I do, you know." He preened himself a bit. "I'd soon outrank the plebeian James, could I but control my impudence. What are you doing up here, my girl? Isn't this somewhat out of your way?"

"I'm looking for the Long Gallery. I wanted to see the big pictures."

He made her a courtly bow, gesturing down the corridor. "Pass then, fair one. Until your return I will but 'dwindle, peak and pine.' "

Mary told him coyly not to be an old silly and hurried along. It did not occur to her in time to ask him how he came to be upstairs. A minute later, she walked into the gallery and stopped, overwhelmed, Edgemont forgotten.

The gallery was truly long, at least three hundred feet by perhaps forty wide. Tall, narrow windows flanked by wine-velvet drapes separated the over-life-size portraits in their heavily carved gold-leafed frames. The inner wall was solid, broken here and there by great unused hearths. More paintings hung between the fireplaces, a mural-size battle scene, men in lace and satin standing by elegant horses, and ladies in shimmering gowns.

One space was vacant as though a painting had been removed. Mary walked toward the empty space, curious, and then the huge portrait next to it caught and held her eyes.

She stared up into her own face.

The Countess Beatrix. She had no need to read name and date on the bronze plaque attached to the ornamental frame. She moved closer, irresistibly drawn to the lovely dark-haired lady—for Beatrix had been painted wearing the Rushmoreland rubies.

A tiara, necklace, earrings, bracelets, and brooches gleamed from the canvas. Mary tried to count the stones and lost track.

Pigeon-blood red, they were depicted so real-
istically that they glowed and lit up the painting. Catching her breath, she stepped close to
examine a huge ruby pendant surrounded by diamonds. Never had she beheld such beauty. She
knew a moment of real regret that they would
have to be sold—but never would they deck
that orange-haired hussy! A wave of fury rose
in her breast at the thought of her rubies on a
commoner like Rowena La Fleur. The Rake
should not have them! Looking up at Beatrix,
she swore to her, quoting her father's favorite
lines from Homer.

" 'The day shall come, the great avenging day
—which Troy's proud glories in the dust shall
lay!' "

And behind her, a deep, amused voice completed the couplet. " 'When Priam's powers and
Priam's self shall fall—and one prodigious ruin
swallow all.' And am I Priam, my well-read
housemaid? Is that a reference to my ruinous
career?"

Mary gasped and shrank back. Lord Harborough stood a bare yard away. His eyes were still
blue, she realized hazily, though now more than
a trifle bloodshot. She tried to recover her lost
ground.

"Me lord, I never knew you was come in!"

"Oh, no." He shook his head, then held it between both hands and moaned before he spoke
again. "I seem to recall that you promised to call
me Rake, not my lord—and what has happened
to bring such a vulgar accent to your tongue?
You spoke as a lady last night."

"I didn't think you'd remember!" Mortified by her carelessness, she realized she had once more forgotten to guard her tongue.

"And what is a housemaid doing quoting Homer?"

For a second, Mary felt petrified. Homer! Could he know the secret of the letter? No, how could he?

Lord Harborough folded his arms and leaned his shoulders against the wall in the empty space next to Beatrix and regarded her. She fought to control a rising panic.

"You are out of place, my child. How does a lady of your quality come to be working as a domestic?"

He didn't know! She sagged, relieved. *To steal back my rubies,* she thought. What else? But this she could not say.

"It is quite simple, my lord—"

"Rake."

She ignored the interruption. "I am in sadly reduced circumstances, my lord, and obliged to take any employment I can find, not having the training to become a governess."

"You promised me," he accused. "I thought you at least would stand my friend."

She looked up, questioning his words, and for a moment lost herself in his smiling gaze.

"Rake," he supplied. "We are alone, you know."

Her face must have changed expression, for his mischievous little-boy grin spread across his face. "I never seduce friends."

Now her face flamed and she turned away,

wishing she hadn't such fluctuating color. Or at least that she could converse only with gentlemen. Without thinking, she said these last words aloud, and he threw back his head and roared with happy laughter, only to groan and press both hands again to his forehead.

"Don't do that," he complained. "I am not exactly in plump currant this morning."

Mary regained her composure. "You drank too much last night."

"You needn't tell me, I know. I wasn't feeling happy." He looked down at her, a growing wonder in his eyes. "I am, now. I like being with someone with whom I can be myself instead of continually striving to preserve my image. Why do I feel this way about you?"

"Probably because I do not give a snap for your image. You have no need to impress me, my lord."

"Rake," he interposed mechanically. "That must be it. You don't care that I am a disreputable lord, do you? My little housemaid, you do not know your place and I am very glad of it. But what is your place? You are obviously quality born and well educated."

"And penniless," she finished for him. "And quality cannot be sold for food and shelter."

"It can, but you would not, I can see." He grinned again. "If ever two beings were reversed! You and Rowena. A lady in the scullery and a scullery maid for her mistress!"

Mary flared up at this. "I am a housemaid, I am not in the scullery."

"But you do admit you are a lady!"

She clamped her lips shut, and turned back to the portrait of Beatrix. It would never do for him to start investigating her background. Already she had given away too much.

He followed her gaze. "Quite something, are they not? I mean to turn this castle upside down, brick by brick if need be, for the pleasure of seeing my family when Rowena wears those rubies."

Mary, her eyes on the glory of red jewels against the dark beauty of the Countess Beatrix, suddenly succumbed to a fit of the giggles at the picture Rowena would present.

"Oh, surely you must not, my lord! Can you not see? Rubies with that orange hair!"

He laughed outright. "Henna, bleach, and rubies. By God, she will look a clown!" He glanced down at Mary's charming face. "But you—you are the one to wear them. With your dark curls and sapphire eyes, the effect would be sensational!"

Feeling her quixotic color rise, Mary turned away, but he swung her back, looking from her to the portrait.

"By the gods, you'd look exactly like the Jacobite's wife!"

Mary froze in sudden panic, but he dropped his hands.

"It's criminal of me, I know it. Rowena has no business wearing jewels that belong to a countess. She isn't cut out to be a lady."

He paced a few feet down the gallery, and returned to her side. "I erred," he admitted, "in bringing her to the ancestral castle only to spite my family. Never seek revenge, my pretty housemaid. It drives you to make a fool of yourself. But I cannot back down now. I promised Rowena that if she came with me, she would be a lady and some day wear the Rushmoreland rubies. Whatever faults I have, I keep my promises. Besides, Rowena is a good sort and she deserves to get back a bit of her own."

But not my rubies, Mary vowed again silently. Tonight she'd get that book and translate the clues. She'd been here far too long already. The fact that for some reason she would regret leaving Rushmoreland—and its rakish earl—she refused to accept.

Harborough broke into her thoughts, suddenly visited by inspiration.

"You—" he began. "What is your name, anyway?"

This time she was prepared. "Mary Migglesworth," she said, holding her head high.

He gave her a startled look. "Good God. Well, no matter. Mary–whatever, you are no longer a housemaid!"

"What? Why—what do you mean?"

"You have just become a lady's maid. I promised Rowena she should have a personal abigail and you will be ideal. Perhaps you can teach her to speak and act in an acceptable manner in company and relieve part of my shame. Come, I'll take you at once to your new mistress!"

He grabbed her hand and pulled her along the gallery toward the stairs before she could reply. Down one flight, they approached Rowena's drawing room and Lord Harborough paused outside as they heard a male voice respond to the actress's shrill laugh.

"She has a guest. Wait here, Mary, while I see who it is."

He entered, leaving the door wide and Mary standing on the threshold. The visitor had his back turned, but she detected something familiar in the set of his shoulders and the gorgeousness of his raiment. He was a true Pink of the ton. His coat boasted long tails and a nipped-in waist, with sleeves gathered at the top and peaked upward with wadding. The brilliant yellow of his skintight stockinette pantaloons contrasted vividly with the pale mauve of his coat. His starched shirt points were so high he could not turn his head and when he stepped around to greet Lord Harborough, she was treated to all the splendor of his embroidered waistcoat. It rioted with color: rose, purple, and royal blue, embellished with saucer-size basket-work buttons of silver. A single huge jewel—not a ruby —glinted in his snowy neckcloth.

Mary was in no position to appreciate his magnificence. She recoiled in horror as she stared at her father's raffish crony, Sir Archibald Andover.

Would he know her? She pulled the ruffles on her mobcap down to hide as much of her face as possible. There was a slim chance he might not recognize her at once, for Clarence had always sent her upstairs when Andover's like was to be present at one of his card sessions. She knew him mainly as a figure to be peered at from between the rails of the landing banister—but he might have seen her on the rare occasions she walked in the park with her father or shopped with him on Bond Street. For some reason she made no attempt to fathom, it was quite important that the Rake should not know she could be acquainted with such a libertine.

She need not have feared. Andover was far too absorbed in playing off the airs of an Exquisite for Rowena's benefit to notice the presence of a mere servant.

"Well, Andover! What the devil brings you here?"

The Rake strode forward, greeting him as an old friend, and Mary was struck by the change in the man. He swaggered, his attitude that of a supercilious care-for-nobody; his mouth was drawn down in a smile that more closely resembled a sneer; and his eyes, so open and laughing only minutes before, drooped with ineffable boredom. *This* was his image? The guise he felt obliged to present to the world? No wonder he had such a reputation! The man underneath, the one she knew from the library and the Long Gallery, was far more to her taste. A bit too much to her taste, in fact. The sooner she left Rushmoreland Castle the better for her peace of mind!

He had taken Andover's extended hand and given it a limp, perfunctory shake. "What are you doing here anyway, you gudgeon? I'm meeting you for lunch in less than an hour!"

Andover took a step backward, spreading both arms. "But behold! I have come to take you up in my chariot! And incidentally"—he dropped his pose—"to take a gander at this bounteous windfall of yours."

Rowena unfurled a chicken-skin fan and flourished it. "Ain't it grand? Never have I laid eyes on so many rooms! But dark! And that gloomy! What this plaice needs is some cheery furnishings."

Andover sat down on the sofa beside her, gallantly kissing her fingers. "And you shall have them, my pet, if I have any say in the matter. What about it, Harborough? Thought you might be doing up the apartments for your little lady and perhaps you'd like a guiding hand."

"Harborough, that would do me a treat!" Rowena peeked up at the Rake over her fan and simpered. "Do let's! Andover has a real turn for such matters, knowing as he does what's in fashion in all the great houses."

The Rake shrugged. "As you will. I daresay the rooms could use a new touch."

"Then it's settled." Andover slapped his knee. "Suppose I move in tomorrow and spend a few days looking it over?"

Rowena squealed with delight. "Do, ducks. I've been that tedious here you wouldn't believe. You'll bring a bit o' life into the place!"

Slouching to a chair, the Rake seated himself and raised his eyebrows at Andover. "What, are you not afraid of our ghost?"

"Ghost!" Rowena shrieked, and he laughed—but not the happy sound Mary had heard in the gallery.

"Yes, my dear, I'm told I've inherited one.

They say the Jacobite we deposed walks the halls swearing vengeance on all usurpers."

Rowena gasped and rose slowly to her feet.

The Rake waved a languid hand. "Sit down, you silly wench. I'm only hoaxing. There is no truth in the tale."

"But I have heard it too." Andover shook his head. "Nothing in it, of course," he assured Rowena. "An old wives' tale meant to frighten off treasure hunters. They were his rubies, you know."

Rowena rallied at that. "My rubies," she declared. "Harborough has promised them to me."

Out in the hall, Mary clenched her fists and gritted her teeth, striving to keep silent and not give vent to her feelings. How she'd love to tell that painted jade a few home truths!

"The way I heard it," Andover went on, "he's not after vengeance but only searching the bedrooms for his wife so that he can tell her where he hid the stones."

He did tell her; Mary hugged the knowledge to herself. *He told her, and now I shall find them, for rightfully they belong to me.*

"Well." Inside the room, the Rake crossed his long legs at the ankles and settled back. "Then I shall certainly wait up for him and try to worm out his secret."

Rowena reached across and slapped his wrist with her fan. "Have done, both of you. I know you're bamming me, but you're making me that nervous I shan't sleep a wink!"

"Aye," Andover agreed. "Enough to make

one's blood run cold. Moaning and footsteps, you know. All humdugeon, of course."

The Rake grinned. "Then you're coming to stay? Sure you wouldn't be afraid to spend the night here—say in the Long Gallery?"

"Of course I would," Andover answered promptly. "Afraid of catching an inflammation of the lungs in this drafty barrack."

"A-aow, no!" Rowena hastened to reassure him seriously. "We have a fire in every bedroom. A real palace, this. Good as the best hotel! Now, what are you laughing at, Harborough? You know I speak truth!"

Andover got to his feet and bent to kiss her hand. "Till tomorrow, fair fatality. I shall be with you, bag and baggage, by teatime."

Mary slid away down the hall, looking frantically for cover. Before she could escape, the Rake appeared at the door and called her name. Mentally commending her chances to fate, she pretended to adjust her mobcap, in order to hide her face, and walked past the departing Andover as casually as she could. To her immense relief, he didn't spare her a glance.

The Rake winked at Mary as she entered. "Here she is, Rowena, the maid I promised you."

Mary curtsied. "Good day, madam. I shall endeavor to do my best while in your service."

Obviously impressed by Mary's language and ladylike bearing, Rowena beamed at her.

"Eh, but you must have worked in a real quality house!"

"Yes, madam," Mary replied with truth, "I have."

Rowena leaned forward confidentially. "Dearie, I don't mind saying—on the quiet, now —I'm not regularly at home here. You have real class manners. Mayhap you could give me some pointers now and again, like what your former mistresses wore when they stepped out and how they went on."

"Yes, madam, I will do my best." Mary curtsied again, having noted that the action went over far better with Rowena La Fleur than with Mr. Wesson. In fact, that lady seemed highly pleased.

Rowena dismissed Mary with instructions to return in time to dress her for dinner, and Mary, deciding she'd best find Sarah and tell her of this development, headed for the servants' area. She would not be sorry to see the last of those chamber pots.

Below stairs, when her new situation was learned, Mary was amazed by the enormous step upward she had taken in the domestic hierarchy. No longer would she dine in the Servants' Hall with Sarah, Holly, and the footmen. They clustered about, regarding her with a new respect.

"You are now Miss Migglesworth to us," Sarah explained with a touch of envy.

Mary sighed. Drat Clarence! She might have known that name would come and haunt her!

Holly knew more than envy. She hugged Mary, near tears. "Amanda and Jane will be that angry!" she wailed. "They don't care a bit for three in a bed, but they cannot expect me to sleep alone!"

"But I'm not leaving," said Mary, astonished. "I'm only changing positions."

"Oh, but you can't sleep with a housemaid now!" Holly wiped at her eyes with the corner of her apron. "You're an upper servant, quite one of the upperest. Why"—she stepped back, round-eyed with awe—"you'll sup in the Housekeeper's Room and you'll go in right after Mr. Wesson and Mrs. Greenfield. And on the arm of Mr. Guimper!"

"Who on earth is that?"

"He's valet to the earl! Oh, Mary, you are now too great to speak to the likes of me."

"Aye," put in Edgemont. " 'Forever and forever, farewell. If we do meet again, why we shall smile.' "

Mary did smile. "I am no longer Juliet? Now it's—Cassius, is it not?"

He kissed her hand, for once serious. "Truly, I shall miss you at our revels. No one else speaks or understands my language in this abode of ignorance."

"Take heart." Mary retrieved the hand he seemed reluctant to release. "You must associate more with your new master. He also is conversant with your bard."

Edgemont's eyebrows rose. "Rake Halliburton? A scholar? That I cannot accept!"

"He's not at all what you think." Mary flew hotly to his defense, and caught herself wondering why. "He—he has had an excellent education." A lame finish she knew, and far from what she could have told.

All eyes, she saw, were upon her. Edgemont broke a growing silence. "How come you to know so much about the man?"

Mary felt her betraying color rise. "I—I had opportunity to observe him while in attendance on my mistress. He seemed most intelligent." She nearly added, "In contrast to Rowena La Fleur."

Sarah helped her gather together her few possessions. "Belinda's uniforms will never do for you now; leave them for the next girl." She frowned. "Mrs. Greenfield will be in a great state, replacing you so soon. Have you nothing in black? Well, your gray uniform must make do for now. No doubt Mrs. Greenfield will see to dressing you properly in a few days. Come along, I'll show you to your room. James will see to having your trunk moved."

She led Mary to the opposite wing and up to the third floor where she opened the door to a rather charming tiny cubbyhole—containing a single bed. So she was to have a room all to herself! Mary fairly hugged herself with glee. This would simplify her search immensely. Tonight, for sure, she could look for Pope's translation.

Sarah pointed out a bell that hung over the door. "This room is directly above the countess's suite and the bell cord goes inside the wall and down to the bedroom so that the—the occupant may summon you at any hour."

At Mary's urgent request, Sarah showed her

the way to Rowena's quarters before leaving her.

"Dinner for the family is at eight o'clock, Mary—I mean Miss Migglesworth. You must be here to dress Miss La Fleur by seven at the latest. Then come to the Housekeeper's Room for your own meal. No doubt your mistress will require your assistance upon retiring, so you will wait for her here in your room until she rings."

Alone at last, Mary sank down on her new bed to make plans for her evening. A candle and tinderbox sat on her table, ready to hand. Now if only the hours would speed by! Even as she thought, the bell began to ring.

Helping Miss La Fleur to dress for a simple dinner at home came as a revelation to Mary, whose wardrobe could only be called sparse. Satins, laces, brocades, and lustrings crowded gowns of crepe and gauze in Rowena's dressing room. It was with some difficulty that she persuaded Rowena to don a fairly simple robe of figured nile green satin over a ruffled undergown of creamy net.

"Surely," she explained with what diplomacy she could muster, "you will wish to save your more formal attire for the many dinners and balls over which you must soon preside."

"Lawks, dearie, you are quite right." Rowena handed back a beaded demi-robe. "I declare, you are going to be a real treasure. I would have brought along me old dresser from the theater, but she wouldn't leave the show. Born and bred on the boards, she was, and grown old in the business." She heaved a melancholy sigh. "I miss her that you wouldn't believe." Mercurially, she cheered. "But I see you'll do fine, ducks."

After talking her out of wearing the entire contents of her jewelry box, Mary sent her flamboyant charge down to the dining room with only a rope of pearls and an emerald brooch adorning her gown. Except for her orange hair and painted face, she appeared almost respectable. As Mary went along to her own meal, she wondered what the Rake would think of her labors.

The cuisine of the Housekeeper's Room far exceeded that of the evening before, but she found dining under the austere eyes of Mr. Wesson a chilling experience. In that rarefied atmosphere, she missed the cheery chatter of the Servants' Hall. Only Mr. Guimper, who accepted her as his social equal, seemed inclined to friendly banter, but he soon subsided under Wesson's quelling gaze. Mary slipped away as quickly as she could, once more on the excuse of unpacking. Thank goodness, she'd not be here long.

Perhaps, this very evening . . .

It was late before Mary finally settled Rowena for the night. The Rake did not put in an appearance and Mary felt an inordinate relief at not having to see the pair together in a bedchamber. Rowena apparently had a different feeling. She was pettish as Mary brushed out her orange curls and scarcely spoke a word other than to complain of a tangle. The warming pan passed between her silken sheets should have been warmer, and Amanda, whose duty it was, received a sharp scold and retired in tears. Mary felt herself lucky to be summarily dismissed after blowing out the candles.

For nearly an hour she sat in her room waiting for all sounds in the castle to cease. Then, taking candlestick and tinderbox, she crept out and down the massive split staircase, heading for the library.

A beam of light came from the dining room door. She paused, uncertain, then tried to slip by in the dark, only to be accosted by Edgemont in a rollicking mood. He stood by the sideboard, draining the last of a decanter of brandy.

"What?" he cried. "A maid unafraid of our ghost? Ah, well, 'Some say no evil thing that walks by night . . . hath hurtful power o'er true virginity.'"

Mary's galloping heart began to quiet. "Good God, you frightened me more than any ghost! Is that more Shakespeare? I don't recognize those lines."

"Well, no," Edgemont apologized, tilting up the decanter to drain the last drops. "Merely words of Milton, but so appropriate. Perhaps our last housemaid lacked the necessary chastity."

Mary perceived him to be a trifle on the go and forgave his lack of reticence. In fact, she saw reason to encourage it. He seemed in a talkative mood.

"Tell me," she coaxed, "what exactly happened to her? What did she see?"

He replaced the empty decanter and tried another. "Our host has an uncommon capacity for after-dinner brandy."

"The ghost," Mary prompted.

He succeeded this time in obtaining almost half a glass and leaned back on the sideboard, contented and ready for conversation. "Why, she claimed to have encountered the Jacobite in the Long Gallery close on midnight. All cloaked in white, she said, and he walked toward her moaning 'Beatrix . . . Beatrix . . .' He then disappeared, she said, fading right into the portrait of his wife."

Mary shivered, all at once in the grip of that uncanny sensation said to be caused by someone walking on one's grave.

"Silly girl fainted on the spot," Edgemont finished. "She left first thing in the morning."

"But what in the world was she doing up there at that hour of the night?"

Edgemont balanced his now-empty glass on the edge of the sideboard. "Well, as a matter of fact, she had come to meet me. Luckily, I heard her shriek while I was still on the stairs. I knew she'd rouse the house so I hid on the landing until old Wesson had trotted by."

Mary eyed him with some skepticism. "Did you believe her? That she really saw the Jacobite? You don't seem to be afraid to walk the halls at night. Has no attempt been made to lay this ghost?"

"What, and destroy a tradition? We take pride

in the tenacity of the old gentleman. Except for a rapid turnover in maids, he gives us no trouble. Never seen him myself. Old Wesson claims our ghost is a figment of overactive imaginations, but you know what?" He leaned toward her confidentially, breathing brandy fumes in her face. "You know what? He keeps a loaded shotgun by his bed and says he'll blow a hole through our specter should he dare to penetrate his quarters."

A sudden gust of laughter convulsed him. "Wouldn't I like to see fat old Wesson chasing a ghost through the halls!"

Mary giggled. It was an appealing thought.

Edgemont pulled down his waistcoat and straightened with dignity. "I must leave you, fair one. 'The deep of night is crept upon our talk, and nature must obey necessity.'"

As he spoke, a blast of gunfire echoed through the Great Hall.

Chapter Five

Dashing out of the dining room after Edgemont, Mary ran directly into the Rake, who had come bursting from the library. He stared at her —and then at Edgemont, and she felt her color rise. He turned away abruptly as excited shouts came from the servants' passage and the Great Hall suddenly filled with people.

Down the broad curving staircase, stepping with lordly tread in a pool of candlelight, came an apparition. Wesson, his vast bulk cloaked in a tentlike dressing gown of wine velvet splashed with orange flowers, carried before him an ancient fowling piece in one hand and a branched candelabrum in the other. Hot on his heels came Rowena, clutching a purple negligee over her rose-colored nightdress. Like the audience at a melodrama, the assembled company stared up.

The Rake broke the fascinated silence. "What the devil is going on?"

Rowena dashed past Wesson and threw herself into Harborough's arms. "Burglars!" she shrieked. "Murderers!"

Wesson continued his stately passage to the foot of the stairs, where he placed the candelabrum on a table.

"I heard Furtive Sounds, my lord, on the back stairs. Suspecting a Miscreant, I took up my gun and followed someone up to the Long Gallery." Carried away by his story, Wesson abandoned capitals. "There I seen him, my lord, plain as a pikestaff, in the moonlight from the window. All garbed in white, he was, and when he turned at me, I fired. I fear I must have missed for he vanished."

Edgemont nodded. "Into the portrait, like Belinda said. 'Vex not his ghost: O! let him pass!' "

Rowena promptly screamed, clutched at the Rake, and fainted theatrically in his arms.

"King Lear," Edgemont explained. "Thought it suited."

Remembering her new province, Mary ran to Rowena's side and helped his lordship carry her to a settee, where she lay, moaning and rolling her beautiful eyes.

Relieved of his burden, the Rake rounded on Wesson, furious. "Now look what you've done! Shooting at shadows! You might have hit someone and I'm damned sure you've severely damaged the wainscoting! Put that beastly cannon away!"

"If you say so, my lord." Wesson cradled his gun, his tone injured. "I was only acting Pursuant to my Duty."

"Well." Somewhat mollified as Mrs. Greenfield came to Mary's aid and released him from the job of reviving Rowena, the Rake looked up into the dark staircase. "If there's anyone up there, we'd better find out. Take James and—and that one." He pointed at Edgemont. "Search the rooms."

Wesson picked up the candelabrum, shouldered his gun, and beckoned imperiously. The trio ascended to the upper gallery.

No one seemed to want to leave the Great

Hall. They milled about, waiting for the three men to return. Rowena, sitting up shakily, professed her intention of never returning to her room alone and pouted when Harborough suggested in that case Mary should sleep on a cot in her dressing room.

It was some time before Wesson and his satellites returned, announcing that they found no one. A check of the ground floor assured that all doors and windows were bolted.

"Too much port before bedtime," the Rake diagnosed, thoroughly insulting Wesson. "Enough, let's have no more freaks this night. You may all return to your quarters."

Mary caught his eyes resting on her. She and Edgemont were the only ones other than himself still dressed in their daytime attire and she felt the heat rise in her cheeks again. Surely when he saw her come out of the dining room with Edgemont he must have thought the worst —but what could she say?

He frowned and turned back to reassuring Rowena. His arm about her slender waist, he took up a branch of candles and led her toward the stairs. Mary watched them go, an unwelcome sinking sensation in the pit of her stomach.

Everyone began to depart for their rooms, seemingly disappointed that the evening's entertainment ended on such a tame note. Wesson went stiffly, muttering to himself, trailed by his staff. Mary followed the Rake and Rowena and, as Rowena cheerfully dismissed her, continued up another flight in the darkness to her own

room. Never mind, she told herself sternly. You
are here for only one purpose, and you'd best
stick to it, buckle and thong. But she found herself victim to unease. It would no longer be a
simple task. If Wesson were going to prowl
about the halls with his shotgun at night, it
would somewhat hamper her activities.

There were no more provocations that night.
In the morning, after a breakfast in the Housekeeper's Room, Mary went in search of her mistress to complete her dressing for the day. As
she hurried along the second-floor corridor,
male voices below in the Great Hall caught her
attention. Visitors. She slipped quietly down
one floor to a landing where she could peer over
the banister.

Three men stood barely inside the front entrance: Wesson faced a tall, middle-aged gentleman with a pompous air while the third,
much younger, hung back and stared covetously
about the hall. Mary disliked him on sight. The
older man appeared only annoyingly toplofty,
but the younger had the face of one eating a
lemon—or equally sour grapes, Mary decided.

"I understand the earl is now in residence."
The gray-haired man spoke in a cold, haughty
voice. "You will inform him at once that his uncle and his cousin are here. Mr. Jameson Halliburton and Mr. Kendrick Halliburton."

From the rigidity of Wesson's back, Mary suspected that he shared her sentiments. "I will Ascertain," he pronounced in frigid tones, "if his
Lordship is at Home." He turned and trod majestically into the dining room.

The older man looked about, his expression that of one smelling a long-defunct fish. "Unfortunate," he remarked in a thin, dry voice. "Most regrettable. We can only hope his wild ways will bring a rapid end to his career before he has wasted our entire estate."

The young man moved away from the suit of armor he had been inspecting. "Or found those damn rubies."

Mary gripped the banister. More ruby hunters!

The younger Mr. Halliburton jerked a shoulder, fretfully. "Oh, God, if only things were better managed, it would be we who were in residence here, and free to hunt for that treasure trove at will!"

"Kendrick—" his father began ominously. He broke off as Wesson returned.

"His Lordship will See you, in the Blue Drawing Room." The butler spoke as if the words were distasteful. "Please follow me."

Mary left her post as the trio walked away. A disagreeable set of relatives the Rake had, for sure. That Kendrick, in particular, was a nasty piece of work. No wonder poor Harborough disliked his family!

Rowena was not in her rooms when Mary arrived there and she finally discovered her in the Long Gallery. She stood before the portrait of Beatrix, posing and playing off the airs of a great lady—but wearing a negligee that put Mary to the blush.

"Just look at them jools!" She sighed in ecstasy as Mary approached. "It's the dream of me life to wear them rubies. Won't I look lovely, ducks?"

Mary, her mind filled with quite a different picture, held her tongue and Rowena rambled on.

"I'll be as grand a lady as any of them high-in-the-instep females. They'll all envy me, they will. Harborough is going to find them rubies and put them all back in the gold sets and then I'll traipse down the corridor by their boxes at the opera house and their eyes will start out of their heads. They won't look down on me no more!"

In spite of herself, Mary felt a rush of sympathy for Rowena. She'd never be a lady. She had neither birth nor breeding—and she lacked something else. Not just taste, though that certainly was missing; it was more an innate sense of what was done and what was not. She shook her head; Rowena would never win the acceptance she craved.

"I was a star, you know." The actress posed again, orange head thrown back and her voluptuous figure on display. "They all come to see me. Me uncle owns a touring company and I'm his leading lady. That is, I was, until I left with Harborough to become a real lady. It's a good thing to be a real lady, all respectable." She sounded a bit doubtful and Mary sensed a feeling of loss behind her words.

"I kind of miss it all," Rowena went on wistfully. "The camaraderie, don't you know, and being the most important person in the company. Here I got luxury and everything a girl'd want, only it do get a bit lonesome. I'll be real glad when Andover comes. He's a bit o' cheer, let me tell you." She took Mary's arm and steered her down the gallery. "Come along, ducks, time to get me dressed."

As they completed her toilette, Rowena chattered on. She seemed quite happy this morning and Mary was annoyed to find that she herself was not. How much of this cheer was due to the Rake's taking her up to her bedchamber last night? she wondered. Not, of course, that it was any of her concern!

"I liked treading the boards," Rowena said as Mary coaxed her orange hair into curls with a hot iron. "Until I met Harborough, I was going to act forever. When I got too old for ingenues, I'd be a character actress like me ma and me gram before her. Only that's sort of out of the social world, if you know what I mean. We on the stage is different. Not part of the ton like I am now. Like I'm going to be."

Like you'll never be, Mary thought with sudden pity, and realized, surprised, that she felt an odd sort of bond with Rowena, being a little of an outcast herself due to Clarence's regrettable life-style. Surprised, she found she liked Rowena. She was, basically, a good sort, as the Rake had said. She took extra care to make Rowena look as genteel as she could.

Later that afternoon the servants, Mary among them, lined the lower windows of Rushmoreland Castle to view a most impressive entourage—the arrival of Sir Archibald Andover. First came a hired fourgon, loaded with baggage, and bearing a formidable gentleman's gentleman on the forward seat beside the driver. A groom followed, leading a showy chestnut hack. Last, a curricle drawn by a pair of matched bays brought Sir Archibald himself.

Mary, effaced behind the drapes on the landing she had once shared with Edgemont, took no part in his settling in other than to ascertain which suite he would occupy so that she could keep out of his way. She peeked out, observing from behind the scene, as Edgemont and his superior, James, struggled with innumerable boxes and satchels. It looked as though Andover intended to stay for months! Mary plucked at the velvet drapes with nervous fingers. However was she to keep out of his way? It seemed her fate to meet with constant hazards.

It was well after midnight before she could creep down to the library, for the three principals spent a riotous evening, leaving an incredible mess in dining and drawing rooms for the morning maids. Mary couldn't help feeling a trifle smug that it was no longer part of her duties.

She had already lit her candle, holding it high, and therefore failed to notice the dim strip of light seeping out into the Great Hall. Too late. She opened the library door to find the room alight from a branch of candles on the table by the hearth. Her heart sank. Not again—not his lordship!

But it was. The Rake sat waiting in the wing chair before the dying fire, an empty brandy glass in his hand. He leaned back with a sigh of relief. "Ah. Do you know, I had nearly given you up, my nocturnal confidante. I could not be sure you regularly kept these late hours. Come, talk to me. I feel a need for sensible conversation after this evening." His brows drew together suddenly. "Or do you come to meet our domestic Adonis?"

Ladies do not curse, but Mary remembered certain phrases let drop by her careless father and they trembled on her tongue. He could not think her enamored of his second footman! Worse, how was she ever to search the library for the Jacobite's book if his lordship persisted in sitting up all night?

"I missed you last night," he complained. "You went to the dining room to meet my footman instead!"

"I did not!" Mary denied it vehemently. "He caught me while I was on my way here—I mean, he—I—" Lord, what could she say? How could she explain without his thinking she came in hopes of meeting himself?

It was just what he did think. He grinned. "I'm glad. I was afraid he had cut me out, and I like being with you." He considered her for a moment. "I like looking at you, Mary Migglesworth. Sit down, and tell me how you go on with Rowena."

Once more, Mary sat at his command. "We seem to suit," she said. "I believe we'll get along quite well, but I'm afraid I can never teach her to be acceptable in polite society."

"Good God, no need for that. What polite society would come here? I'll be quite satisfied if you can make her a little less—er—gaudy and possibly clean up her speech."

"I can only try." Mary shook her head. "It may be hopeless. Even if she does remember the words she must use, she may not pronounce them correctly."

He chuckled, that deep happy sound that awoke a chord within her. "A sow's ear, eh? I feared as much, but there is a bright side. Only think how furious my family will be when called on to meet her in public! My great-aunt Emily in particular. She's my grandfather's youngest sister, seventy if she's a day and not enough of her to fill this cushion."

"She sounds a dear."

His blue eyes opened wide, shocked. "She's an ogre! And what's more, she's bound to descend on me and try to bring me back into the fold."

"I see, and you are terrified."

He grinned and ran a hand through his tousled dark hair. "I am. If she only gives me warning, mayhap I can persuade Andover to make a bolt into town with Rowena. She is very anxious to blow some of my new blunt to replenish her wardrobe and brighten this gloomy rabbit warren."

"Are you sure your great-aunt will come?"

He refilled his glass. "Oh, yes. If only to observe me in my new glory. I'm the black sheep, you know." His mouth twisted into the sneer she had so disliked when he spoke to Andover. "They all expect me to act the Rake. They are sure I'll sell this great pile and waste the fortune in six months—and so I shall."

Mary sat up straight. "You shall not!"

"What, give them the satisfaction of learning I'm not as bad as painted?"

She frowned, assimilating this. "Are you sure that is what you meant?"

He sipped at his glass, thinking over what he'd said. "It didn't come out quite right, but you see how it is. How can I recant without losing face?"

"Well, you needn't become a veritable paragon, a pattern card of rectitude." Mary smoothed her skirts and looked up with a quirking smile. "Surely this estate grants you enough income to continue living as you have."

"Oh, more than enough."

"If that's what you really wish to do," she continued.

He glanced at her with a weary sigh and set his empty glass on the floor beside his chair. "Not really. I'm devilish tired of it all. No fun anymore now that I can afford it. And Rowena is a dashed problem. She's a lovely bit of muslin, but I'm tired of her, too."

Familiar as she was with many unladylike cant terms from living with Clarence, Mary felt a small rush of pleasure that he didn't seem obligated to mind his speech but treated her as an equal. She found him touchingly vulnerable as she realized how much the snubs of his family must have hurt him.

"Why do you act as you do then?" she asked

gently. "Why strive so hard to incur their disgust?"

He smiled, but it slipped somehow awry. "Do
I do that? Yes, I suppose that's it. Rebellion. I've
always been a rebel. You should have known
my father. Or, no," he corrected himself.
"Thank God you never did. My mother died
when I was in leading strings and my father was
a cold man, uncaring. I was much in his way. He
resented me, I believe now, as much as I did
him." He turned and raised questioning eyebrows. "Have you a father, little one?"

Indeed she had, and was suddenly thankful
for Clarence with all his eccentricities. Without
mentioning names, she regaled the Rake with
some of her father's wilder schemes for their
survival, and they sat together laughing and
talking in quiet contentment for nearly an hour
more until she remembered who and where she
was. They walked companionably up the wide
front stairs, parting on the landing.

Mary went to her bed, a prey to new and very
sympathetic thoughts about the rakish usurper.

Life at Rushmoreland Castle suddenly took
on a different turn with Sir Archibald Andover
in residence. A man who liked his company long
and cheerful, he coaxed Harborough into holding card parties every night. Mr. Wesson and
Mrs. Greenfield did not approve and breakfast
in the Housekeeper's Room took on a doleful
air. Mr. Wesson went so far as threatening to
retire, but only halfheartedly.

"As you well know, Mrs. Greenfield"—he sighed deeply—"I have served Rushmoreland All my Life, Man and Boy, starting as a page to the present incumbent's grandfather."

Her sigh echoed his. "Aye, that we should live to see the castle come to this pass."

"Last night's guests, now! A Shabbier set of Fellows you'd be hard put to find. And Her, presiding over the whole like a Madam." Mr. Wesson bent his head in deference to Mrs. Greenfield's shocked gasp. "I beg your pardon, ladies all, but it is More than Man can Stand!"

Mr. Guimper, on Mary's right, harrumphed as though about to speak up on his master's behalf but thought better of it. Both he and Mary left the table as soon as politeness permitted.

In the hall, they encountered James and Edgemont, the former in a towering rage.

"You!" he howled at Edgemont. "Why does she send for you? Yesterday, the day before, and now again today! I outrank you—it is my job!"

"No, really," Edgemont explained equably. "You are his lordship's personal footman. It is my place to accompany his—ah—guest."

James simmered down. "Well, she needn't send me after you like you was the Duke of England."

Edgemont shrugged. "She knows no better, and I doubt you would care to be seen following in her train. Do you truly wish to spend your days traveling to and from London on the rumble of her coach? You will arrive only in time to drive in the park at the hour of the promenade and then spend an hour with the modistes on

Bond Street where all your compatriots may see
you carrying her purchases—which would
astound you by their number!—and then arrive
here barely in time for dinner. Dear James, you
would hate it."

James glared at him helplessly and stomped
off.

"That took the wind from his sails right
enough, eh?" The valet poked Mary in the ribs,
startling her into an involuntary squeak.

Edgemont seemed to be somewhat exercised
in his mind. "Tell me, Guimper, why does your
master not accompany her? Why does he risk
such loveliness alone but for her footman in the
streets of London? Surely, 'Beauty provoketh
thieves sooner than gold.' He should have a
care!"

"Hah." Guimper laughed. "He's nothing to
fear. That one's not likely to whistle a title and a
fortune down the wind. He's safe as houses, he
is." He grinned down at Mary. "More than you
be, missy, if she's getting ready to drive out
again. You'd best hop it."

Mary hopped.

The servants might be unhappy; Rowena was
not. At last she had opportunity to wear all her
gowns, and the means to order more. Mary's
duties were light as Rowena spent her third day
shopping in London. She walked in the garden,
out of sight of the house, and wondered how
she was ever to be alone in the library. Andover
and his parties severely cramped her efforts, for
the castle rang with merriment until the wee
hours, and when the guests finally departed, the

maids were up and about cleaning grates and laying fires.

Once, when an outside engagement called an early halt to the evening's festivities, she made an attempt. The Great Hall for the moment was empty; the library door stood ajar. She slipped inside. Candles still burned on a side table and the wing chair sat by the fire.

Mary's heart gave a sudden lift. Someone rested in the chair. She hurried forward, aware of how much she had missed the intimacy she had shared with the Rake. Did he wait, hoping to talk to her again? The man in the chair moved slightly, the candlelight fell on his face, and Mary nearly cried out in shock.

Andover! Not the Rake!

He hadn't seen her, and she ran silently back out the door, shaking inside.

After that harrowing experience, Mary decided on an open daytime raid. Too much time had been wasted already; and it seemed that, with the continued presence of Andover, her friendship with the Rake, if it really was such, was over. The Pope translation of the *Iliad* lay so nearly in her grasp and she, fool that she was, had not given her best efforts toward securing it. Never mind that his eyes were blue and his smile glinted in the candlelight at night. He was not for her—or she for him—and the rubies were not for Rowena!

Sir Archibald, Rowena informed her in the morning, was taking her for a drive in his curricle, and after nearly an hour of debating the appropriateness of various gowns, Mary finally saw her off. Relieved to know they were both out of the castle, she made her way down to the Great Hall. It was deserted and she walked into the library—for once empty of his lordship—and closed the door. If she were to be caught, she could always say she was looking for a book for Rowena—although what type of literature that lady might enjoy was beyond Mary.

An hour passed and Mary, absorbed in reading the titles of the hundreds of books on the shelves that lined the walls, quite forgot the delicacy of her situation. She heard the rattle of a carriage drawing up on the cobblestone drive at the front entrance, but thought only that Rowena must be returning. Neither she nor Andover were likely to enter the library, for Wesson would be serving refreshments in the upstairs drawing room. Not until the sounds of an arrival filled the Great Hall did she realize she was trapped in the library and the visitor was being ushered in upon her.

She dived precipitously behind a pair of heavy drapes and struggled with the latch on the full-length French window behind it. It wouldn't budge. One of Clarence's riper exclamations sprang to her mind, but she bit it back and tried with all her strength to force the stubborn catch. She had to get out!

It was no use. Frozen by the ages, the window had probably not been opened in the last hundred years. She flattened herself against the ancient mullioned glass, praying that her toes were not visible beneath the curtains, and waited, thinking as she did so that she had spent overmuch time lately concealed behind the window decor of the castle.

Then, with a creeping feeling of horror, she saw that the drapes had not completely closed; a crack before her gave a clear view of a narrow strip leading to the door. She could only hope the person coming in would not see a narrow strip of her.

The door opened and the Rake held it for a tiny woman in an old-fashioned poke bonnet. She was dressed entirely in black, outmoded but quality, both in cut and rustling silk fabric. Her white hair framed an imperious little face, sharp-eyed and beaked as to nose.

"I am amazed at your fortitude, Aunt Emily," the Rake was saying as they came in. "Daring to enter this den of iniquity."

The lady seated herself stiffly upright in the chair he set for her, in Mary's plain view, and waited until his lordship apparently sat down himself across from her, before she answered.

"I am certain my consequence can sustain a visit to my great-nephew and"—Mary saw her shudder—"the Head of the Family."

The Rake roared with delight. "Good God, so I am. If that isn't a leveler for Uncle Jameson and Cousin Kendrick!"

She smiled, thin-lipped, in agreement. "I can't but feel it is an excellent thing for them. They both stand in need of a set-down, and you may be sure this unforeseen development has upset them greatly. However, your uncle is next in line. If I were you, Harborough, I would take precautions if I were to step out alone at night. I certainly do not approve of you, but I would not care to see your cousin Kendrick in your shoes one day."

The Rake sounded much struck. "My God, no. Odious little beast!".

"It is your clear duty, Harborough," she continued, seeming to take pleasure in using his new title, "to marry at once and set up your nursery. It is essential that you produce an heir before you meet with an unexplained accident. And I mean a legal heir. I quite understand the motives that prompted you to bring that—that female here, but she will not do!"

Mary, who had no recourse but to eavesdrop, now did so avidly. Not, of course, that this conversation was in the least way any of her business. . . .

She could not see the Rake, seated across from his great-aunt, but from his tone she could imagine that quick drawing together of his brows as he frowned. "You know very well, Aunt Emily, that I have no intention of marrying Miss La Fleur."

The black poke bonnet bobbed once, decisively. "Certainly I know that. The purpose of my visit here today is to invite you to dine with me a sennight from Thursday."

"Invite?" His voice rose satirically. "Or command?"

She ignored his question. "There will be in the party three unexceptionable young ladies, all eminently suited for the position of your wife. I wish you to look them over."

"I am not purchasing a goose for my dinner," the Rake replied coldly.

His great-aunt Emily gave an imperturbable sniff. "Much the same thing," she said. "It is high time you made such a purchase. You must be all of five and thirty."

"Only thirty-three, ma'am."

"Quite old enough to settle down. Since you are now the Head of the Family, I am determined to bring you into fashion. A great deal will be forgiven a title and a fortune."

He stretched his long legs out before him and crossed his ankles, bringing his feet into Mary's narrow line of vision. "I fear I am beyond redemption."

"We shall see. If you but contract an eligible alliance, I have high hopes." She rose to take her leave, smoothing the black mitts she probably never removed in public.

The Rake rose also and she deigned to smile briefly up at him. "Yes, Harborough, I have hopes. In the meantime, however, I cannot quite approve of your friendship with Archibald Andover. That young man is really not the thing. Very bad *ton*."

He demurred. "Andover is a harmless fribble, Aunt Emily. He's a bit wild, perhaps, but his family and the Halliburtons have known each other forever. Why, his father and my uncle played together in these halls as children."

Mary could not hear her reply as they left the library, closing the door, but what she had overheard disturbed her. Why, she would not admit to herself.

Of course, he had to marry someone, but it didn't help that it would not be Rowena. It was only that she hated to think of him snared into a life of misery with some shallow little fortune hunter after the unhappy life he had already led. He needed someone who understood him, someone he could talk to . . . all at once, the direction in which her thoughts were leading became all too clear. She broke from her hiding place behind the drapes and fled to the servants' wing. Tea. That's what she needed. A good strong cup of tea.

As she neared the kitchen, she heard raised voices, one of whom she knew only too well. Filled with a sudden misgiving, she opened the door. A boisterous game of silver-loo was in progress, the group seated about Mrs. Beecham's scrubbed oak worktable. Mrs. Beecham was there, her rosy face beaming. So also were James, two kitchen maids, a man she thought to be a groom, Harry, the man who drove her from the station, and three others she did not recognize. The one remaining gentleman, his back to her, she had no trouble identifying at all.

"Father!" she cried. "What are you doing here?"

"Ah, here is my daughter!" Clarence rose from the table, his face wreathed in smiles. "Mary, my dear, you are come at the right time! You must excuse me, the company." He scooped up a handful of small coins and dropped them into a capacious coat pocket.

"Here, now!" James complained. "You can't

pike off when you're all ahead. That ain't right-ful!"

Clarence waved an affable hand. "Later, my friends, later. You shall have your revenge, I promise, but now I must speak to my daughter alone. I shall return anon."

He took Mary by the elbow and steered her back out into the hall.

Oh, lord, she might have known he'd come!—oversetting all her careful plans—but what could she do? She shook off his hand. "Been physicking the domestics, have you, Father?"

Clarence laughed. "Looed the board three times. The old skill hasn't failed me." He seemed to note some disapproval in her glance and reassured her. "Not trifling, my dear. Far from it. I'm putting up at that wretched pub in the village and I have to pay my shot. No help for it."

"Why have you come? Father, you will ruin everything!"

"Why are you still here?" he countered. "I came because you must need my help since you've accomplished nothing on your own. Besides, I thought I'd like to take a gander at the old pile myself." He looked up and down the stone-flagged hall. "Where can we be private?"

"I'll have to take you up to my room, I suppose. The castle teems with people down here."

"Then come along." He took her arm again. " 'Lead on, I say, where you go, I follow.' "

"Oh, Father, not you too!"

"Eh?" He shifted to a lower tone, almost apologetic. "Ah, Mary, my dear"—he considered a bit of fluff on his sleeve—"Mary, I fear I may have inadvertently let you in for some trifling unpleasantness."

Mary paused, aware of a vast and familiar sinking sensation. "Now what?" she asked, resigned.

"Oh, nothing, really." He urged her on, far too casually. "It is only that when I arrived, I introduced myself as your father. To gain admittance, you must see. Couldn't use my own name, of course, so I said I was Mr. Brown. Damme if I could remember what ridiculous name you finally chose."

She gasped. "*I* chose? It was all your doing!"

"Ah, well"—he brushed this aside—"that's as may be. The thing is, rather than get into complicated explanations, I let it ride. They seem to have leaped to the conclusion, since our names were different, that you were my ill-begotten child." He peeked at her sideways, and hurriedly looked away.

Mary stared at him, dumbfounded. Her first irrational thought was that this was the last thing she wished the Rake to think of her. Her next, far more rational, was that it was exactly like Clarence.

"Not that it matters a whit," Clarence assured her. "You shan't be here long now that I've come to assist you and we've neither of us given our right names."

The fact that he was right unaccountably depressed her even more. After all, why should she care what gossip she left behind? She'd soon

be gone—and soon forgotten, even by one who
claimed to need a friend.

"Come on, Father." She led him to Wesson's
private staircase. "Three flights up and across a
mile of corridor."

As they rounded a second-floor landing, a female figure enveloped in the embrace of the am-
orous Edgemont gave a startled shriek and broke
away, her orange hair flying in disorder.

"Rowena!" exclaimed Clarence happily. "By
all that's holy, Rowena La Fleur! What the devil
are you doing here?"

"Clarence! Can I believe me eyes!" She patted
at her hair. "Lawks, you gave me such a scare!
Thought you was his lordship come upon us!"
She spotted Mary behind him, trying to shrink
into the wall, and immediately jumped to the
wrong conclusion. "And with me personal maid!
You shameless old reprobate!" She gave Mary a
broad wink.

"Oh, no!" Mary spoke up quickly. "It's not
what you think!"

Rowena smiled, obviously not believing a
word. "Sure, dearie. Go along with you now!"

Mary gave up. This would be the end. What
more could happen? She answered herself: with
Clarence on hand, anything. Meanwhile, explanations to Rowena would have to wait. If only
the woman would keep her mouth shut!

Clarence showed signs of wanting to remain
to chat, demanding an introduction to Edgemont. She dragged him away and on up the
stairs, foreseeing an interesting interview with
her mistress ahead, for above all she must dis-

abuse Rowena of the mistaken conclusion she had drawn—by hook or by crook—before she mentioned it to Harborough! There seemed to be no end of things she did not wish the Rake to think of her!

Chapter Six

Up at Mary's room, Clarence stopped short inside the door. "Hah!" he exclaimed. "They do you well here for a housemaid!"

Mary pushed him on in. "I've made some progress, Father. I'm now Miss La Fleur's—dresser, I believe she called it. Quite a step up and it has eliminated my biggest obstacle. As a housemaid I had to share a bed with another girl and it was difficult to get out at night."

"Yes, Rowena—how comes she to be here? Only last week I saw her at the opera house."

"Harborough brought her. To annoy his family, I believe."

Clarence crowed, delighted. "By the gods, that would do it! Those Halliburtons are as consequential a gang of stuffed shirts as it has ever been my pleasure to avoid."

He had been prodding her mattress experimentally, and now stretched out full length.

"You're far better off than me. That tavern! My humble cot is stuffed with corn cobs. I see now why you don't have that book yet. You've been up here lying around in luxury. Time I showed up."

"There have been problems, Father. That library is a very popular place, even after midnight."

"Balderdash! Anyone with a bit of gumption can find a few moments when a room is empty! I begin to think you plan to discover our rubies on your own without including me in the fun!"

"I would that I could! You've no idea what a complication you add. I can't have my old father —legal or not—wandering about the halls. If you get caught, old Wesson will discharge me at once, and I must be here in the castle, free to move about, if I'm to search for our rubies. Getting the book from the library is only the first step, and a much larger one than I expected."

Clarence turned on his side, plumping her pillow. "I fail to see why."

"Harborough," she exclaimed. "I believe he lives in that library at night. He is there every time I go in."

At this, Clarence sat up. "You're not to be in his way, my girl. I warned you of him. He is a loose fish who has gone his length in every extravagant folly and I'll not have him eyeing my daughter!"

"Oh, Father." Mary sank into her only chair. "He is quite the gentleman at home. I don't fear him."

"You should."

He was right again, Mary realized ruefully, but for the wrong reason. The man was far too attractive when behaving himself.

"If he is there at night, then you must go earlier."

She laughed, but not happily. "I just did. This afternoon. And I was trapped when he came in with a guest and I had to hide behind the draperies."

Clarence nodded approval. "What I would have done myself."

"No doubt. At any rate, I couldn't get out through the window and had to remain hidden while he entertained his great-aunt Emily."

"Old Emily Halliburton? I know of her."

"Yes? She's trying to marry him off so he'll have an heir before his cousin kills him for the title or some such nonsense."

Clarence lay back, stretching his arms over his head. "Aye, she would. Hates that branch of the family like poison, and she has reason. That Kendrick Halliburton is as queer as Dick's hatband. And the old lady is a harridan. If she has her hooks into the new earl, he hasn't the chance of a snowflake in hell. She'll have him leg-shackled before he knows what hit him."

"Not if he can help it! He is against the whole scheme." And so was she, Mary added to herself. Definitely against it.

Her father had lost interest in Harborough's matrimonial problems. "Tell me, when do you dine here? May I join you? The food at that tavern is indescribable."

"You certainly may not. I'll have you know I

am now a fixture in the Housekeeper's Room, one of the elite. I go in right after the butler, and on the arm of his lordship's valet."

"Hoity-toity. I'm that impressed." Clarence grimaced, obviously not. "Well, if you will not accommodate me, I shall return to the kitchen. I suspect Mrs. Beecham of having a warm spot in her heart for me."

"Very well, Father. Only for goodness' sake, don't let anyone see you up here in the halls."

Clarence gave this warning the dismissal it deserved. "I'll meet you back here after dinner and we shall go down to that library together and put an end to this farce. It's high time you came home. I'm not comfortable without you."

"What a taradiddle! That's doing it too brown, Father. You hardly know I'm there."

"Yes, I do!" He caught himself growing sentimental, and rallied. "Who's to see to my laundry? And my breakfast? You keep out of that Rake's sight. I need you at home."

"Oh, and he's not all, Father. Andover is here!"

"What? Sir Archibald? Actually staying in the castle?"

"Yes, Harborough invited him, but I rather felt he invited himself."

Clarence rubbed his nose with a thoughtful finger. "Now why . . . can he have an ulterior motive? His father and old Harborough were close as inkle weavers when they were boys. Mary, my girl, we'd best keep an eye on that boy."

"Pish-tush, Father. He cares only for the

combing of his hair and the set of his coats. He
spends his time showing off his fancy raiment to
Rowena. Our only fear from him is that he may
recognize me."

Her father shook his head. "Do not underestimate him, my dear. I have played cards with
that gentleman too often. For all his decorative
front, I have found him to be needle-witted.
Well, be that as it may." He rose, slapping his
knees. "I grow hungry. Should you not be about
your duties? I cannot imagine Rowena dining in
an afternoon gown."

"Oh, dear, I'd better go down." Mary
bounced out of her chair. "There's no telling
what she'll put on if I am not with her." She
glanced at the bell over her door. "It is odd that
she has not rung for me."

They walked down one flight of the main
staircase together and Clarence whistled as he
took in his surroundings. "They do themselves
well, those usurping upstarts! This is quite a
place!"

Mary giggled. "That's the first thing Rowena
said as she came in the front door." She mim-
icked the actress's vulgar tones. "A-aow, what a
plaice! A regular palace!"

"To think this might be our home but for that
idiot Jacobite!"

"Be careful how you address our ancestor, Father. You may bring down retribution. They say
his ghost walks these halls."

Clarence shrugged. "He's welcome to it, for
all of me. I daresay I'd walk too if I'd lost my
head."

"As well as all our rubies? According to Edgemont, he's looking for his Beatrix to tell her where he hid the jewels. He's been seen in the Long Gallery, where her portrait still hangs. They say he moans and calls her name."

This aroused Clarence's interest. "Her portrait? The Countess Beatrix? I must see that. Is the Jacobite hanging there also?"

"The empty space! There is a painting missing beside hers; I wonder if they removed him after his disgrace. Only Beatrix hangs there now—and she's wearing the rubies, Father. All of them. I'll take you up to see her after dinner. Speaking of the rubies, Harborough is after them, but I don't believe he has any idea where to look. He means to find them for Rowena!"

"Lined her little nest with gold, has she? Well, she's a grand gal. All luck to her, but not our rubies."

Mary eyed him, curious. "Do you know her—ah—well, Father?"

"Wouldn't say that," he hedged. "Mutual friends in common, you know. Just an acquaintance."

"I see."

"Truly. Never one of my light skirts. Too expensive," he admitted frankly. "Couldn't afford the likes of her."

Mary felt it best to leave it at that and pointed Clarence toward the back hall leading to the servants' stairs.

Rowena was donning a cerise domino when Mary tapped softly at her door and entered. She dropped a black velvet loo-mask and gave a startled shriek.

"Oh, it's only you, ducks." She patted her ample bosom with a sigh of relief. "For a minute there, I thought you was Harborough come home unexpected. I don't need you tonight, dearie. Harborough and Andover are gone to the clubs and there's a masquerade on at the opera house. I'm sure no one would think it wrong if I go by meself as long as I take a footman to walk behind."

Edgemont, Mary surmised. Well, why shouldn't Rowena have a bit of a lark? She hadn't seen her look so happy and excited since her arrival.

"You take the evening off too, ducks." Rowena winked broadly. "Give my love to Clarence."

Mary started to speak, but Rowena shoved her out the door. "Go along, now do. Have a good time; I shall!" The door closed with a decisive click, shutting Mary out in the hall.

There was nothing for it but to go down to her own meal. So the house would be empty tonight. She felt a little ripple of excitement. Things were coming to a head at last. A free evening in the library and she'd have the *Iliad.* Then she and Clarence could translate the passages—and maybe, maybe they would have the location of her rubies!

Now when she was finally so close, doubts began to assail her. Would the book still be there? It had been over seventy years, after all. And would the cryptic message really be the clue she hoped for, or was it merely an intimate, beautifully crafted farewell to his beloved Beatrix? Clarence held no confidence in the letter— and Clarence, annoyingly, was often right.

She hurried up to her room after the evening meal, expecting to find him waiting. It was she who waited. After half an hour she went in search, straight to the kitchen. As she suspected, the loo game was in full swing and she was sorely tempted to leave Clarence there. It had occurred to her that if they encountered Wesson in the Great Hall, her father would be hard to explain. But again, if he should come up to her room and find her gone, nothing would prevent him from walking straight down the front stairway and opening every door in the Great Hall until he found the library. Oh, why could he not have stayed at home!

He didn't want to wait in her room, either, when she finally lured him away.

"What matters it if we are seen, once we've our hands on that book?" he demanded.

"Oh, Father! The book will only give us the clues! I must be able to remain here and hunt for our rubies."

Clarence grumbled, "I want to see something of the place beside the back halls."

"If I find our rubies, Father, you shall live here," Mary promised. "Now, with all gone from the castle but the servants, no doubt the library will be dark. I shall need to light the candles when I get there. Do lend me your Pocket Luminary, it will be so much quicker than my tinderbox."

Still complaining, he handed her the small bottle and she left him once more stretched out on her bed.

The Great Hall lay in darkness except for a single wall torch that threw wavering shadows on the tapestries and made a single broad pool of light on the stone-flagged floor. Mary tiptoed down the stairs, reminding herself that the huge chamber was subject to sudden cold drafts that caused eddies flowing along the ancient banners as though an unseen hand brushed their length. Wesson, or someone, had banked the fire in the gigantic hearth but the smoke that had blackened the stone mantel and the beams above it came out in thick puffs like spectral wraiths awakened by the gusts of wind down its old chimney.

Mary clung to the shadows along the wall, skirting the pool of torchlight and telling herself over again that she knew her ghosts were only the drafts blowing intermittently through the vast chamber. But which door was the library? How far along had she come? She reached a table, and her questing hand found a candelabrum. All the domestics, off the leash so to speak, were behind the green baize doors, no doubt rioting in the Servants' Hall. She could safely risk a light.

Selecting a long taper from the branch, she opened Clarence's Luminary, the little bottle lined with oxide of phosphorus, and rubbed in one of the chemically treated splints. She pulled it out with a quick jerk and flinched as she always did when it burst into flame, though it was

far less dangerous than the French Etherial
Match that Clarence had prided himself on before the invention of the Luminary.

Her taper lit, she snuffed out the splint and
tucked the bottle back in her apron pocket.
There was the library door, only a few steps
away.

Suddenly, she felt a prickle of fear and knew
she was not alone.

She whirled around and the flare of the candle
revealed the figure of a man coming toward her.
Oh, the devil! She had waited until too late and
the Rake had returned. But it was not the Rake
—it was Andover! Her first thought was that he
had recognized her and had come to catch the
spy in an act of thievery and expose her. He
reached out and seized her wrist. She struggled
frantically to escape, dropping her lighted taper.

He laughed and twisted her arm behind her.
"Little vixen! Here, all I want is a kiss."

Mary kicked him sharply in the shin, relief
granting her extra power, and he howled.

At the sound of his cry, the library door
slammed open and the Rake charged into the
hall. In an instant, he took in the scene in the
beam of light from the door. Leaping at Andover, he grabbed him by the collar and pulled
him away from Mary, landing him a facer that
caused him to measure his length on the stone-
flagged floor.

Andover sat up, holding his jaw. "What the
devil did you do that for?"

Furious, the Rake stood over him, fists

cocked. "Well, what the devil did you think you were doing?" he countered.

"I only wanted to kiss the gal, dammit, not rape her here in your hall." Andover tried to scramble to his feet.

"Oh, devil take it." The Rake ran his fingers through his hair, his eyes confused. "Sorry, old man. I didn't think. I don't know what got into me." He offered a hand and helped Andover up. "But you can't go around seducing my maids."

"Why not?" Andover rubbed his sore jaw. "You do it yourself."

"Well, you're far out if you think my maids are fair game for my guests."

He did not add "particularly this one," but it seemed to be apparent to Andover from the knowing look on his face. He glanced at Mary, who cowered in the shadows.

"Ah, your property. I beg your pardon, Harborough. Hands off. I understand."

Mary, scarlet-faced and thankful for the near-darkness, turned to run but the Rake caught her arm.

"Stay here," he ordered. "I want to talk to you." He kept his grip on her as he faced Andover. "I thought you were going to retire early. What brings you back downstairs?"

It seemed to Mary that the man hesitated for a perceptible second before he answered.

"I heard noises in the hall outside my room and came out to investigate. Footsteps, you know, so I followed them down the stairs. Only trying to lay your ghost, my friend, not your maid." He leered at them and Mary was suddenly aware that the Rake had pulled her close beside him. "How was I to know the ghost had an assignation with you?"

Harborough let go of her arm and gave Andover's shoulder a friendly buffet. "Take yourself off, you gudgeon, before I floor you again."

Mary started to hurry away but the Rake stopped her, steering her before him into the candlelit library. He pushed her into a seat by the fire and sat down in his favorite wing chair.

"Now, my pretty little maid, you are going to tell me why you roam about at night—can it be you hoped to find me down here?"

Mary half rose, shocked. "That's the last thing I wanted!"

"Then, if not me, what is the attraction of my library?" His dark brows drew together. "My handsome footman?"

"No!" Mary denied it vehemently. "Never! I —I just couldn't sleep and I came down to find a book to read." This at least was the truth.

The dark brows rose, over eyes once more heavy lidded. "Now why do I have the feeling you are lying to me?"

"I am not! I did come to find a book."

Her sincerity must have been evident, for he clapped his hands to the arms of his chair and pulled himself to his feet. "Then I shall help you find one. What do you prefer? We seem to have a preponderance of sermons and Greek and Latin texts on our shelves. Or do you care for poetry? How about some Shakespeare?"

Mary shook her head, but his brows had drawn together again.

"That's right, little maid. I must not forget that you are on intimate terms with my Shakespeare-spouting footman. Are you telling me it is to find appropriate quotes with which to answer him that you come down in the middle of the night?"

"It is not the middle of the night! And that is not why I come! But what are you doing home so early?" She flared with righteous wrath and accused him: "You went out to the clubs; I had no reason to expect you back so soon!"

"Blame Andover for that! He made me return." He selected a candle from the branch on the table. "What sort of book do you prefer?"

The candle he held up lit the side of his face and Mary gasped.

"My lord—Rake, what has happened to you?"

A red-and-purple bruise swelled on his temple, dangerously close to his eye. He touched it gently. "Does it show so much? A trifling misadventure."

Mary felt her heart grow cold. His great-aunt Emily had hinted—no, told him—that he might meet with a fatal accident. Could this have been an attempt on his life? "You were attacked by someone?"

"A common footpad only. As we left White's, on our way to Almack's, we passed a dark alleyway and this brigand sprang out and clubbed me down. If it hadn't been for Andover, he'd have finished me off and taken my purse."

"Andover!"

"I tell you, I was mighty thankful he was along. He may look a useless dandy, but he carries a sword cane. We got off easily."

The color had drained from Mary's cheeks. Surely, the hand of his uncle lay behind this. How could she warn him without revealing her presence in the library?

"You were the one attacked, not Andover."

He shrugged. "Only as I was a bit in the lead."

"I pray you will not walk out alone at night! Your uncle . . ."

"Now what do you know of my uncle? Uncle Jameson! That's ridiculous." But an arrested expression crossed his face as if he too must be remembering his great-aunt Emily's words. If only he would take them to heart!

He turned to the book-lined wall behind them, abruptly changing the subject. "For what do we hunt if not for Shakespeare? I cannot believe any of these sermons are entertaining—though undoubtedly soporific if you wish to read yourself to sleep. How about a volume of poetry?"

Mary hesitated. Could he know about Homer after all? Dared she tell him for which book she searched? She took a breath and risked all.

"The *Iliad*. I want Alexander Pope's translation."

This drew no reaction from him other than raised eyebrows. "What, not in the original Greek? Almost you disappoint me."

In her inordinate relief, Mary giggled. The

Rake paused in his perusal of the shelves and looked down at her. "Do that again."

"What?"

"That funny little chortle. I like it."

Mary primmed her face. "You appear to think me a figure of fun, my lord."

"Rake," he corrected, stopping his search. He tipped up her face with a finger beneath her chin and pretended to frown. "If you cannot refrain from using that beastly title when we are alone, I shall—I shall call you Miss Migglesworth!"

In spite of herself, Mary giggled again and his sleepy eyes glinted with laughter in the candlelight.

"Thank you."

He went back to reading the names on the book bindings and Mary, conscious of an odd disappointment as he turned so easily away from her, picked another candle from the branch and began on a different shelf. After a few minutes, he spoke again.

"I am not at all sure I want to help you find your *Iliad.*"

Mary's candle wavered. What did he mean?

"If we find it, you will stay above stairs reading. You will not come down at night to talk to me anymore." His tone was light and teasing, but she sensed a note of seriousness behind it. "You know," he went on, "you are the only person with whom I can be myself. I have missed you these past evenings."

"What a plumper! Why, you have partied here every night!"

"But I have not enjoyed it. I am tired of acting the part of a depraved peep o'day boy."

"Then stop!" Mary so far forgot herself as to scold him. "I have no patience with false pretenses. Why do you not just drop this image you feel constrained to perpetuate? Why keep it up?"

"To aggravate my beastly family, of course."

Mary turned a chilly shoulder. "It is your choice, then. Do what you will. You do not need me."

He touched her arm. His hand felt warm and oddly gentle. "I hope you do not mean to desert me, little housemaid."

She swallowed a lump that formed unaccountably in her throat. If only she had the right to never desert him! "I—I am no longer a housemaid," she informed him with an attempt at nonchalance. "Remember? I am now a lady's maid. Quite a step upward."

He threw back his head and laughed. "We progress! The gap narrows!"

Now what could he mean by that? She felt her traitorous blush stain her cheeks. He flirted with a maidservant, of course. She'd be a fool to misinterpret his words. She hurried over to another shelf without answering and silence reigned for several minutes.

"Aha!"

She jumped, and turned to see him pull out a volume with a brown marbled cover.

"Here you are, Miss Lady's Maid. One *Iliad*, by Homer, out of Pope, as ordered."

For a moment it felt as though her heart

stopped. At last! The Jacobite's book! Her hands shook as she reached for it and she carefully restrained her tumultuous emotion.

He held it above his head. "I suppose you now intend to leave me?"

"My lord, it is grown late! I must leave. Please give it to me!"

"Rake," he said, still holding the book out of her reach.

"Rake, then. Oh, please R–Rake, let me take it and go."

Reluctantly, he placed it in her outstretched hands. "Only if I may walk you to your room. Where have they put you?" He led her from the library.

"Above Miss La Fleur. On the third floor. But truly there is no need for you to accompany me."

He shook his head. "Oh, but there is every need. According to Wesson, these halls are not safe. More than Andover walks here at night."

"Do you mean the Jacobite's ghost? Oh, but it is all right because I am a virgin. Oh!" She realized what she had just said and hid her flaming face in her hands.

He stopped at the foot of the stairs. "I am sure you are." His voice was alive with amusement. "But why should that be of interest to our ghost?"

"Oh, dear, my unruly tongue! It is merely a quotation from Milton told me by Edgemont. He—he said I was quite safe because 'no evil thing that walks by night hath hurtful power o'er true virginity.' "

The Rake gave a delighted howl of laughter. "Miss Migglesworth, you are a treasure! You are indeed safe, but Rowena had best have a care!"

He was still grinning when they arrived at Mary's door. She knew a sudden fear that he might attempt to enter with her but instead he made a courtly bow. Catching her hand, he kissed her fingertips. Then, the smile gone from his face, he turned her hand over and his warm lips brushed her palm.

He looked up at her, his expression enigmatic. "Good night, Miss Migglesworth." He bowed again and vanished down the hall.

Shaken, Mary stood for a moment looking after him. She became aware that she clutched Pope's *Iliad* to her chest and turned quickly to open her door.

The candle burned low on her dressing table by the bed, but it gave enough light for her to see the room was empty. Her heart leaped to her throat, and then sank.

Clarence had disappeared.

Chapter Seven

Mary set the precious book on the bed, hiding it with her pillow. It was of the first importance to locate her wandering father before he was found by someone else.

She was saved the trouble. Even as she turned toward the door, it burst open and Clarence bounded in.

"Did you know there was a tomfool ass of a butler parading around out there with a dashed great elephant gun?"

"Father, he didn't see you?" Mary ran to shut the door he'd left wide open.

Clarence pulled down his waistcoat and shot his cuffs. "Of course he didn't, but it was a near thing. Why didn't you warn me?"

"I told you to stay in here and wait for me!"

"I merely wished to go to this Long Gallery and see the portrait of my grandmother." He sat down on the bed with an injured air. "Barely got outside your door before I nearly ran into the fattest butler I've ever seen, wearing a most regrettable dressing gown, too, and pacing up and down with this junior cannon on his shoulder for all the world like one of Prinny's Horse Guards!"

Mary burrowed under her pillow and retrieved the *Iliad*. "He's watching for our ghost. But, Father, only see! I've got it!"

"About time. Here, give it to me." He held out a casual hand.

"You're mighty calm about this!"

"Why should I not be? It is no great discovery. We knew where the book lay; I can only wonder why you did not go down and get it at once." He opened the volume. "Well, let us see if your theory holds water or if this has all been a wild-goose chase for nothing."

He turned past the flyleaf and gazed thoughtfully at the frontispiece, a steel engraving of a bust of Homer, while Mary fairly hopped with impatience.

"Get on with it, Father! Is it the right book?"

"Let me see." Holding the volume at arm's length, the better to decipher the small print, he read aloud from the title page. " '*The Iliad of Homer*, translated by Alexander Pope, Esq. . . . A New Edition, with additional notes, critical and illustrative, by Gilbert Wakefield, B. A. Volume I. London, 1806.' " He threw it down. "Eighteen-oh-six! This is not the Jacobite's edition! This one is quite new."

Mary collapsed in the chair, dismayed. After all she had gone through . . . but surely it would read the same! She rallied. All the lines would be numbered as in the original.

"It will suffice, Father. Here is my copy of the Jacobite's letter." Mary pulled the crumpled sheet from the bosom of her gown and unfolded it with suddenly shaking hands. To come to this at last! "The first is line three hundred eighty-three in Book Twenty-three. Look it up quickly!"

Clarence began to leaf through the pages. "Over half the volume is taken up by this damned Wakefield! A Preface, an Essay, a General View of the Epik Poem, then General Observations by the Editor, one Gilbert Wakefield, B. A., of Hackney, September 21, 1795. Ah! Finally, the First Book—no, preceded by The Argument and Notes Preliminary. Here we go, Book One, 'Achilles' wrath to Greece the direful spring of woes unnumbered, heav'nly goddess, sing!' By heaven, Homer must have known what his readers would have to plough through in later centuries to find him! And that is all there is on the page! The rest is a damned footnote!"

He thumbed rapidly ahead. "And still on. Every page is half or more of footnotes! Mary, this volume contains only Books One and Two; it is part of a set!"

"What! But I thought . . . oh, dear, are any of our clues in this one? Let me see—no! Our earliest is in Book Three." Here, Mary forgot herself. "Damn! I shall have to go back down."

"You've brought us a useless volume!" Clarence slammed the book shut in disgust. "Surely I have trained you better than that! All you had to do is bring up the ones we need and you come with one paltry volume that does us no good whatsoever!"

"It was not my fault!" Mary's temper sparked. "I had no choice, this is the one Rake—Harborough—handed to me. I could not stipulate specific editions I should know nothing about!"

"Harborough! What was he doing with it?"

"I told you, he's always in the library and he

helped me search. He's the one who found this copy."

Clarence scowled. "Didn't I warn you to keep away from that man? And now see what's come of it!"

Mary picked up her brass candle holder. "He's not there now. He's gone upstairs. I'll try again—only this time," she begged, "please stay put, Father."

Clarence had already settled himself on her bed, his head propped on the pillow. "How this does take one back." He opened the *Iliad*. "Pope's Essay on Homer. So this is where my old tutor got his lectures. Demme, almost word for word!"

Hoping he'd remain absorbed, Mary left him and started down the front stairs. The castle now lay in complete silence. She wondered briefly if Rowena had come home—and if not, if the Rake had discovered her absence. Did he go to her rooms at night? And why should she care?

She ran down the last flight in the dark and entered the Great Hall, still dimly lit by embers in the huge hearth. As before, the errant drafts, like cold, unseen hands, ran the length of the threadbare banners and puffed phantom wraiths from the fireplace. She knew what they were now and steeled herself to cross to the library door in the shadows.

No one was inside. Taking out the Pocket Luminary, she pulled another splint and lit her candle. Now that she knew right where to look, it took only moments to secure the other vol-

umes. There were four more. Before leaving this
time, she checked the last pages in Volume Five
and made sure she had the ending. She snuffed
out the candle and flitted, like a specter herself,
through the great hall and back up to her room
on the third floor. Now why hadn't her first ex-
cursion been as simple? Clarence would never
let her forget.

He glanced up as she came in. "You have
them all? Good. Do you know, I've a mind to
read the poem again. I'd forgotten how interesting the story is. I can't see why you didn't just
get all the volumes long ago. Nothing seems to
get done properly unless I rouse myself to take a
part." He shook his head slowly, wondering.
"Most curious. I've noticed it often of late."

Mary dropped the books on the bed beside
him and selected the second volume.

He took it from her at once. "Here, give it to
me. You'll only make a mull of it. Let's see, what
does this contain? Book Three and up to"—he
checked the back pages—"Book Eight. I'm not
surprised it took this Wakefield so many volumes to contain one poem. Half of every page is
taken up with his confounded footnotes and
paltry comments!"

"Book Three, Father, there are two entries in
Book Three!" Mary ran her finger down the list
from the letter to Beatrix. "Look up lines two
hundred eight and three hundred twelve." She
found she was trembling with excitement. She
stood on the threshold of her treasure hunt! If
only Clarence would hurry; but then he had
never believed in the letter as a genuine lead to

the rubies. In fact, he seemed convinced that the stones themselves were long gone.

The unbeliever spoke from the bed. "Here we are. Line two hundred eight, on page twenty-nine. 'She moves a goddess and she looks a queen.' Ah, well." He closed the book. "It's all a love note, my dear. No clue there."

"Don't give up now, Father!" She could not be wrong! The Jacobite would not have gone to such pains for merely a tender letter of farewell. "Please, find line three hundred twelve."

With a condescending air of humoring his little daughter, Clarence opened the book again. "Line three hundred twelve . . . page forty-three, I believe. Yes. 'Wrapt in the cold embraces of the tomb.' I declare, a fine thing to write to one's bereaved wife. Daresay he was feeling a bit sorry for himself."

Mary, who had found a quill and ink bottle in the dresser, quickly turned her copy of the letter over and began to write down the quotations. "No indeed, we must be right! Oh, I can feel we are close! Now Book Five, it is in the same volume. Look up line three hundred seventy-one."

Obediently he located it. "Page one hundred ninety-three. 'Not two strong men th' enormous weight could raise.' " At this, Clarence's interest picked up. "That's not a thing one says to one's wife often."

"Another volume, father! We need Books Twelve and Thirteen." Her frayed quill spattered ink on the page. "Oh, no, wait. We are going about this all wrong! We should read the lines in the proper order, the way the Jacobite

wrote them. He would not have skipped about
so unless the quotes were meant to go a certain
way." She flipped the letter back over. Her
throat had gone dry and her voice came out in a
squeak. "Number one, Book Twenty-three, line
three hundred eighty-three."

Clarence, who enjoyed any game that had
rules and the promise, if not of remuneration, at
least of a definite conclusion, now entered into
the spirit of the thing. "Book Twenty-three,
that's almost the end." He picked up the last
volume. "What's the line?"

"Three hundred eighty-three!"

A minute later, Mary nearly fainted with excitement as Clarence declaimed in ringing tones:
" 'It is not strength, but art, obtains the prize!' "

"Father! We have the secret!" She shivered,
ecstatic. "This *is* our map to the rubies—we
have but to follow the clues!" She held up the
letter with a trembling hand. "I'll read the references and write them down as you find them.
The next is Book Twenty-four, line six hundred
sixty-two!"

Clarence pawed through the volume he held
and Mary took up the pen, ready to write.

"Page two hundred ninety-five—two hundred ninety-six—here! Line six hundred sixty-
two, 'Two urns by Jove's high throne have ever
stood.' Urns? Where are there urns hereabouts?"

Mary thought rapidly. Not inside the castle,
unless it referred to vases—and a throne? "In
the garden, perhaps. There are urns full of flowers and stone benches that might be called
thrones. Go on, Father, I can't wait!"

Clarence put down the book. "And I cannot find the lines," he said mildly, "unless you tell me for what I should look."

"Book Three, line two hundred eight. We have that already. The one about the goddess and the queen. Now, how could that . . . of course! The rose garden! It must be full of statues and they are probably all of Greek gods and goddesses." She waved the letter. "And we have the next! The enormous weight two strong men cannot raise—oh, Father, it is in the garden for sure. Everything out there will be of stone and far too heavy to lift."

Clarence rubbed his nose. "I can't see any reason to rejoice about that. How old is this rose garden? Could it not have been redone since the Jacobite's time? If the rubies were there, someone must have found them."

Mary shook her head impatiently. "If they had been found, I'm sure it couldn't have been kept a secret. At least not in the Halliburton family, and the Rake means to look for them. No, I'm sure they wait for us! Come, we are almost there. Book Thirteen, line one hundred six is next. Do hurry, Father, don't fumble so!"

"I have to find the right volume. Not Four, this has Books Fifteen to Twenty. Must be Volume Three. Ah, here we are. Book Thirteen."

"And line one hundred six."

"Line one hundred six—page two hundred twenty-three, 'and seem to walk on wings and tread in air.' Now what . . . ?"

"A winged goddess, of course." Mary scratched down the words hastily. "This will be easy! We find a stone statue of a goddess with wings standing by a bench with two urns—and what next? Book Three, line three hundred twelve. Oh, we found that, it is the one about the tomb." She hesitated, doubtful. "I have not seen any tombs in the garden."

"Are none of the benches ornamental?" Clarence looked up. "Might not one look like a sarcophagus? I believe many were brought up from Italy for decorative purposes."

"Are you sure that is the right line?"

He picked up the correct volume and found the line again. "Yes, it can be no other."

"Let us go on then. Book Twenty-two, line four hundred eighty-four."

"The last volume. Here it is on page one hundred fourteen. Ah, the tomb must be correct. 'Unwept, unhonour'd, uninterr'd he lies.' That sounds like we'll have a skeleton in our sarcophagus!"

"I'm sure none of the benches would have been left occupied. Are there graves on the grounds?"

"Oh, yes." Clarence nodded. "All our ancestors are here somewhere. But this says, whoever it is, he is not buried. Could it refer to the stones themselves? That they lie above ground?"

"Maybe it will tell us. There are two more. Book Twelve, line two hundred eighty-three."

"I cannot see his reason for fiddling about so," Clarence grumbled, putting down the volume he held and hunting for another. "Not this one. Ah, Volume Three again. What was that line?"

"Two hundred eighty-three." Mary fairly

danced with impatience. "Do hurry. I want to go out to the garden at once!"

Always contrary, her father immediately moved slowly, pretending to be unable to find the page. Recognizing the symptoms, Mary subsided into an aggravated silence until he found the proper page.

" 'Without a sign his sword the brave man draws.' Now what could that mean?"

"A statue holding a sword?"

Clarence sat back. "Bound to be. No doubt the place is infested with copies of great pieces from sixteenth-century Italy. All those Greek heroes were sculpted holding swords, from David to Moses."

"I don't believe he was a Greek, Father. Or either of them, for that matter. There is only one more, one we missed in Book Three. Line three hundred fifty-seven."

This proved to be a facer, for it read: "plough the watery deep."

"The estuary?" Mary pondered. "Or could it mean a pool or fountain? Could he have hidden them underwater?" Another thought, a disheartening one, shook her. "But there is no mention of the secret passage!"

"Of course not." Clarence smiled pityingly. "I told you not to take those old tales seriously. No, my dear. That was sealed up long before the Jacobite rebellion."

Reluctantly, for it was dear to her heart, Mary relinquished her secret passage.

"Come, Father. It is not really late. We can go out in the gardens at once while no one is about.

It is still moonlight outside my window, enough to see our way, and we know what to look for. Two urns by a carved stone bench near a winged goddess and a warrior with a sword. At least one of them may stand in a pool as a fountain and be too heavy to lift and we'll have to feel about under the water for a box or a bottle! Come on, let's hurry."

But even as Mary spoke, she became aware of strange sounds in the vicinity of her door. Scratchings, the knob rattling, and the hinges squeaking a bit as though the door were being pushed.

"Someone is trying to get in!"

With Clarence, it was the work of a moment to make a practiced leap into her wardrobe and disappear. His daughter was made of sterner stuff.

"Who is out there?" she demanded, standing her ground. Could it be Andover? She gripped the brass candle holder, ready for him. Not the Rake, she knew. She suspected he would knock and walk right in.

A meek voice spoke from without. "It is only me."

Mary relaxed. "Come in, me." She pulled the door open and the maid Holly slipped inside.

"I'm that sorry you heard me," she said. "I didn't mean for to disturb you, only to stuff this garlic into your keyhole."

Mystified, Mary stared at the bedraggled clove filling her room with its fragrance. "What on earth for?"

"Why, to ward away the ghost! I've been that

worried about you, you being up here alone so near the Long Gallery. I'd have come earlier but I was afraid of Mr. Wesson. He's prowling about with that great gun of his, and I'm already in trouble with Mrs. Beecham for burning nutmeg in her best skillet. For a wish, you know. You write it on a bit of paper and burn it with the nutmeg and then bury the remains. Only she caught me and never let me collect the ashes, so it won't come true."

Mary sat on the edge of her bed, surprised to find how pleasant it was to see Holly's cheerful rosy face once more. And she was deeply touched by the girl's bravery in daring the ghost-ridden halls at night to bring her a charm. She held out her hand, accepting the garlic, knowing she'd regret it until she could wash away the persistent odor.

"Were you not terrified to come up here after dark?"

"Oh, no." Holly seated herself in the chair. "Not now. See?" From her apron pocket, she took a little square of cheesecloth tied into a bag with a scrap of ribbon. It seemed to be filled with crumpled dried flowers. She took out another and added it to the garlic in Mary's hand.

"This one is for you. You must keep it close upon your person, for you never know when you may meet the ghost! I'd have brought it sooner, but I had the greatest trouble finding all the herbs. There's Adder's-Tongue, Bloodroot, Loosestrife, Feverbush, and Dogstooth Violet. A combination bound to keep you safe! I added a clove of garlic to be sure and on the bit of paper inside, I wrote a warning message to all evil things. No, don't open it!" she added as Mary, ever curious, began to investigate the little package. "It is a very powerful spell and you must not weaken it."

Mary smiled. "To be sure, I won't. I collect you are no longer afraid to sleep alone."

"Oh, I am to have a new bedfellow. Amanda and Jane are that happy to get me out of their room, you won't believe! They are angry with me anyway. You see, I broke the glass beads left me by my grandmother and it seemed such a fortuitous happening! I'd been wanting to try a love spell, you know. Before restringing them, I laid them out in a three-foot circle on the floor of our room, and then I stood in the center, and spun three times to the left while I scattered a jar of bay leaves and some thyme all around. They said it was a heathen waste and created a mess. I had to clean it up all by myself."

"But did it work?" Mary giggled suddenly. "Do tell me, have you found someone to replace Edgemont in your affections?"

"Oh, him." Holly sniffed. "I gave up on him long ago. Besides, there's to be a new footman!"

This brought a quick frown to Mary's face. "They are not letting Edgemont go?" Had they caught him with Rowena? Would that have so angered the Rake? He must have gone straight to Rowena's rooms after he left her. But Holly was shaking her head.

"No, oh, no. Mrs. Greenfield is that pleased, you can't imagine. Besides a new footman, we are to have *three* new maids and help in the kitchen for Mrs. Beecham. And you'll never guess! James is to be under-butler at last! Edgemont doesn't mind at all and told him something about his greatness ripening. They are only unhappy now because Mr. Wesson has set them to guard the landing by the long gallery. He takes the first hours himself, then it's James's turn and Edgemont has to stay from three in the morning until we all get up."

So that was how Clarence came to encounter the butler with his gun. A watch on the landing might make their escaping out to search for the rubies a problem—no, they could always creep down the hall to Wesson's stairwell while he was otherwise occupied and go out through the kitchens. She remembered Clarence hiding in the wardrobe, by now probably cramped both in muscle and temper. She rose.

"You'd better hurry back and get some sleep. It's very late."

"Oh, it's all right. I have only my apple left to do."

Mary walked with her to the door. "And what initial are you trying for now if not an E?"

"I've given that up. I'm counting the seeds instead. You know, one I love, two I love, three I love I say, four I love with all my heart, but five I cast away. And last night I had six! Six *he* loves! I do wish I'd get an apple with many seeds, for the verse ends with 'ten he tarries, eleven he courts, and twelve he marries.' And there's to be a new footman! Now don't forget to put the garlic in your keyhole."

Holding her cheesecloth bag of herbs before

her like a shield, Holly scampered down the dark hall. Mary watched her go, conscious of that warm feeling of awe one gets on realizing one has discovered a friend.

Behind her, Clarence clambered stiffly from the wardrobe. "I thought that female would never leave. Why did you not signal for me to come out?"

"Because she is completely scatter-witted and her tongue runs on a trolley! Everyone in the castle would know there was a man in my room." Mary shut her door and pushed the battered garlic clove into place.

"I'm your father," he complained. "Nothing wrong in that. And what the devil are you doing to foul up the place with that stench?"

Mary smiled, a tender thought for young Holly. "Warding off the ghost, of course. And keeping tryst in a way."

"Well, it's your sleeping chamber, not mine, thank God. Get your cloak, girl, and show me the way to the garden. I need to walk off a cramp in my left leg."

In a rush, her excitement returned. The rubies awaited! But now, so close to the end of the trail, she knew an odd reluctance to hurry the search. It might so soon be over, and she'd leave Rushmoreland—and the Rake. She would never see him again until possibly the day he had to sell up the castle to cover his—and Rowena's!—debts, and she'd turn him out into the streets. It was Clarence who now hurried things along.

"Come along, girl. I've no mind to spend all night at this."

Mary went out first, looking both ways up and down the passage. She could see no one, but at the far end, on the landing next to the long gallery, a faint light glowed. She patted the apron pocket in which she had put Holly's ghost-warding herbs and tiptoed toward it. If Wesson waited there with his fowling piece, the front stairs might be blocked, but his passage would be clear.

Not Wesson, but James, guarded the landing —if guarding was the word. He slept, his back against the wall, his head on his chest, and the ancient gun across his sagging knees. This ruled out leaving by the servants' entrance, for Wesson might still be awake. She returned for her father and together they slipped silently past the sleeping footman and down into the Great Hall.

The huge front portals were locked and bolted with heavy iron bars. Even could they open them, the ensuing racket would rouse the castle.

"How do we get out of here?" Clarence asked in a normal voice that echoed through the silence of the vast chamber.

Mary shushed him with a finger to his mouth. "Quiet!" she whispered. "Do you want to bring them all down upon us?"

She felt him shrug in the darkness, and pointed him toward the area where she remembered the dining room. "I think there is a door to the terrace over here. It's no use trying the French windows in the library. I've already tried them and they are frozen shut."

For once she had remembered correctly. There

were double doors opening on the terrace, and the latches worked easily for they must have been opened often for alfresco meals. She drew the bolts back quietly and pushed out one side of the doors. Together, they stepped out into the black night.

Mary realized at once that she had been too optimistic in her view of the moonlight through her window. The moon had vanished behind thick clouds and there was more than a hint of rain in the air. She hung back. "It's too dark, Father."

"Nonsense," said Clarence sturdily. "I'm here now, so let's get on with it."

They made their way across the terrace, stumbled down a few steps, and felt soft moss beneath their feet.

"This must be the shrubbery," Mary whispered. "I think the rose garden is just beyond."

The path they followed lay in darkness, a darkness that deepened as they passed beneath some trees. A stiff breeze had sprung up and rustled the leaves above their heads.

"This is no rose garden," said Clarence, coming to a stop. "We are in a yew alley."

Mary tried to peer through the trees. "We should have brought a candle."

"No good. This blasted gale would blow it right out." Drops of moisture fell on them, shaken from the dew-damp trees by the wind. "Or it would drown in this rainstorm," he added sourly. "What we need is a shielded lantern. Where the devil is this dratted rose garden of yours?"

She hesitated. They had been following a winding path, first walking between the hedges of a shrubbery and now under trees. "I'm not sure. I only saw it once, from a distance as I drove up in the cart. I'm all turned around."

"I might have known." Clarence seemed cheered by the fact that she could not lead the expedition. "Follow me, I'll find the way."

Mary caught at his coattails. There was something entirely too eerie about wandering around in the darkness. The rubies had waited over seventy years; they could wait a bit longer. "We'd better go back. I cannot see my hand before my face. This is no night to search for anything. Let me spy out the ground in the daylight and we will try again tomorrow if you can obtain a lantern."

"Oh, no. I know you, you mean to hunt by yourself and cheat me out of all the fun."

"Nonsense, Father. How can I feel about in the pools in broad daylight? Someone would certainly see me and then where would we be? I only mean to try to locate the proper statues and then we shall know exactly where to look. I can only hope that we are not completely lost out here and forced to wait for daylight to find our way back!"

"Not to worry," said Clarence, airily. "I've eyes like a cat."

He took her hand and felt his way along the tree-lined alley.

"Hah!" Triumphantly, he pointed to a break showing a lighter gray against the black trees. "Here we are, my dear, just as I told you."

Mary came up beside him, still clinging to his hand. Indeed, they seemed to have located the elusive garden, for the odor of roses hung lightly in the damp air. And there were statues, looming like paler shadows in the darkness.

They started forward. The thorny bushes caught at Mary's skirt as she stepped cautiously along and once Clarence swore when he walked straight into a particularly vigorous shrub.

"Confound all roses," he muttered. "Ought to be dug out and replaced with civilized plants. Never did care for the paltry things. All spikes and smelly blooms."

Mary grabbed his arm. "Look, Father! There to the right. Is that not a figure of Mercury? I think I see a raised arm, and is that not a wing on the foot that is in the air? Could that be the one we seek?"

Clarence bounded ahead. A winged statue . . . and if there should be a pool nearby . . .

There was.

He blundered into an ornamental bench and with a wild yowl, fell over it, grabbed vainly at the bushes, and went headlong into the water with a resounding splash.

Chapter Eight

Immediately, someone shouted from the house. James, Mary thought, awakened by Clarence's howl. She heard the back door creak open and seized one of Clarence's flailing arms. Yanking him out of the pool, she helped him to his feet.

"Father, are you all right? Are you hurt?"

"I fear my enthusiasm is somewhat damped." He shook himself like a dog, spraying Mary with algae-stained water. "Why you undertook this foolhardy expedition on such a foul night, I'll never understand."

Mary refrained from the obvious riposte. "Are you hurt?" she asked again.

"Only my dignity." He attempted to wring the water from the tails of his coat. "I believe I shall leave you now. I am going back to that paltry customhouse in the village and get dry clothes, a hot toddy, and a heated brick for my bed."

"Yes, Father, do so at once. And take care," she added. "I think both Wesson and James have come out to see what made such a noise. Go quickly."

Remarking that he had no desire to remain in gardens about to be overrun with zealous butlers armed with shotguns, even if they were fat, Clarence went, dripping. He headed toward the front of the castle and the main gates while Mary, wondering if she should create a diversion to protect his retreat, sank down behind a large rosebush. It was too dark to see the actual pursuit, but she was amazed to note that it sounded as though it headed the wrong way. And surely that was Edgemont in the fore! Rowena must have returned. But why did he lead the hunt away? He could not know who hid among the roses.

She began to creep toward the looming darker mass of the great castle, and as she neared the cobbled drive, she met the reason. Rounding a curve in the path, she came up against a large soft object that shrieked like a startled mouse. It was Rowena.

"Miss La Fleur!" Mary held her voice to a near-whisper, and Rowena clutched at her gratefully.

"A-aow, ducks! Am I that glad it is you! I cannot get in—they've bolted the door!" She listened for a moment to the row in the back gardens. "Whatever shall I do?"

Mary reached for her hand. "Come on with me."

Rowena held back. "I can't go in that way, not through the servants' door like I meant to. They are all up and running all over the place. Luckily Edgemont could just join them like he'd never been gone, but how am I to get in without beating on the front door? Not that anybody'd hear me. They're all out here!"

"I'll get you in." Mary pulled her toward the side terrace. "There's a door unbolted here."

Hanging on to Mary's hand, Rowena

crouched low and followed her along the beds of roses, her usual spirits miraculously restored.

"I say, dearie, was that old Clarence we passed as we come in? He looked all wet!"

Mary giggled, reprehensibly. "You should have heard the splash. He fell into one of the pools."

This tickled Rowena. "I'll wager you pushed him in. That's the way to cool off the old bastard!"

For a moment, shock held Mary silent. She had always known Clarence to be somewhat rackety, but she was beginning to get a new view of her parent.

"You needn't have waited up for me, ducks, but I'm right glad you did!" Rowena prattled on. "Here, dearie, take me domino and loo-mask in case we meet someone. It won't do for me to be seen coming in dressed like this. Is he home?"

Mary, rolling the garment into a ball and tucking it under her apron, had no need to ask whom she meant by "he." "Yes, he came home early." Remembering the reason for his sudden return, she felt a sharp pang of fear for his safety. Would he heed his great-aunt's warning? His devil-may-care features rose in her mind, laughing at her with those challenging sparkles in his eyes. But he had hesitated. . . .

"Oh, dear." Rowena hurried her steps. "Well, I can only hope he hasn't come to me room. Not that he's likely to," she added, bitterly. "If he has, I'll just say I took a bit of a nap over a good book in the library and forgot to come upstairs."

"Oh, no." Mary stopped her. "That won't serve, for it's where he has been himself."

"Whatever for?" Rowena sounded startled. "He's never one for reading, any more than me."

This Mary did not answer. "Perhaps you could say you were out walking in the garden," she suggested, "and came in when you were frightened by an intruder—who fell in one of the pools."

They had reached the terrace where the door Mary had unlatched still stood open. Rowena turned and gave her a quick hug. "You're a real love, dearie." She scurried in and Mary followed more slowly.

At first relieved that Rowena had not questioned her presence in the rose garden, Mary suddenly remembered why. She really must explain Clarence to Rowena as soon as possible, before the garrulous actress made some casual remark to the Rake that would destroy his apparent good opinion of his housemaid.

The goings-on of the night before constituted the sole subject in the Housekeeper's Room at breakfast. Wesson, as well as both footmen, had not slept much, and as a result the butler was more than usually austere. Mary listened closely to the speculations of the upper staff as to the identity of the intruder; but Clarence, in his person as her father Mr. Brown, did not come up, and she was thankful that he had kept his activities to the kitchens. She escaped immediately after eating, on the pretext of seeing if Rowena awaited her morning chocolate.

The Servants' Hall was abuzz with excited voices as she passed the door. She paused and listened. Here at last was something more solid than a specter, and she sensed a feeling of relief behind the wild conjectures hazarded by James and Edgemont. Edgemont in particular made impossible suggestions and she grinned as she realized he was covering for himself and Rowena. Could it be possible he thought it was Rowena who fell into the pool? Giggling to herself, she turned to hurry away.

"Miss—" one of the grooms had seen her by the door. "Miss—ah—Brown?" Mary recognized him as one of the loo players. He came out and thrust a twist of paper into her hand. "This here was left for you this morning."

The note must be from Clarence. She felt a modicum of surprise that he had arisen so early in the morning. Perhaps, finally, he took their search for the rubies seriously! She thanked the groom and walked away, unfolding the missive as she went.

She read it as she passed back through the Great Hall. It was from Clarence, as she had surmised. He would meet her, he wrote, at moonrise, by the same door to the terrace.

And this time I shall wear my top boots and borrow a lantern from my host at this blighted inn. Do you make a reconnaissance of the grounds and mark

*carefully where we must go. And to be sure this
message does not fall in enemy hands, may I suggest
that you chew it well and swallow it at once?*

She grinned, crumpled up the sheet, and
threw it into the huge hearth, where a blazing
morning fire consumed it far better than she
could have done.

Rowena, when she peeked into her room, still
slept. She rarely arose before noon. Mary, having time on her hands, decided to fulfill Clarence's instructions since it was what she had intended to do anyway.

The rose garden proved amazingly easy to
find in the daylight. They had merely turned
right instead of left at the foot of the terrace
steps the night before. No one was about, the
castle being abustle inside with morning chores.
She was free to stroll where she would.

She wandered up and down the rows, pretending to inspect the colorful blooms. Several
of the statues she passed might possibly do, but
none of them were exact. The Mercury had no
sword. A triumphant David stood in a pool and
leaned on a sword, the tip pointing downward
at the water. This seemed most promising, but
no urns stood near him. A Venus covered herself
coyly by a coffinlike bench, but she had no
wings.

The only wings she found were on a pair of
cherubim hovering over the entrance to a sort of
gazebo. Possibly Clarence would come up with
the solution. It might be that some of the figures
had been moved about. Either the gazebo or

possibly the David in the pool . . . She turned back to the castle.

Holly, encountered in the lower hall, informed her that chocolate had been carried up to Sir Archibald and tea to his lordship, but Miss La Fleur had not yet rung her bell. She obviously disapproved of such sloth, and of Miss La Fleur in general.

"Too free and easy, she is. Doesn't know her place. Why, she calls Mr. Wesson 'Cocky' and I'll wager she uses your first name instead of Migglesworth!"

This Mary could deny, at least the part about using her first name, for Rowena greeted her always as "ducks" or "dearie." Knowing how this would affront Holly's sense of social decorum, she kept quiet and changed the subject.

"Have you a bedfellow yet? I have seen no one new in the halls. Do we also still await the new footman?"

Holly flushed, her face as crimson as ever Mary's had become. "Oh, Miss Migglesworth, I do have the greatest hopes! He is not come yet, but only this morning I held a buttercup to my throat and Amanda said she saw the yellow glow reflected all around my chin! And then I blew the fluff from a dried dandelion, and seven seeds remained! Seven babes, that means. So you can be sure I'll have a long marriage! All my signs point to a lover coming my way!"

Mary, startled to discover she had a tempting urge to try some of Holly's divinations, excused herself and hurried up to Rowena's quarters.

Edgemont dallied in the upper hall outside

her door, his aspect so tragic that she went up to him at once.

"Good heavens, Edgemont, what is betide?"

He looked down at her, so woebegone that he could converse only in the language of the Bard, his native phraseology unable to do justice to the strength of his emotions.

" 'Fie, fie upon her!' " he quoted miserably. " 'There's language in her eye, her cheek, her lip, nay her foot speaks: her wanton spirits look out at every joint and motive of her body!' "

This somehow sounded a bit indecent to Mary, whose horizons were broadening every hour.

"I love her," he declared. "And what can I offer her to compare with a palace and a title? I —'a poor player that struts and frets his hour upon the stage and then is heard no more'?" He threw up his hands in despair. "Truly, mine . . . 'is a tale told by an idiot'!"

Mary's sympathetic heart went out to him. She caught one of his hands and pressed it warmly. "Oh, surely not. Does she hold out no hope?" Should she, she wondered, tell him to apply to Holly for a love spell?

" 'This is the very ecstasy of love . . . Oh, cursed spite that I was ever born . . . !' "

From Romeo to Hamlet! And out of context as well! Mary felt helpless in the face of such despair for, of a certainty, his case must be hopeless. Nothing, she was sure, would move Rowena from the pinnacle she had reached, especially with the vision of the rubies ever dangling before her. She patted the hand she held, silently, and was rewarded by a tremulous smile on the handsome face above her.

"You're a good lass." Edgemont lapsed at last into colloquialism. "I know she could never give up Harborough for a second footman. I am resigned." He turned away and walked off down the hall, his final words trailing back to her. " 'Past hope, past cure, past help! . . . My dismal scene I needs must act alone.' " She felt a bit encouraged. At least he had returned to *Romeo and Juliet.*

She tapped on Rowena's door and a cheerful voice bade her enter. The lovely Miss La Fleur sat at her dressing table, resplendent in a negligee of peach satin and Chantilly lace. A gift, Mary was sure, from Harborough. Now why should that thought occur to her?

Her mistress winked as she entered the room. "Good morning to you, ducks. I was just on to ringing for you. I'd like me hair brushed. Give it one hundred strokes, me old ma always said, and no cheating. That's what keeps the shine on it."

"And she was right, ma'am." Mary came forward at once and picked up the brush. Rowena turned to face the mirror and Mary looked at the beautiful reflection. Flamboyant, yes, but her features were perfect even though their colors were artificial. She unpinned the ribbon-bedecked lace nightcap and picked the curl papers from the incredible orange hair. With long, even strokes, she began to smooth out the kinky curls.

"Ah, and if that don't feel good." Rowena

sighed with pleasure. "Always had to do it meself before. Me old dresser couldn't be bothered. Above all that, she said, though she did the final arrangements something grand."

She fidgeted in her chair as though something were on her mind. "About last night," she began at last. "I know you'll have no call to speak to my lord, but I thought it best to tip you the nod. It won't do to upset Harborough."

Would Rowena also keep quiet about Clarence? Mary wondered. Aloud she assured Miss La Fleur that she would never run sly. "I am no tattlemonger. You may rest easy on that score."

"There now." Rowena beamed at her in the mirror. "I knew you were a right one when I saw you with old Clarence. We girls must stick together, but let me give you a word of advice, dearie. You steer clear of Clarence and his like. No money, ducks. Not worth the effort."

Now was her chance to straighten this out. "Oh, it wasn't what you think, really! He—he is a relative."

She realized all at once that she couldn't admit to being the should-have-been Earl of Rushmore's daughter—and remembered almost thankfully that below stairs they thought her illegitimate. Could she tell Rowena that? But would not the Rake suspect her of being after the rubies anyway if he learned of Clarence's presence in the castle and their questionable relationship?

"Please," she begged. "Do not tell anyone that he was here or I shall be discharged!"

Rowena's face grew pink with indignation

under her paint and rouge. "Over me dead body, you will! Neither Harborough nor that overstuffed butler has any business with one that's me personal servant. You'll stay with me, dearie, come hell or high water. But there, don't you worry none. Me lips are sealed—as I trust yours will be!"

Mary resigned herself. Rowena apparently knew her father all too well. She would believe Mary had an assignation with him and was sneaking him up to her room and no amount of explaining would change her mind. Just so she didn't mention it to Harborough as a casual bit of gossip! She could only hope Rowena would be as good as her word.

The actress was a sociable creature and she needed a friend to confide in. Mary discovered that she was not at all displeased to be so chosen. Rowena clearly was lonesome in the big castle. Harborough and Andover spent much of their time at the clubs in London and rarely took her out where she could be seen by all the people she wished to impress. Mary listened with a secret and entirely uncalled-for pleasure to her complaints of coolness and neglect from the Rake.

"For you must know, he has not once come to my bed since we arrived here!"

Mary made suitably sympathetic noises as she brushed. Did the Rake truly regret his rash defiance of his staid family? She hoped suddenly that he did not mean to expel Rowena until that lady decided herself to leave. She had become fond of Rowena. For all her flash, the actress was oddly vulnerable beneath her gaudy exterior. And, Mary suspected, far more in love with Edgemont than she knew, for he soon became her main topic of conversation.

The wonders of the evening before filled Rowena's mind to the exclusion of all else. She raved about the masquerade—and about Edgemont.

"Did you ever behold a more beautiful man? The way he quotes Shakespeare! He must know every line of every play ever wrote. I declare, if it didn't mean he'd leave the castle, I'd write me uncle to take him on. There was talk of doing *Romeo and Juliet* next season." Her voice took on a wistful note. "I can just picture Edgemont in them velvet tights and long curls. Romantic? I tell you!"

Mary agreed that Edgemont was indeed the picture of a romantic hero.

"And me his Juliet . . . Oh, ducks, sometimes I do miss treading the boards, but I never had it so good as now. I know when I'm well off, all right and tight, but I could fall in love with that man did I not want more to live in a castle and be a lady and wear those rubies . . . A—aow!"

"I beg your pardon, ma'am! An unexpected tangle!" In more ways than one, Mary thought, carefully brushing out the offending curl.

"Think nothing of it, dearie." Rowena rambled on about the masquerade, the friends she had met, and how she had shown off her new gown and jewels. "And me new footman. The handsomest cove they'd ever cast their daylights on." She sighed happily as she watched Mary's busy hands in the mirror. "We shall deal famous, you and me, ducks. Only I'm not to call you that. What's your last name, dearie? For I do know that a lady's maid is an upper servant and should be known by her surname. Harborough explained that to me."

Oh, did he! Mary could imagine only too well the unholy glee in his dark eyes as he explained this, straight-faced, to Rowena. Well, there was no getting out of it. She sighed. "It's Migglesworth, ma'am."

"Miggles—! Lawks, ducks! Why haven't you changed it?"

"Believe me," Mary said sincerely. "I'd like to do so, but it is too late."

Rowena clapped her hands, causing her many rings to strike rainbows in her reflection. "Nothing is never too late! And a name is easy as a ha'penny. Why, I don't shout it abroad now, but I was once Sadie Mucker." With the delight of one bored to tears, she entered into the game of choosing a new name while Mary listened with a growing sensation of déjà vu.

"Now, let me see. Grovemont? Beneville? Casterleigh?" Rowena mused. "Them names is all too hard to say."

"And too fancy," Mary agreed.

"I played a maid once," Rowena recalled dreamily. "Me first step on the boards, that was. Me first lines, too. Semple, that was m'character. Maybe I'll call you Semple."

It had gone far enough; Mary felt she had too

many names already. "Why not just Mary? I'd feel ever so much more comfortable."

"And so would I, ducks." Rowena beamed into the mirror at her. "I declare, the highfalutin airs in this castle are fair getting me down! Backstage, now . . ." She rambled on and Mary sensed a strong feeling of homesickness as Rowena reminisced of old friends and happier times. Being a lady was not what she had expected.

"I thought it would be all fancy clothes and pretty jewels, dearie, and so it is, but where am I to wear them? A lady don't go to masquerades, or even theater parties at the opera house with the actors. And I miss all the excitement, don't you know, and the crowds cheering and calling me name. I'd almost go back," she added wistfully, "if I could just once wear them rubies and have all them top-lofty females see me in all that glory!"

But that, Mary vowed to herself, would never happen. Not if she could help it. Rowena was doomed to a life in the castle—at least as long as Harborough held on to it.

Mary had almost convinced herself that Andover's staying in the castle would pose no problem for her. As a servant, she could easily stay out of his sight—she thought. She dropped the hairbrush as Andover himself came in the door without knocking, walking right into Rowena's boudoir.

Rowena greeted him with delight and he seated himself on her chaise longue, watching while Mary heated the iron and began to touch up the orange curls. She kept her head down and her face turned away, but he kept glancing at her. Did Andover think it ironic that the maid he thought of as the Rake's newest conquest was the servant of his mistress? Or did he recognize her as Danforth's daughter? She gasped with relief when instead of accosting her, he leaned over and attempted to pinch her bottom.

She blushed and jumped away, while Rowena laughed uproariously.

"Give over, Archibald. None of your games now! I'll not have you upsetting me abigail. See, she's red as a beet. Go along, ducks," she ordered Mary kindly. "You needn't put up with the likes o' him. I'll ring your bell when I'm ready to dress."

Mary went thankfully, but she lingered in the hall as she caught Andover's next words, casually spoken though they were.

"I say, Rowena, have you happened to hear Harborough make mention of a secret passage somewhere in this old pile?"

Rowena first gave a little scream, then laughed again. "You're trying another hoax on me, I know. I'll not rise to that fly. I don't believe a word of your ghost stories."

It seemed to Mary that Andover's answering chuckle had a smug and self-satisfied sound.

She was in a fever of impatience the rest of the day, waiting for Clarence, to tell him someone else knew of her passage—and might be looking for her rubies!

The Rake must have been talked into driving Rowena and Andover into London for the day, for when the actress next summoned Mary, it was to select the proper garments with which to dazzle all onlookers as she rode by in the open carriage with the Harborough crest on the door.

They were gone barely an hour.

Mary, brought at a run by the commotion in the Great Hall, was called upon to soothe her near-hysterical mistress with a vinaigrette and cologne water.

"A highwayman, ducks!" Rowena shrieked when she saw Mary. "We was fired upon right outside our gates!"

Mary felt the blood drain from her cheeks, leaving her far paler than the highly painted Rowena. Fired upon! Surely an unmistakable attempt on Harborough's life this time! She turned to him blindly. "My lord—Rake, are you hurt?"

He smiled, a quick, tight grimace. "No. Missed us all, but gave our horses a devil of a scare. Thought for a minute they'd overturn us!"

Rowena moaned and pushed away the vinaigrette Mary had retrieved from her reticule. "Take that stuff away, dearie, what I need is a shot o' gin!"

Andover entered from the dining room, carrying a brandy decanter and a number of goblets.

"Try this, my lovely. You're above the gin these days."

The Rake took the tray from him. "Come, let's repair to the library." He met Mary's stricken eyes over Rowena's head and smiled again, just for her. A reassuring smile of complete understanding, she noted with some relief. He knew, and perhaps he'd take care. "I'll not be going out again for a while," he added, for her benefit she was sure.

Wesson and Mrs. Greenfield both hovered in the background and the Rake nodded to them. "Dinner at home this evening. For us all."

"Yes, my lord."

Wesson's imperturbable mask had not slipped, but Mary could see by Mrs. Greenfield's trembling lip that she was about to have a fit of the vapors. She took the woman's arm and led her back to the Housekeeper's Room, after which she found Holly and sent her for tea. The trio in the library would want nothing so mild, but she could certainly do with a cup. Her thoughts were in chaos. However could she keep the Rake safely inside the castle? And how could he circumvent a murdering uncle?

It seemed forever until moonrise, but at last she slipped outside to meet Clarence. The clouds of the night before had cleared away and the moonlit garden lay in eerie silence under the pale light. Odd shadows seemed to move along beside her as she walked around to the terrace doors. It was after midnight: the witching hour, Holly would say.

She felt in her apron pocket and knew a foolish sense of comfort at finding the cheesecloth bag of herbs still there. With a slight effort, she stifled an urge to hold the bag before her like a shield as Holly had done.

Ghosts did not exist, she reminded herself, suspiciously eyeing a statue of Rebecca at the

Well on the edge of one of the pools. And even if they did, the local incumbent walked inside the castle, not out in the rose garden. These pale figures were of solid stone, not an amorphous specter among them! Strange, she thought, how one's imagination took over in proportion to one's lack of ability to see clearly. Wandering about in dark gardens with Clarence by her side was one thing; walking all alone—she hoped!—was quite another.

She made her way cautiously past a row of lighted windows, the anteroom behind the dining hall, where Wesson and James were clearing away the debris from the party's extended evening meal—and probably draining the half-empty decanters as Edgemont had done. The terrace lay ahead of her. A figure, paler than the dark walls of the castle, sat on the lower step and as she approached, it rose slowly to its feet.

Was it—? Yes, it was her father, waiting as he had promised. She ran to meet him, flinging herself into his arms in her relief to meet another living soul.

The terrace doors behind them swung open and an angry voice addressed her accusingly.

"That's not my footman! Now who the devil are you carrying on with?"

Chapter Nine

Harborough! Mary cast her eyes heavenward. Did the man never sleep?

"What are you doing here?" she demanded.

This did nothing to assuage his temper. "I live here, remember?"

"You know what I meant. Why aren't you inside with—with Rowena?"

"Who is this?" asked Clarence.

The Rake ignored him. "You didn't come to the library and I knew you met that confounded footman in the dining room, so I came to find you there."

Mary, so indignant at this charge that she could only sputter, stood there stammering. "I—d–do not m–meet Edgemont anywhere! I d–don't!"

Clarence raised his quizzing glass and haughtily inspected the Rake from head to toe. "Who is this?" he asked again. "One of the footmen?"

"No," said the Rake, and went on to Mary. "You weren't there, and then I looked out the window and I saw this sinister figure sneaking through the shrubbery and I thought . . . I mean . . . I expected someone, so I watched and then you came dashing up and hugged him!"

"And you thought I'd hug your beastly uncle!" Mary was now rigid with anger.

"How am I to know which side you are on?" A miserable note crept into his voice. "The way you go on, being so mysterious! You can't imagine how I felt until I saw it was not him! Anyway, I'll not have you hugging strange men in the garden after midnight! The footman I can understand, but—"

Clarence interrupted. "See here, my girl, I'll not have you carrying on with footmen!"

The Rake deigned to notice him. "What right has this frumpety old counter-coxcomb to object to your actions?"

"Sir, this is my daughter!" Clarence tried to clasp Mary in his arms again, but she eluded his grasp. He recalled the epithets just applied to him and squared off, fists raised. "Take back those words, sir, or I'll draw your cork!"

The hurt tone in Harborough's voice had melted Mary's wrath. No wonder he'd been upset, thinking she'd gone to meet his uncle. And he cared that she had not! She forgave him on the spot and pushed her father back.

"You two are acting like a couple of spoiled children. This really *is* my father," she assured the earl. "Truly it is."

The Rake blinked at Clarence in the pale moonlight. "Mr.—Migglesworth?"

"Good God, no!" Clarence exclaimed, revolted. "But this young lady is my daughter. Nothing wrong with hugging your own daughter, I believe, even under a full moon. I am trespassing, however." He added more mildly, "I trust you will not squeak beef."

"To whom?" the Rake asked. "Myself? Or my footman?"

"Oh, God," Clarence muttered aside to Mary.

"Now we are in the suds. I collect this is Harborough?"

Mary threw up her hands. "Naturally, Father. This is what I was complaining of. One cannot stir a foot in this castle—or out of it—after midnight, without encountering him."

Clarence sketched a polite bow. "How do you do? Sorry, I failed to recognize you in the dark."

The Rake seemed to have forgotten his role as the host, as well as his manners. "What the devil are you two up to?" he demanded. "And who the hell are you? I've felt from the start there was something mighty smokey about you, Miss Mary Migglesworth!"

" 'Something . . . rotten in the state of Denmark,' " she corrected.

"Never mind that, I want to know what is the meaning of all your nocturnal wanderings. And why must you drag your poor old father into your schemes?"

Clarence drew himself up again, insulted. "Young man, that is no way to speak of your elders—and betters!"

"Betters! A pair of sneak thieves perhaps, or who knows what!"

"We have no intention of robbing you!" Mary exclaimed, somewhat rattled by being accused so baldly, and she spoke before she thought. "If you must know, we are only looking for my great-grandmother's rubies!" She clapped her hand to her mouth, realizing her stupid mistake.

The Rake stared at her, openmouthed, and Clarence shook his head. "Now you've gone and done it, my girl. Nothing for it but to introduce ourselves." He extended his hand. "Danforth here, Clarence. I know of your great-aunt, Emily Halliburton."

"So that's it! The ex-Rushmore, eh?" Harborough pumped the offered hand heartily. "Thank goodness! I really didn't feel I could ally myself with a Migglesworth!"

Now what did he mean by that? As her employer . . . or . . . Mary, already unstrung, now felt thoroughly disconcerted. Her heart began to behave in a very unorthodox manner and she felt her cheeks flame as she met his eyes. Was that a warmer glow, glinting in the moonlight as he looked down at her—or was it only amusement?

He went on quickly. "No wonder I thought you resembled that portrait! I should have tumbled to it at once. And I was right, those rubies were meant for you to wear. Too bad they now belong to me."

"To you!" Mary gasped.

"Certainly. They belong to Rushmoreland, to the current earl, and that's me."

Mary's heart still pounded, but for an entirely different reason. "Oh no, they do not!"

The Rake shrugged. "Well, they are not up for grabs, that is certain. If they are located, they belong to the estate."

"That they do not!" Mary stamped her foot. "My great-grandfather had no right to take them for Prince Charlie. They were not his to give. Those rubies were never heirlooms of the estate, but the personal property of the Countesses of Rushmore."

"She's correct," Clarence interposed, digging out his snuffbox. "Listed as such in all the family records."

He offered the box to Harborough, who absently took too large a pinch and began to sneeze.

"Bless you," said Mary. "The possession of those rubies was established more than eight generations ago as a financial safeguard for the countesses. Bless you," she repeated as he pulled out his handkerchief. "It's always been that way. Each successive Earl of Rushmore added another stone to the collection."

"Not me." Clarence dusted snuff from his neckcloth. "Couldn't afford it. No point in it anyway. Everything all gone to the devil by my time."

The Rake had found a loophole and pointed to it. "If they went with the female line, how could they stay in the Rushmore family?"

"By tradition the dowager countess handed them to the bride of the new earl. If she died before her son married, they went to the eldest daughter to be held in trust for the next female on her marriage to the head of the family. The Countess Beatrix, had she found them, would have given them to my grandmother, who in turn would have handed them to my mother. At her death, ownership passed to me." She paused, triumphant, but the Rake shook his head.

"Now how do you figure that?"

"My father had no son and I am the last of

the Rushmore women and therefore the final owner of the rubies."

The Rake's eyes held that mischievous gleam. "Only until I marry! I'm the earl now owning Rushmoreland. They will belong to my wife."

Clarence replaced the snuffbox in his pocket. "I fear there is something wrong with that statement."

"Oh, no, they will not!" Mary exclaimed. "You are not a Rushmore. You are merely an upstart Harborough!"

"Ah," said Clarence. "That would be it."

"We shall see about that!"

Mary stamped her foot again, since being a lady she could not kick the Rake. "You cannot claim my rubies!"

The moonlight glinted on white teeth as he grinned. "They say some women are more beautiful when they are angry. Do you know, they are absolutely right."

Mary gasped, struck speechless, and he added more seriously, "But one thing I promise you, Rowena shall not have them. I don't know quite how I shall tell her." He sounded unhappy. "I have been trying to think of a way."

Clarence, left out of the argument long enough, cleared his throat for attention. "Is not all this rather premature? We do not have the rubies, nor do we know they still exist."

The Rake and Mary both turned on him. "Do not be a mar-plot, Father," his dutiful daughter reprimanded. "We certainly know they are here somewhere."

"I have this odd feeling," said the Rake, "that

you two possess some clue to their whereabouts." Mary and Clarence both looked at him
in dismayed silence. "And now I am sure of it."

The silence continued.

"Let us place our cards on the table," he suggested. "A friendly game. You have a clue. I can
top it. This is, after all, my castle. I can have you
both removed bodily and put an end to your
activities, or you can include me." He sat down
on the moonlit terrace steps. "Think about it—
and, please, do decide to include me. You must
know, this is the first time I have not been bored
in years and I have no wish to terminate our
acquaintance, little housemaid."

This last was said in such a humorously
pleading vein that Mary nearly succumbed. But
he would claim her rubies! No! Clarence saw her
decision in her stiffening back and took her arm,
drawing her a little way down the path.

"This calls for a conference, my dear."

She faced him, her countenance stormy. "He
shall not have my rubies!"

"It will do us no good to have the clues if we
cannot be here to follow them."

"I don't care."

"Mary, my girl, he cannot claim them. They
are yours by legal right. Somewhere among my
grandmother's papers I am sure we have the
documentation to prove our ownership. I am
afraid he holds the upper card for the moment."

Mary hesitated. It did seem as if they had no
choice. If the Rake should forbid them entry to
his grounds, they could not search. That pause
was her undoing, for she began to think about

what he had said before. He did not want to
terminate their acquaintance. And what had he
meant by being thankful he need not ally himself with a Migglesworth? At the time she
thought . . . but could he have meant just in
this venture? And that look in his eyes—was it
only the moonlight? Or could he mean . . .
Her thoughts raced in chaos; her heart began
again its erratic behavior. Did he mean to join
them to keep her near? Or only to use their
clues to find the rubies?

She took herself firmly to task. He flirted with
her. Rakes always flirted with housemaids. He
only wanted to be in on their game. He meant
nothing by what he had said. Never would he
look so or say such things to a lady of quality as
he had said to her those evenings in the library.
After all, he was the Rake! Treat it in kind, you
stupid girl!

Nevertheless . . .

"Ah," said Clarence, who had been watching
her expressive face. "We agree." He turned back
to the Rake, once more extending his hand.
"Welcome to our hunt. I have no real faith in
running our fox to earth, but we shall have the
exhilaration of clearing a number of fences. Tal-
lyho!"

He plunked himself down on the step and
picked up the lantern he had brought from the
tavern. "I'll have this alight in a moment."

Mary still had reservations, but she found it
impossible to resist the appeal of this closer relationship with the Rake. Unfortunately, he had

raised hopes she could not deny. The man held a far too great attraction for her.

Clarence mastered the lantern. He set it on the step beside him and bade Mary tell Harborough all. Briefly, she recounted the finding of the letters, the cryptic clues, her subsequent trip to Rushmoreland, and her attempts to locate the needed Pope translation in his library.

"I am crushed," he mourned as she finished. "So that is why you came to my library. It was not my fatal charm that lured you down night after night." He found a bright spot. "Or my footman's. Do you know, that is a load off my mind."

"What's all this about footmen?" Clarence demanded. "You keep talking about footmen. I will not have you flirting with the domestics, Mary, it is not at all the thing!"

"Rest easy, Father. I do not know enough Shakespeare."

He eyed her with suspicion. "What's that to say to anything? It is Homer we are interested in."

The Rake was grinning appreciatively. "And now you have the book."

"Books," supplemented Mary. "You gave me only one. There are five volumes. I had to go back down."

"It is your library." Clarence spoke with more than a hint of censure. "One would think you'd know your own books and have given her all the volumes at once."

The Rake attempted to appear contrite. "I bow before your superior classical knowledge."

"He didn't know either," said Mary.

Harborough grinned again. "Almost I have hopes of this expedition. Where are these cryptic clues? Have you translated them all?"

Mary took her copy from its hiding place in the bosom of her gown and unfolded it. He bent to study the paper in the light from Clarence's lantern.

"Now why did I not think to look in there?" he murmured in her ear.

She flushed. "You probably did." Her reply was tart.

Sadly, he shook his head. "You wrong me, little housemaid. Where you are concerned, my motives are pure."

Now she blushed for sure, feeling the heat creep over her cheeks. Truly, the man was a menace! She moved away, leaving him to read alone.

"Two urns," he mused, "a heavy winged goddess, and a tomb. Obviously, this refers to a cemetery. Could he have had the stones buried with himself? No, hardly," he added hastily. "But they may be in with someone else."

Mary came back, objecting. "He would not subject his Beatrix to a search of a dead body!"

"And then plough the watery deep," he went on thoughtfully. "A burial at sea? No, that will not do either, for she could never have retrieved them in that case."

"The grave of a sailor," Clarence announced. "There are sea captains among our ancestors. Must have been."

"Then I know the very place!" The Rake

folded the paper, started to put it away, and then those devils danced in his eyes. "Here, Miss Migglesworth, you keep this. I'll watch to see it safely stowed."

Mary made a face at him and put it in her apron pocket beside Holly's bag of herbs.

He led them around behind the castle, following the route Mary had taken from the kitchen door. From there, he struck out past the gardens, down a long branch of the yew alley, and finally to a broad meadow sparsely dotted with tombstones. A huge square vault, the size of a small church, stood in the very center.

"Ah, yes." Clarence sighed sentimentally. "The home of my ancestors. All the Earls of Rushmore sleep here except my grandfather and my father." He turned to Harborough. "You must see about bringing them here, my good man. It is not right that they should lie so far afield."

Mary frowned. To so address the Earl of Harborough! Her father was getting above himself. All this past glory had gone to his head. The fact that she ordered the Rake about was quite beside the point.

The Rake, however, nodded. "Why not? From the size of this place there must be room."

They were near enough now to see the building in some detail in the moonlight, and Mary caught her father's arm. Two huge stone urns guarded the entrance, and above the open arch that served as a door, a marble winged angel hovered entwined in a wreath of vine leaves.

The Rake stopped and spread his arms expansively. "You see? One ruby storehouse, as ordered." They scrambled to be first within.

Clarence swung his lantern from side to side. It glowed eerily, highlighting life-size stone figures reclining on the raised sarcophagi inhabited by their dead inmates. Two rows ran down the walls and several more coffins were set as though scattered in the central space. Clarence remained, transfixed, at the entrance and Mary wandered down a row, awestruck.

The Rake grabbed the lantern and began systematically checking each statue. The sleeping figures seemed to smile and open their frozen eyes as the lantern brushed wavering shadows across their carved features. Mary shivered. They looked so real—and they were! At least, beneath them lay real people. Her ancestors, great-great and more great. Fanciful thoughts crowded her head. Could they know that the last of the Rushmores stood among them, for with Clarence, their name would die? She was jerked back to reality by the Rake.

"Hah!" he shouted triumphantly. "I knew there would be one. See here!"

He held the lantern aloft, lighting the figure of an ancient knight who lay on his back, full length on his stone coffin, with the hilt of his sword between the hands folded on his chest.

Clarence came up and scrutinized the bronze plaque set into the carved shield by the knight's side. "Sir Cuthbert of Rushmore. Well, well. I've heard tales of his daring during the Crusades. He was a younger brother of the earl. His body was brought back from Turkey, not in very good condition, I believe, but given a place of honor."

"He has the sword!" Harborough exclaimed. "We have the two urns, the winged goddess, the tomb, and the sword."

Mary voiced a few objections. "He won't do, I'm afraid. He does not fulfill the requirements, for he's both honored and interred and possibly even wept for. He is not a sea captain, and his sword merely points at his own toes."

Clarence, too, sounded doubtful. "Aye, where is the watery deep to be ploughed?"

The Rake was not to be discouraged. "At least he must be too heavy to raise. We are the two strong men; perhaps with the help of Miss Migglesworth we can pry him up and have a look."

"You look," said Mary. "I cannot say that I am fond of skeletons."

She was overruled. Struggling and panting together, they managed to slide the lid several inches to the side, enough to shine the lantern within. Mary shrank back from the odor of mold and dust, but the Rake and Clarence peered in with interest, her father even reaching in an arm to poke about among the bones and flaking scraps of dry leather garments.

"A cross between his hands and blackened silver buckles," the Rake reported at last, disappointed. "He wears a chain with a stone of some sort, but no rubies. No bag or box that might hold them."

Mary, with admirable restraint, did not say "I told you so." She still held hopes for her secret passage. "Let us go back," she suggested with a shiver. The uncanny atmosphere of the vault had begun to grow on her. "If we read over the quotes again, perhaps we shall discover a new avenue to search."

The Rake, however, continued to wander about among the huge coffins. "I suppose this is where I'll be one of these days."

"That you will not," Clarence informed him. "These are Rushmores. My ancestors. You upstarts are buried outside. Probably because there is not much room left in here," he added magnanimously.

"Then I shall construct another building, just like this one, next to it. Here, give me a hand, both of you, and let's put old Cuthbert back to bed."

The idea of bed appealed to Clarence. "A false trail. Enough for tonight." He was beginning to get bored. "It's a wild-goose hunt. If our rubies were ever here, they are long gone by now."

They shoved the lid back into place, and Mary dusted her hands on her apron, patting Holly's charm. If any ghosts dwelled in this mausoleum, so far they had been well warded.

"I'll not give up, Father. It is we who have the letter. No one else could have the clues."

Clarence shrugged. "Then they were found by accident. I feel the need of a glass of port and a comfortable fire."

The Rake smiled down at Mary. "I'll not give up. After all, this is only my first attempt. Come, Miss Mary Migglesworth, we shall go study your clues once more and try another tack."

They trooped back to the castle and Mary felt warmly grateful for his support. Clarence might always be ripe to try any lark, but he was a weak reed to lean on for he lost interest rapidly in any project that did not instantly succeed. And he was far too self-centered and conscious of the needs of his own comfort. She knew him too well to persist in the hunt this night.

At the Rake's suggestion, they got all the volumes down from her room and set up a study in the library, well supplied with decanters of brandy and wine, while they rechecked the numbers of the lines.

Clarence appropriated the wing chair and leaned back, sipping delicately from his glass. "Not a bad vintage, this, quite acceptable, but I had a better one in the kitchen. Did you know you have in your cellars some bottles of as soft a Dijon port as I've ever had the privilege of tasting?"

The Rake glanced up from the volume he held, his brows snapping together. "No, I did not know it."

Clarence twirled the liquid, watching the play of firelight on the wine. "Your butler does."

"Oh, does he?" The grim note in Harborough's voice boded ill for Wesson. "I see I shall have to check more closely into my new possessions."

"It's your own fault," Mary told him. "You have refused to take your new consequence seriously. You deserve to have your butler hold back the best."

He stared at her for a moment, an arrested

look in his eyes, before turning back to the volume he checked. "I see I must mend my ways, whether I will or no."

Clarence clapped his book shut. "There's the last and we've made no errors. The lines stand as we have them."

The Rake joined him by the fire, comparing the list he held with Clarence's. "Let us start over, from the top. Art, not strength. Two urns by a throne. A weight. A winged goddess—or queen. A tomb. An unburied man or object. A sword, and a watery deep." He ran his hand through his hair, tousling his Windblown combing beyond repair. "There are urns on the terrace . . . no." He dismissed them out of hand. "Someone recently has planted them with shrubs and there are no statues."

He threw himself into a chair, deep in thought, and Mary watched him hopefully. She was rewarded.

"Aha!" He jumped up, grabbing Mary's arm with one hand and with the other the lantern by which Clarence, once more engrossed in Homer, had been reading. Clarence yelped a complaint, but the Rake and Mary were already through the door into the Great Hall.

Harborough stopped in front of the huge hearth and held the lantern high. "Art," he announced, gesturing with his free arm toward a dark canvas that hung above the smoke-blackened mantel.

Mary considered the painting, doubtfully. It depicted a number of embattled sailing ships of a bygone era, their cannon blasting one another's collapsing masts during an unbelievably rough and wild storm at sea.

"Excellent marksmanship considering the inclement weather," she remarked.

"You're not looking at it!" the Rake complained. "Read the names on the sterns of the two ships in the foreground. *HRH Elizabeth* and the *Francis Drake!* There is our queen and the watery deep. And there is an urn on each end of the mantelpiece and even swords."

There were two rusting swords, crossed, hung beneath the painting. Mary eyed them critically. "They point in different directions," she observed. "Not a very good sign. And the ships are not treading on air although the painting does hang rather high."

"Admit it's a possibility!"

"A very thin one." She raised another objection. "Has anyone ever been interred in your hearth? I doubt my great-grandfather referred to the oxen that must have been roasted here."

He lowered the lantern, exasperated. "Just like a female, always finding fault!" They started back to the library, passing under the banner-hung gallery. Suddenly, he paused and doused the lantern.

"Listen!"

They stood close together in silence, the darkness wrapping around them. "I thought I heard a door open."

"Hush!" Mary reached for his hand.

Stealthy footsteps crossed the gallery floor above their heads and a dim glow as of a single wavering candle traveled along toward the landing.

"Our ghost walks!" the Rake whispered, and they flattened themselves against the wall, waiting.

Mary became too flat, hitting her head against the lower corner of one of the ancient shields ornamenting the wall. It slipped from its rusted nail and fell forward. The Rake lunged and caught the top edge, easing it toward the floor before Mary could be crushed by its weight, but it made a clatter as it landed.

The candle in the gallery went out and they heard running footsteps heading for the staircase.

Their ghost was getting away.

Chapter Ten

Dropping the shield the rest of the way to the floor with a crash, the Rake took off for the staircase at a run with Mary, holding up her skirts, right behind him. A pale shadow fled before them, up yet another flight to the second-floor landing.

Mary panted as they followed the sound of

pounding feet in the nearly complete darkness. "Heavy feet . . . for a ghost!" she gasped.

The footfalls turned at the second-floor landing, ran down the corridor across the front of the castle, and veered off into the oldest, unused wing. And stopped.

Harborough stopped too, listening, and Mary sank to the floor, catching her breath.

"Hell and the devil confound it!" he whispered. "There's a thousand places to conceal oneself in this dratted barrack!" As he spoke, a stealthy, scraping noise came from a room ahead.

Reaching down, the Rake found Mary's hand. "Come on, he's here someplace close!"

He felt along the wall, found a door ajar, and they slipped silently inside. Through a vine-covered window, a faint moonglow lit the room, creating ghostly mounds of the shrouded furniture. Mary grasped the hand she held tighter and pressed close to him.

He bent his head toward her. "Afraid?"

"Not with you here."

He released her hand and his arm went about her waist instead with a reassuring hug. It stayed there.

As far as Mary was concerned, he could hug her forever, but the spell was broken by a muffled clump in the next room as if someone had fallen over a footstool.

The Rake charged to the door in the opposite wall and jerked it open in time for them to see a pale figure leaving by the other side. In this oldest section, the rooms led into each other without access to a corridor, like dens in a rabbit warren. They scurried from chamber to chamber, the pale shadow ever flitting ahead of them like a will-o'-the-wisp, insubstantial as a specter —except for the sounds of his passing. The rooms appeared to be used for storage, and obstacles for the unwary abounded.

Once when they lost sight of their quarry, it almost seemed as though the shadowy figure waited for them to catch up.

"I have this odd feeling we are being led astray," the Rake muttered, once more catching Mary by the waist.

She stopped, leaning against him, for a moment almost forgetting why they were alone in the darkness of a deserted wing of the castle— until a frightening thought struck her.

"Do you think—could we be running into an ambush? Could it be your uncle?" She clutched at his lapels. "Let's go back!"

Harborough laughed aloud. "My Uncle Jameson is nearly as high in the instep as Wesson! I can just see him leading us on such a chase."

A door farther away creaked on rusty hinges, and the Rake was off again, pulling Mary along by the hand.

It was the last sound they heard from the intruder they pursued. Harborough slowed to a stop. A stillness settled over the ancient stone walls and they waited, uncertain.

"Is he gone?" Mary tried to see ahead but her eyes met only impenetrable darkness. "It feels oddly like we are alone." She found herself whispering.

Beside her, the Rake straightened and she sensed in him the same uneasy consciousness of isolation. "Confound it, I wish I knew where we are. If his purpose was to get us lost, I fear he's succeeded!"

Mary squeezed the hand that held hers. "We cannot be lost! This is a building, after all. We have only to reach an outside wall and follow along it to the front."

It sounded easier than it proved to be, for they had no way of knowing if they wandered in circles through the endless rooms. Not that Mary cared. She could feel the glow of warmth emanating from Harborough. Her shoulder brushed his arm as they moved along and a funny, shaky sensation bubbled within her. When his arm encircled her waist once more, the blood quickened in her veins. A strange lightness, compounded of excitement and happiness, flooded through her like an elixir, and she wondered if he, too, felt the compelling tug of awareness between them.

They walked slowly, as if neither wanted the journey to end, and it was with a decided regret that she at last recognized the back passage at the head of Wesson's stairwell. From there, it was disappointingly easy to reach the grand staircase that rose from the Great Hall.

"There's no light up there." Mary pointed toward the landing by the Long Gallery. "Do you suppose Wesson has given up and placed no guard tonight? Now, when one was needed!"

As she spoke, a cataclysmic crash of flying

pots and pans echoed from the stairs above and Mary shrieked like Rowena.

The Rake threw his head back and roared with laughter. "The crafty old buzzard! Wesson's set a trap and our ghost has fallen into it! Come on!"

They raced up the first flight and a veritable fusillade of shots screamed past them. Harborough caught Mary, hauling her down as Wesson and his two footmen charged down the corridor toward them. Yanking her after him, the Rake dove behind a huge oaken chest on the landing. They crouched, holding their breaths as the armed brigade labored past and on into the Long Gallery.

Mary became suddenly aware that besides holding his breath, the Rake was holding her— rather tightly—in his arms. He spoke softly into the hair by her ear.

"Now where the devil can he have procured all that weaponry? I fear I shall have to replace the lock on the gun room if any of us are to survive!"

She was almost certain his lips touched her hair, for she felt the warmth of his breath.

Suddenly nervous, she tried to wriggle free. "Why are we hiding here? You needn't hide! This is your home!"

"I don't care to be shot by my own butler, even if it is Pursuant to his Duty." He cuddled her closer. "This seemed a very good idea at the time. It still does."

Mary found she couldn't rise. "We—we'd better go."

"Why?" he asked. "I like it here. We should do this more often. Do you know," he continued conversationally, "my footman has kissed you, Andover has kissed you—"

"They did not!"

He ignored her interruption. "And I have not. And you are my housemaid."

"You wouldn't dare!"

He grinned. "Oh, wouldn't I!"

Mary found suddenly that he would, and the sensation was altogether delightful. The lips that brushed her cheek before pressing hers were warm and firm, sending little quivers of bliss through her whole being.

But this was not at all the thing! He had no business treating her like a servant girl—or—or one of his bits of muslin! She tried to become quite indignant and pull herself free.

"Really, my lord!"

"Rake."

"Oh, bother! No wonder that is your nickname. Why do you not go to see what is happening upstairs instead of—of—oh, do go!"

He grinned, released her, and rose slowly to his feet. "Yours to command, Miss Migglesworth. I go, but I shall return."

A world of meaning hung in his tone, and Mary, thankful for the darkness, felt her color rise. Very much on her dignity, she scrambled to her feet and straightened her skirts.

They could still hear shouts in the hall above, and running footsteps, but no more shots. The Rake listened for a moment and then turned to her. "I think it best that you go back down to the library and remain with your father until the upper halls are clear. I shall see you into his care."

Undeniably, it was nice to have someone considering her welfare. Mary accepted his proffered arm, resting her fingertips on it daintily, and as regally as if she were a princess, he escorted her down the grand staircase. She pretended not to see the mischievous gleam in his eyes as they passed beneath the wall torch in the Great Hall.

The library, when they entered, was empty. Naturally Clarence had not remained where they left him. Volumes of the *Iliad* lay scattered about and the candles guttered on the tables. Mary turned to Harborough in sudden panic.

"Rake—my lord! If he is roaming about the castle in the dark, Wesson will think he is the ghost and shoot him!"

"Stay here." He pushed her into the wing chair. "I'll stop them."

"How? Oh, how can you? If you go up those stairs, you will be shot!"

He laughed. "Watch me." Before Mary could stop him, he ran out into the Great Hall and headed for the green baize doors. Just before them stood Wesson's huge dinner gong with the hammer hanging beside it. He caught it up and beat the gong a hefty blow, sending bell-toned echoes vibrating through the cavernous chamber.

The baize doors burst open and Mrs. Greenfield, flanked by a timorous gaggle of maids, peered out.

"My lord!" she cried. "Is it fire? Are we attacked by bandits?"

"No, no," he soothed. "Merely our ghost."

She squealed and fell back into the cluster of maids, all of whom retreated in disorder as the doors swung to.

Wesson, trailing behind James and Edgemont, waved his fowling piece as he puffed down the stairs.

"Do you have him, my lord? Have you Caught the Miscreant?"

The Rake raised his eyebrows. "Do you mean you have not? I made sure he'd be dead by now, or have you merely been using my ancestors' portraits for target practice?"

The pop-eyed butler was spared an answer by Andover, who drifted down in his wake, dressed in a brocade robe and nightcap.

"What, is the evening's entertainment not quite done? You must know poor Rowena is practically cowering beneath her bed."

"Well she might." Mary, behind the library door, heard a grim note in his lordship's voice. "Someone was in here tonight. We gave chase, but he escaped. If he is still within the castle, we shall have him."

He turned to the butler. "Wesson, do you check all the ground-floor doors and windows. Make sure all are bolted. James, up one flight with you, and Edgemont take the second. I will do the third myself. When all below is secure, we meet at the Long Gallery and go together on the upper levels and even the battlements if need be. I see you are all armed, but may I beg you not to fire? Enough damage has been done to the paneling on my walls."

He waited until the three men were on their way, and clapped Andover lightly on the shoulder. "Perhaps, man, you will comfort Rowena for me. Assure her we are doing all possible to keep her safe."

Andover did not move. He eyed the Rake thoughtfully. "Know what I think, Harborough? It occurs to me that uncle of yours may be having a shot at the title."

"Now what put that daffish notion in your head?"

His words were light, but Mary caught a serious note in his voice and felt a tiny shimmer of relief. Thank God, he realized his danger.

"I may be daffish," Andover said as he turned to mount the stairs, "but I suggest you keep your pistol handy and bolt your bedroom door at night."

The Rake's laugh was short and mirthless. "Go to Rowena. I'll have a care, Archie, but only to humor you."

Mary watched Andover depart. So he, too, believed the Rake to be in mortal danger. But she remembered seeing his uncle Jameson, and he was an elderly man. The figure they pursued this night was quick and agile.

Harborough returned to her. "Come, Mary. I believe the coast to your room to be clear. Let me see you there, and then I shall search for Clarence. No doubt he has gone to ground, hiding from the hounds."

Mary shook her head. "Not my father. He is

far more likely to have gone to determine the cause of the commotion. Hiding is not his way."

"Then I'd best find him." He took her arm and hurried her across the Great Hall and up the stairs to her room. He threw open her door— and they discovered Clarence lying on her bed with his boots off, immersed in a volume of the *Iliad*.

He laid it down as they entered. "Ah, my dear, there you are at last. Only think, I have found it!"

Mary ran to him. "Father, what?"

"Right here." He exhibited the volume he held, proudly. "In Book Four, line one hundred ninety-six. 'The day shall come, the great avenging day—' "

"Oh, Father," Mary interrupted, disgusted. "I thought you meant the rubies!" Clarence looked past her and deigned to notice the Rake.

"Hallo, Harborough. Brought her back safe, have you? No end of ruckus going on out there. I started to follow you but lost sight of the chase almost at once. Waited awhile and then took a candle and went up to the Long Gallery to see if my ancestors still hung. Did you know someone piled a beastly stack of pots and pans on your stairs? And threaded them through with a length of twine!"

Mary collapsed on the edge of the bed. "Oh, no! Was it you who sprang Wesson's trap?"

"A trap, was it? No, not I. Had a light so I stepped around it. Thought when I saw it that somebody would fall over it. Dangerous," he informed the Rake, disapproving.

"I'll have it all cleared away at once," Harborough promised meekly. He leaned his shoulders against the wall and shoved his hands in his pockets, prepared to stay and be amused.

"Too late, I'm afraid." Clarence picked up his book. "I had barely inspected my grandmother Beatrix, my great-grandfather, and two great-great-uncles when I heard the devil of a crash. Knew what had happened."

Mary rose and patted his stockinged toes. "How is it you were not caught?"

"Oh, I doused my candle at once. Should have left it lit, for in the dark someone ran full tilt into me. Felt a rush of cold air and demme if the creature didn't disappear."

"Disappear!" Mary's hand froze above his feet.

The Rake's shoulders came away from the wall and his eyes sparked with sudden interest.

"Do you mean he ran out of the gallery?"

"Oh, no. I'd have heard his footsteps. One moment he careened into me, the next—gone."

He refused to be shaken from his story. Mary's eyes met the Rake's and she repeated Holly's tale of Belinda and the Jacobite's ghost. "There is something odd," she finished, "about that Long Gallery—"

"Indeed there is!" Clarence complained. "In only minutes the dashed place was overflowing with butlers and footmen all shooting guns! I barely managed to escape up the back stairs."

The Rake was of a more practical turn of mind than Mary. "Our ghost must have climbed those same stairs."

"That he did not." Clarence was firm. "No one on those stairs but me. Whoever—or whatever—it was, disappeared right in front of me. In the pitch blackness, I couldn't see where he went, but I felt this blast of chill air and then got that feeling one has when you know you are alone. Oh, it was the Jacobite, all right." He glanced at them sideways to see if he was believed.

Mary shuddered and the Rake's arm went about her protectively. Clarence observed this with a paternal eye and swung his legs to the floor.

"Time I was getting back to that infernal pub." He fished around for his boots and located them under the bed. "Things seem to have quieted down. By the by, Harborough, my grandfather's portrait is missing. Please see it is returned at once. A Jacobite he may have been, but he was a Rushmore."

The Rake grinned. "I'll have it replaced."

"Do so. No wonder he walks. Probably misses his wife, hanging there by herself. If he is trying to find her to tell her where the rubies are, we ought to see the old boy has all the help we can provide. Give me a hand here, Harborough. Shove and I'll stomp."

Mary looked on, mildly scandalized, while the earl knelt and lent his aid with her reprobate father's boots. He left with Clarence, apparently intent on leaving no doubt in her father's mind that he did not mean to remain with her. His final words were an admonition to lock her door.

* * *

Bleary eyes were the order of the day at breakfast. Mary learned that nothing and no one had been discovered during an all-night search. Not surprising, she felt, considering the ease with which she, Clarence, and the Rake had moved about.

Wesson, however, was determined to continue the guard on the landing since his trap had failed. Ignoring their wails of dismay, he assigned Edgemont and James to stand shifts with him.

Mary herself had not a moment of peace, for soon after breakfast a parade of milliners and mantua makers descended on Rushmoreland Castle. Rowena was in her heyday, reveling in the results of her shopping trip in London with Andover.

After one look at the mounds of bandboxes, Mary knew she could never cope alone and sent for Holly, much to that damsel's delirious delight. Mary was kept at Rowena's side, aiding her in the trying on and fitting of every gown and every bonnet, while Holly sat on the floor, trembling with excitement as she opened the boxes and peeled back the layers of silver paper to reveal more treasures.

Rowena, preening herself in the mirror as she held up a cerise satin ball gown that fought with her orange hair, noticed the little maid's round eyes in the reflection.

"Lawks, ducky, you should be a lady's maid, loving the pretties like you do."

Holly's face flamed. "A-aow," she said, in

an unconscious mimicry of Rowena's tones.
"Who'd ever hire the likes of me!"

"She has a real feeling for color and fabric,"
Mary put in. "Perhaps she could be my assistant
at times such as this."

Holly's eyes and mouth formed a trio of O's.

Rowena clapped her hands. "I've got a wardrobe full o' real nice things I'll never wear again.
You shall have a genuine flash gown, right up to
the nines! You too, ducks, one for each of you!"
She turned to the open cabinet overflowing with
flamboyant costumes. "Take your pick, loves,
any one you like—only not this." She caught a
fold of mulberry satin and Mary recognized the
gown she wore the day she arrived.

Rowena ran her hand lovingly down the
gleaming material. "This here is me favorite. I
reckon I'll wear it a few times more, but take
any you want of all the rest."

Holly sat on the floor, surrounded by the
opened boxes, too frozen by the magnificence of
the offer to move. A pair of tears ran down a
face so pale that Mary stooped to her aid, helping her to her feet. With a shaking hand, Holly
touched the skirt of an exquisite ball gown of
ruby-red figured velvet with silver rosebuds and
flounces, open over a creamy pink gauze under-
dress. She pulled the hand back.

"I'd never get to wear nothing like that no
place, not ever."

"Lots of others, dearie, take your time." Rowena began to empty the wardrobe, recklessly
tossing the gowns on her bed. Like a little girl
playing with her dolls, she began holding up

one after another, trying the effect on each of them.

Mary soon selected a soft yellow walking dress of merino, trimmed with a great deal of sable fur that she was sure could be removed. It had three flounces to the skirt and long tight sleeves with exaggerated puffs at the top. The fur, leaving only enough for a collar, could be stitched together into quite a creditable muff. The sable closely matched her dark curls and the delicate yellow accented the soft rose in her cheeks and the deep blue of her eyes.

Holly proved her sense of decorum by finally choosing a celestial blue round gown of figured damask, the very thing, she professed, for going to early services in the chapel. "And won't I look the real lady for when the new footman comes!"

Rowena was as pink with pleasure as Holly, and as pleased by their delight as if she and not they had received a sumptuous gift. She plied them with matching bonnets, gloves, hose, and slippers. Holly returned to her quarters in a daze, fairly walking on air, and Mary thanked Rowena sincerely.

"That was excessively kind in you, ma'am," she exclaimed impulsively. "You may be sure Holly will remember this for the rest of her life."

The pink in Rowena's cheeks deepened beneath their coating of rouge.

"Well, now, dearie, I can't help but remember what a new gown would'a meant to me when I was her age. Looking at her, I declare the Sadie Mucker period o' me life just come to the fore."

By the time Mary was finally dismissed after arraying Rowena for dinner in one of her new purchases, she was exhausted. Giving advice and trying to curb Rowena's desire to choose purple satin, silver gauze, and rose pink lustring for everyday wear had worn her out. Finally, some almost suitable morning attire, carriage dresses, and evening gowns were settled upon, and the more outrageous outfits boxed up to be returned.

As soon as she could slip away after her evening meal, Mary repaired to the library on the off chance of finding the Rake, whom she had not seen all day. He was there, and to her horror, resplendent in the tailcoat, black satin knee breeches, and striped hose that composed a gentleman's correct evening dress.

"My lord, you are not venturing out!"

"Rake," he corrected. "And I am. Rowena is determined to set society back on its heels by the sight of her in her new glory."

"Oh, no, you will not give in to her! Your uncle—"

He shook his head. "Andover has suggested a most discreet card house in Pall Mall and we will take a closed carriage. My uncle Jameson is not a gamester; no danger of encountering him in such a place. He would not be caught dead in a gaming hell."

"Just see that you are not!"

He laughed and chucked her chin with a casual finger. "Do you really fear for me, little housemaid?" His eyes, above his teasing smile, were serious, questioning. "No one else does, be sure."

Mary swallowed, only too aware of her feelings for the man who towered over her.

"My lord—Rake—" she whispered. "Take care."

About to turn away, he paused and touched her cheek, a look of wonder, almost awe, crossing his features.

"Not to worry, Mary Migglesworth, I'll guard my life well. For the first time, it is worth something to me."

She caught his hand, holding it to her cheek. "Please . . . do not go."

He pulled her hand down, kissing the fingertips. "Can you not understand? I'll not let my uncle make me a prisoner in my own house. No man will be my jailer!"

She let him go; there could be no way to hold him. Oh, why, she wondered, must the men in my life be so difficult? Clarence was bad enough and now the Rake, childishly clinging to his principles when all logic and reason demanded a compromise! Why could men not be as sensible as their female counterparts?

He would not let any man have such a hold over him. He would not hide. But was he safe even here? That may not have been his uncle Jameson they pursued through the castle, but could it not have been a minion? A hired assassin? In which case, her annoyingly realistic mind demanded, why had the man not attempted to kill them off in the far reaches of the oldest wing where their bodies might not have been discovered for days or weeks? No, it seemed rather the purpose had been to lure them off, to lose them, until some other deed could be accomplished. Well, he had not succeeded. She giggled suddenly, remembering the nerve-shattering crash of Wesson's pots and pans. How frustrated he must have been!

Despite the Rake's assurances, Mary could not rest easy, and she set up a watch on the grand staircase, awaiting his return. Some hours later, as she dozed on the landing, she was awakened from a dream in which a ghostly hand repeatedly thrust a sword at the laughing Rake. A commotion below in the Great Hall brought her to her feet and she looked down to see Wesson carefully divesting Harborough of a bloodstained coat.

A scream died in her throat and she clutched the banister for support. Rowena was weeping loudly and Mrs. Greenfield, pale and flustered, hovered uselessly about her. Mary ran down the stairs as Andover came from the dining room bearing a decanter just as he had before. Again! It had happened again, and this time her lord had been injured.

But he stood, straight and calm, handing the ruined coat to Wesson, and gingerly loosening the back of the linen shirt that stuck to him in a patch of congealed blood.

He saw Mary and beckoned to her. She ran to him, forgetting all else, and in a moment was in his arms. He thrust her gently away and tipped up her white face with one hand.

"I am all right, little housemaid. Barely scratched."

"Oh, I knew you should not go!"

"You were wrong there, Mary Migglesworth; I was very right to go."

She stared up at him.

"You see, now I know." He turned to Andover, who had poured a glass of brandy for the hysterical Rowena and now offered one to him. "Thanks."

Mary realized suddenly that Wesson and Mrs. Greenfield watched openmouthed, and stepped back. Where were her scattered wits? She should be seeing to Rowena, not clinging to Lord Harborough. That lady had ceased her tears and was gulping the brandy Andover had supplied.

The Rake turned to Wesson. "Send Guimper to me, and I think if Miss La Fleur has finished enacting for us a Cheltenham tragedy, she had best be taken up to her room." As he shoved Mary toward her distraught mistress, he whispered two words in her ear. "Library. Later."

With a singing in her suddenly lightened heart, Mary escorted Rowena to the stairs, and they walked up to the accompaniment of a running commentary of the actress's feelings.

"Lawks, ducks, you can't believe the shock it was! When I saw all that blood, I was that staggered I come all over queer! Harborough was the one that got stabbed and it was me got carried to the coach! Whoever could have done such a thing?"

She continued to marvel at the evil in the upper-class world, recounting the events of the evening over and over while Mary sent for Holly to bring a hot warming pan for the bed, the sal volatile, and a glass of Rowena's favorite gin.

"For I can't appreciate that sweet syrupish brandy," Rowena explained. "Only think how it must muddle one's innards! Give me a nice clean tot o' gin every time."

It was long before Mary had her settled and the candles snuffed so she could escape to meet Harborough in the library.

He was there before her, in the wing chair, wearing a dressing gown. Mary noted with a slight amusement that his taste in such garments marched with that of his butler. The deep blue velvet sported a pattern of iridescent peacock feathers. Topped with a fresh white neckcloth, the costume was vastly becoming. He sat quietly sipping a glass of Madeira and as Mary entered, he poured one for her and indicated the chair beside him. She accepted both.

"Now my lord—"

"Rake."

Her smile felt tremulous. She still shook inside. "Rake. Let's have the whole tale with no roundaboutation. How badly are you hurt?"

He shrugged. "As I told you, a mere scratch. I must have moved away as the knife struck for it penetrated a bare half inch, according to Guimper. A dusting of basilicum powder and a patch took care of all."

"What happened? Your uncle—?"

He shook his head. "Not Uncle Jameson. My cowardly cousin Kendrick."

"Your cousin!"

"My uncle was not there, as I knew he would not be, but I saw Kendrick as soon as I came into the room. Odious little beast. I dropped my guard, never thinking he'd have the nerve."

Mary sat up straight. "Then you saw him, you know it was he."

The Rake frowned. "The devil is in it that I didn't see him. The room was crowded, I didn't watch his every move so I had no idea he might be behind me. Apparently, no one saw him strike. All eyes were on the dice; we concentrated on the play. Andover rolled against Fanshaw for an incredibly high stake. Everyone hung over the table and I felt someone hit me on the back, hard, but I didn't know I'd been stabbed until Rowena screamed that there was blood on my back. Kendrick had disappeared by then and I've no proof that it was he."

"It could have been no other!"

"So Andover claims as well. Gossip has it that Kendrick has been inveighing against me at all the clubs. He's very bitter."

"Did Andover win or lose?" Mary's mind took refuge in irrelevancy.

The Rake laughed. "Who knows? Rowena's shriek raised the very devil and I believe someone upset the table, luckily for Andover. The dice are never with him."

He rose and came to her, pulling her to her feet. Uncertainly, she raised her face to his. His arms went around her and she closed her eyes, succumbing to the wonder and warmth of his gentle kiss. Several minutes passed before he put her from him.

He gazed into her eyes, seeking a confirmation he evidently found, for he grinned, hugged her close, and kissed the tip of her nose. "Now, go to bed, Mary Migglesworth. It has been a long day and tomorrow is nearly here."

Chapter Eleven

The next morning, Mary was summoned at the unheard-of hour of ten o'clock to dress Rowena for the influx of the next horde of tradesmen. These were the decorators, furniture dealers, and fabric purveyors contacted by Andover for the remaking of Rushmoreland Castle into an *haut ton* establishment for Miss Rowena La Fleur.

Mary had just started down the hall to her own room, when the Rake came bounding up the staircase.

"Ah, Miss Migglesworth, I have need of you at once. Come along." He took her hand and pulled her back down the corridor.

"What is it? Where are we going?" She hung back, mystified.

"Do you have that list of clues in its usual hiding place? Shall I check and see?"

Mary felt the color rush to her cheeks and drew herself up. "I have it, but if you are to continue in this nonsensical mood, I must beg leave to return to my duties."

For a brief moment, he took on the guise of a scolded puppy, except for the laughing devils in his eyes. "Forgive me, little housemaid. Lifetime habits are hard to break, and you must admit, you are a tempting morsel."

"My lord, I believe you are trifling with me."

"Rake. And I am not. Merely *attempting* to do so, but I will desist if it truly annoys you."

Mary had to admit to herself that his actions were anything but an annoyance, but it would never do to let him know. He was far too free with his teasing familiarities for her peace of mind as it was. She primmed her lips and mustered a tone of hauteur.

"What is it you want with me, my lord?"

Those dancing devils broke loose and his infectious grin spread over his face. "Now if I answered that, you would comb my hair with a joint stool! No, wait!" He caught her arm as she began to march away. "I'm sorry. That was irresistible. Please, Miss Migglesworth, stay and I shall behave. Accept my abject apologies."

She considered his features, alive as they were with ill-concealed amusement, and hesitated a moment too long.

"Ah, that's my girl. Come, I have an adventure planned for us while the household is in an uproar with all these planners." He paused, the

devils back in his eyes. "Take out your list, by
yourself if you must, and let us peruse it once
more. Then we are going to retrace our path of
the other night and find where our ghost was
leading us. That wing may have been in use in
the Jacobite's time. Who knows, our goal may
lie there, and won't that be a nice surprise for
old Clarence!"

Mary giggled and destroyed all her careful re-
serve. "My father will never forgive us if we
solve the riddle without him."

Buoyantly, the Rake took her arm and started
off toward the unused wing of the castle. "His
own fault. He displays a regrettable lack of interest by not being here every minute. Out with
your clues, Miss Migglesworth, and on with the
chase!"

Mary left the precious sheet of paper where it
lay hidden. "I know them by heart."

"Damn," he said cheerfully. "One more of
life's little disappointments, but I shall survive
and look toward another day. Or night," he
added irrepressibly.

Truly, he was getting out of hand, more Rake
than lord every hour. Mary sighed, shaking her
mobcapped head at him, and was rewarded by
the teasing grin that always caused her vulnerable heart to skip a beat. The ghost of the Jacobite was not the only danger inherent in Rushmoreland Castle.

They wandered through room after room, the
windows so overgrown with ivy that they
walked in semidarkness even in broad daylight.
Most seemed to be bedrooms, still containing

enormous beds hung with decaying canopies. Stray pieces of furniture remained wraithlike in the gloom under their dusty Holland covers. Mary shuddered, and realized her mistake when the Rake encircled her waist with a reassuring arm. She moved quickly away, only too aware of his height, his broad shoulders, and something else, intangible, that drew her ever more strongly to him.

The search of the ancient wing proved fruitless as far as urns, winged goddesses, and unburied bodies were concerned. The only trace of the "ghost" of two nights before came in the form of an upset footstool near a door in one of the chambers. They did locate the Jacobite's lost portrait, however, finding it leaning against the wall of a room obviously used for storage.

Dust so layered the eight-foot-tall painting that Mary did not realize whom it represented until the Rake, seizing one of the cloths covering a chair, flapped away the gray covering in a cloud that had them both sneezing. Even then she would not have known but for the bronze plaque set into the ornate carved frame.

"Voilà!" The Rake spread his arms. "The Jacobite!"

Mary studied her ancestor with some misgiving. Knowing Clarence should have warned her not to expect a handsome man, but her great-grandfather gazed down at her with such a forbidding mien that she shrank away.

"No wonder his ghost terrifies all who encounter it!"

The Rake agreed, clicking his tongue in wonder. "How such a line produced a descendant as charming as"—he caught her eye and blandly changed course—"as our Clarence, I'll never understand."

Mary entirely spoiled her dignified image by giggling.

They returned to the main wing and James and Edgemont were summoned to move the painting back to the Long Gallery. They found it quite beyond their strength.

" 'Not two strong men th' enormous weight could raise,' " murmured the Rake, standing close behind Mary. "We are not totally failed. One clue at least applies."

Harry, the odd-job man who had fetched Mary from the village on her arrival, was pressed into service along with one of the grooms. Among them, the four managed to transport the huge painting to its former place, next to the Countess Beatrix; and, after a ladder was brought from the stables, the Jacobite once more hung by his lady. Harborough, announcing that he would query Sir Archibald Andover on engaging a painting restorer for the cleanup job, disappeared like the ghost himself, by the simple means of loping down the staircase.

Tea in the Housekeeper's Room that afternoon was made vastly uncomfortable by the recounting of his tribulations by Wesson, who had the misfortune to be standing by during most of the discussions about the redecorating of the castle. He was quite beside himself with outrage at the plans laid down by Sir Archibald Andover and his crew of creative artisans.

"It is a Monstrous piece of Impertinence!" he proclaimed. "With my own ears I heard them speak of Taking up the Carpets in the Great Hall and Removing the Banners that have hung these four hundred years!"

"Oh, surely not!" Mary was as shocked as he. "Harborough will never allow it!"

The butler turned a questioning eye on her, and Mary realized suddenly that her relations with the earl must be an uncommonly fascinating subject below stairs.

Wesson's brows raised and almost a hopeful note entered his voice. "You think not? You are in a position to know?"

Now all eyes in the room turned on her, alive with expectation.

"I—am sure he would never allow such a desecration of the artifacts of his ancestors." A disappointing answer, she knew, but the best she could manage at the moment.

Wesson sank back in his chair, gloom settling over him once more. "They are not His Ancestors. They are all Rushmores."

Yes, they were *her* ancestors! Mary sat up straight. And Rowena should not destroy her heritage! Before she thought, her unruly tongue said the first words that flew to her mind. "Harborough shall not let them! I'll see to that!"

A general "Aah" breathed through the room as the company received the enlightenment they sought. Mary's fluctuating color rose.

"That is a Great Weight off my mind." The butler stirred sugar into his tea with the air of one performing a ritual. And just what did he mean? Mary wondered. That he was right in his suspicions, or that the Great Hall might be spared?

Wesson turned to the housekeeper. "You must know, Mrs. Greenfield, that I overheard them speak of Reupholstering the dining room chairs in olive green mohair! Those needlepoint seats have been there for nearly a Hundred Years. I am glad to know they will be Spared."

Mr. Guimper, who had thus far been silent, his deeply curious gaze on Mary, set his cup on the table with a small rattle. "No fear of that anyway. The Rake don't hold with green furniture in the dining room. Red is what he likes, and red is what them chairs are."

Ruby red. Chairs were not the only item Harborough preferred in that color. The sooner those stones were found the better—before she, too, began to get the wrong idea. Mary rose and excused herself. Her presence in the domestic area was rapidly becoming untenable.

Rowena, when Mary went in to dress her for dinner, was full of plans for redecorating the rooms *à la* Andover. The names of fabrics such as damask, velvet, chintz, brocade, and mohair tripped off her tongue along with the colors of pale olive green, coquilicot, deep rose, mustard, and straw yellow. She had found only one fault. Andover refused to have the oaken-and-pine wainscoting painted over.

"So dreary, them dark wood walls are! At least, he said we could have some of that new Chinese wall silk in the dining room to go with the new green chair coverings. I wanted all new furniture, but he felt Harborough might object, them old pieces being his inheritance, so to speak."

Mary reminded herself to tell the Rake what a sacrilege it would be to change anything in the Great Hall. However, Andover had apparently had a few things to say about that also, according to Rowena, insisting on keeping "them moldy old cloth hangings" and the suits of rusting armor by the stairs. Only on Rowena's suite had total agreement been reached.

"Three shades of green, ducks, with cabbage roses on the wallpaper and matching damask drapes lined with nile green gauze for me bed. Rose pink satin sheets and a sea green down quilt. The walls will be all olive green behind the roses and Archie says I'll look a mermaid in an ocean bower. He has the loveliest ideas!"

And a bit of sense, too, Mary decided, letting Rowena go all out up here and leaving the Great Hall alone. But the needlepoint chairs in the dining room and the burgundy wall hangings were another matter. He should not take those. Remembering her words in the Housekeeper's Room, she resolved again to speak to the Rake.

She wandered down the hall to the double baize doors and had pushed them open before she became aware that she headed for the library. He could not be there yet. The huge standing clock in the Great Hall struck seven as she came in. It would be hours before he expected her, not until after the evening meal, and perhaps not even then if he and Andover and Rowena made a night of it.

Where would he be now? In the castle, she felt sure, for he would not stir abroad after the other night's adventure. Or would he? Fear that had lain dormant while she believed him to be inside and on his guard awoke, chilling her heart. Suddenly she needed desperately to see him and know he was alive. Without her volition, her feet took her into the library.

She sat just inside the door, leaving it open a crack so she could watch the stairs. What could she say when he found her waiting for him? She thought of an excuse. Harborough had played least in sight all day, having no desire to trail about the castle after Rowena and Andover. He probably had no idea of the horrors they planned, and she meant to disabuse him of this complacency at once. Before he could make one of his teasing remarks, accusing her of being unable to keep away from him, she would give him a round scold about his neglect of the great heritage he now held in trust.

She caught herself up, aware all at once of the enormity of the change in her attitude toward the Earl of Harborough. Positively possessive! But he was the Rake! Tigers did not change their spots. Or was it leopards? Not that it mattered, she told herself sternly, she should remember not to believe a word he says!

A rake belonged to no woman. He dallied where his fancy led him and departed at the first sign of boredom, and she had no intention of being one of the broken hearts thus left behind. Even as she made this resolve, she suspected it was too late.

She rose and paced nervously about the room, trying to pin down her feelings. She could not be in love; she had known the man too short a time. Still, she could not deny her strong feelings of attraction, of friendship, of wanting to care for him and protect him from the covetous ambitions of his loathsome relatives.

But not love, though she admitted at last to infatuation. It was only that he was the romantic, swashbuckling rake of every woman's dreams. He was an outrageous flirt and she'd better remember that . . . and treasure every memory of him, every teasing word, as long as she lived. She sighed. All other men would seem dead bores after her Rake.

But she had not come to Rushmoreland Castle to moon over its ramshackle owner. She stopped before the glass case containing the gold settings that had once held her rubies. They gleamed in the light from the fire burning in the hearth, as bright and polished as the day they were new. So much gold! She marveled, imagining the display the pieces must have made with all the rubies in place. In her mind, she filled them into a tiara for the head of the countess and an empty necklace and pendant for a pear-shaped stone still holding the diamonds and pearls that had complemented them. She visualized them in the rings and brooches and two golden bracelets. One of the rings had a border of diamonds matching those on a pair of earring drops. She wondered idly if they had come as a set. The Earls of Rushmore had spared no expense for their new brides. The whole ensemble must have weighed several pounds! She pitied the poor countesses who had staggered about through long evenings under their weight.

Even without the rubies, the locked case held a fortune in gold and stones, tempting to any thief who managed to enter the castle. She thought of the shadow they had chased through the halls. Could he have been a simple thief?

Voices on the stairs brought her back to her post by the door, and she felt her heart quicken as she recognized the Rake's annoyed tones.

"Oh, devil take it, Archie. You needn't hound my very heels!"

Andover was with him. Mary started back, looking for a place to hide should they come into the library, and then remembered that Sir Archibald was no longer a menace. He could recognize her if he wished, for Harborough already knew she was Danforth's daughter and after the rubies. It seemed so long ago, the time when she hadn't known the Rake . . . the time when they hadn't been friends.

The two men were crossing the hall, Andover trotting behind. "Demme if I'll let you out of my sight until we lay your cousin by the heels! Can't lose you now!"

Harborough stopped and clapped his friend on the shoulder. "Don't act the fool, you gudgeon. I'll be quite safe in my own rooms. Go along, take Rowena out to dine; I promise you I'll stay home."

He reached the library and Mary ducked back. Seeing her, he shut the door in Andover's face and leaned against it. "Let me have some peace!" he called through the heavy oak, and she heard Sir Archibald's reluctant agreement faintly from the hall.

The Rake ruffled his hair and smiled at Mary, somewhat ruefully. "He means well, but he'll drive me to a madhouse with his persistence. You'd think his life depended on my safety!"

Mary started toward him, her relief plain on her face, and he held out a hand to ward her off. "Now don't you start!"

She drew herself up. "I had no such intention. I hope I may believe you intelligent enough to take precautions after all that has happened."

"Then why are you here in my library if not to look for me?"

"To look over the clues again, of course. The books were left in here."

The sounds of a departing carriage came through the heavily draped windows from the cobblestoned drive by the entrance, and the Rake drew a deep breath.

"Thank God, they are gone. Now, my pretty housemaid, to the books. Has it occurred to you that the objects named may be symbolic rather than actual? We'd better recheck the lines."

For some reason, he seemed to feel this best done with both of them seated shoulder to shoulder on the sofa, their heads touching as they bent over the volumes. He made slow work of finding the pages and Mary felt no need to hurry him. Little tingling shivers ran up her arm as his fingers touched hers at every possible time while they handed the Jacobite's list back and forth. They both jumped, startled, when Wesson opened the door.

If the butler saw Mary, he gave no sign. His rigorous training stood him in good stead.

"Mr. Clarence Danforth," he announced, staring at the ceiling.

Clarence elbowed him aside and closed the door after him. The Rake hailed him happily.

"Here's a new come-out! By the front door yet! What's wrong with sneaking up through the garden? You're getting mighty toplofty for a sneak thief."

Clarence grinned. "Why not? Hallo, Mary, my girl. Is that the Dijon in the decanter beside you, Harborough? Ah, thanks." He accepted the brimming glass the Rake handed him and sank into the wing chair. "Not a decent chair in that whole demmed inn."

"There have been developments, Father." Mary slid along the sofa seat, easing away from the earl. "We now know our villain."

Clarence set his drink down with a thump. "Oho! You've caught our ghost?"

The Rake frowned and shook his head. "I cannot believe that. Miss Migglesworth refers to an incident in a gaming hell last night. My cousin Kendrick—I am sure it was he—attempted to end my career with a dagger, but his aim was poor."

Clarence sniffed. "Young Kendrick! Might have known he'd make a muff of it. Blunderheaded weakling."

"My opinion as well." Harborough poured himself a glass of brandy from one of the decanters. No one had offered any to Mary, so she got up and half filled a goblet with the Dijon for herself.

"Now that I know the direction of my danger," the Rake went on, "he'll not have another chance." He sipped the brandy thoughtfully. "Do you know, I almost feel I should write my Uncle Jameson a note of apology."

"No!" Mary returned to her seat by his side. "He still may be behind it all!"

Clarence frowned. "I don't think it. It is not at all like Jameson Halliburton. I believe him to be an honest and respectable man, which is why I've never felt quite right about your suspecting him."

"Not a violent type, is he?" the Rake mused. "Unlike his deplorable offspring. There's not much I'd put past my cousin." He watched the liquid swirl in the glass. "I'm afraid I may have to do something about Kendrick."

The deadly quiet in his voice sent a chill through Mary. She'd come to know such a different side of the care-for-nobody black sheep of the Halliburton family that she'd almost forgotten his reputation. She remembered now that he was known as a crack shot with his dueling pistols and as one who never backed down on a dare or challenge. A new fear gripped her. He must not kill the man and be forced to flee the country!

Clarence spoke from the wing chair. "Damn good wine, this. Could Kendrick have been the man you chased through the halls? Why did he not kill you then?"

"That has been puzzling me. It could have been he, but I felt no menace. We were led away, not murdered. No, somehow I do not believe it was he."

Wesson, at this moment, reentered the room. "Mr. Jameson Halliburton," he announced.

"Speak of the devil!" exclaimed Clarence. "Can he have come into the open? Should you not arm yourself? That is quite a handy-looking battle-ax over the mantel."

Harborough waved him to silence. "Show him in, Wesson." He need not have spoken, for that middle-aged gentleman fairly trod on the butler's heels. He brought up short at the sight of Clarence.

"Danforth! You here!" he exclaimed by way of greeting.

Clarence raised a gently inquiring brow. "Why not?"

"Well, I should have thought—that is, our families—"

"Good evening, Uncle Jameson." The Rake rose, pulling up another chair, and recalled his relative to his manners. "To what do I owe the pleasure of this visit?"

Jameson Halliburton shifted his feet uneasily. "I see you are engaged. Perhaps, another time—"

"No, no." His nephew urged him hospitably to the seat. "Pray sit down. Join us." He seemed to notice that his guest eyed Mary strangely, no doubt wondering at the presence of a housemaid. "Thank you, Migglesworth," he said meanly. "That will be all, you may go."

Mary glared at him but could do nothing. She curtsied. "Yes, my lord."

"Oh, and I see the decanter is nearly empty and Wesson has gone. Please send him back with refreshment for my uncle."

They could whistle for their refreshment! Mary curtsied again and withdrew, not by the door to the hall but to one on the other side of the room, deep in the shadows, that could be left ajar. She saw the Rake wink at her as she left, knowing full well she'd eavesdrop.

Mr. Halliburton had not seated himself. He now frowned at Clarence, and that gentleman, noting Mary's strategic position, got to his feet and stretched.

"No doubt you have business to discuss. I believe you said Andover is in residence. I shall look him up and have a chat if you will excuse me." He ambled across the room to Mary's door, and the Rake grinned as he joined her, leaving an even wider crack. Halliburton, too concerned with the subject of his visit, seemed oblivious of his audience.

"Sorry, Harborough, if I seem uncivil. What I have come to say is for your ears alone, and it must be said." He took the chair the Rake had offered and sat for a few moments in silence, his hands before him, fingertips meeting. Harborough waited, politely silent. Mary and Clarence strained to listen.

"It has come to my attention," the man began at last, "that my son Kendrick has been acting of late in a manner which I cannot condone."

The Rake raised his brows at this bit of understatement and met his uncle's eyes in complete understanding. Clarence dug Mary in the ribs with a forefinger and she nearly squeaked.

"I do not excuse the boy," Halliburton went on, tapping his fingertips together. "There can be no excuse, nor will an apology suffice. While your cousin lived and planned to marry, Kendrick had no thought of succeeding to the title and was content with his lot. But when your elder uncle and his son died and not two weeks after, your cousin also, I am afraid, the earldom of Harborough being so close to his grasp, an unfortunate idea took hold. His intelligence is not strong. He became obsessed with the belief that fate worked in his favor, and I fear the temptation to hurry matters along was too much for him."

Halliburton paused and wiped his forehead with a silk kerchief. "He is an inept bungler, as you have reason to know, but on the off chance that he might have unexpected luck, I have taken steps. I have no wish to see my son hanged for a murderer."

"Nor have I," the Rake agreed irrepressibly, meeting Mary's eyes in the darkness across the room. She closed the door to a slim crack, only to have Clarence push it back.

"No doubt." Halliburton's tone was dry. "At any rate, you should be pleased to know that this morning I had him conveyed to Dover and he is now on his way for an extended tour of the Continent. I have sent him with my own valet, a man in whom I have complete confidence. He has been with me these thirty years. They are also accompanied by an ex-army officer of commanding size and bearing who will keep him under constant surveillance.

"It is my sincere hope that Kendrick may marry abroad and remain there. He has an ample allowance and I believe many of the French and Italian nobility are now short of funds due to Bonaparte. In any case, they are under orders to keep him out of England for two years. Time enough for you to marry, set up your nursery, and produce another heir. May I advise you to do so at once?"

Harborough innocently turned his face toward the study door and his next words were for Mary's benefit.

"As a matter of fact, Great-aunt Emily has commanded me to dine in two days' time with just that in mind. She tells me she has invited three suitable young ladies for me to inspect. No doubt all fubsy-faced, butter-toothed ape leaders, if I know her. Do you know"—he sipped his brandy negligently—"I believe I shall take Rowena with me, that Aunt Emily may make the comparison."

Mary choked and grabbed Clarence's arm, for Jameson Halliburton had turned so purple that he seemed quite likely to go off in apoplexy any second.

"Just funning, Uncle," the Rake murmured lazily, eyeing him with reprehensible amusement. "Only funning. Rowena would not like it above half and no doubt would bore me all the way there and back with her complaints."

Even this qualification did not seem to sit well

with his uncle, who rose abruptly to take his departure. "I cannot order you to do that which will preserve you beyond this two years' time. I have done what I can and I leave you to your own devices. May heaven help you."

The Rake grinned. "I believe it already has. I have given thanks every night these past few days." He winked toward Mary's covert.

Jameson Halliburton merely grunted and passed through the door to the hall. Mary and Clarence tumbled in from the one on the other side.

"I do not much care for that man." Clarence shook his head as he sank back into the wing chair. "Nor for the covetous glances he scatters about your possessions. Could it be other than I thought? Mayhap a matter of like son, like father?"

The Rake frowned. "No, I believe he knows the danger of suspicion in which he and Kendrick would both stand if anything happened to me. He is my heir, you know."

Clarence eyed him shrewdly. "Best change that as soon as possible."

Harborough answered his look rather than his words. "Oh, yes. I have plans in that direction." He threw Mary a mischievous glance. "I have an invitation to dine with my Great-aunt Emily, you know."

"Have you now?" said Clarence. "Well, better you than me. However, you have my blessing. I say, the Dijon is almost gone."

Mary had sunk down onto the sofa, feeling

her face flame as she followed the double entendre. Could he really mean . . . ?

Harborough walked over to the hearth and tugged the bellpull to summon Wesson. He shook his head sadly. "The service here is not all one could desire. I swear I sent a housemaid for a refill near an hour ago."

To her dismay, Mary stuck her tongue out at him before she could stop herself.

"It seems it must have been Kendrick you followed through the halls that night after all," Clarence mused. "I wonder why he did not murder you then. Somehow . . ."

Mary still had her own dark suspicions. "Your Uncle Jameson is not at all decrepit."

"And he is of an age to have known the late earl's father." Clarence looked into the bottom of his empty glass thoughtfully. "I do not credit him with the morals of a murderer, but I scent a strong trace of avarice in his nature. Could he have divined the hiding place of the rubies and be trying to search?"

"It's a possibility, but there is the problem of how he could have gained entrance and how he disappeared. Wesson and his men found no one and all openings bolted safely."

All at once Mary's pulse began to race. Of course! Why hadn't she thought of it before?

"My secret passage!" she exclaimed. "That is how!"

Chapter Twelve

The Rake turned slowly to face Mary, an ineffable wonder lighting his blue eyes. "By all that's holy." He breathed the words. "Do not tell me I have inherited a secret passage as well as a ghost? An embarrassment of riches!"

Mary seized the hand of this kindred soul. "Did you not know? You have not heard the legend?"

"It needed only this. If the Jacobite catches up with me, I shall die happy. Tell me about this passage." He leaned back in the sofa. "Could the rubies be there?"

"No, really," said Clarence. "Nothing to do with our treasure hunt. Merely an old tunnel sealed up over a hundred years ago."

"Anything sealed can be opened." The Rake pressed Mary's hand between both of his. "Where is it?"

"That's just it, we don't know!"

Clarence shrugged. "No one knows. I understand the secret died with my great-grandfather. He considered it an open invitation to robbers and closed it off long before the Jacobite. No chance of the rubies being in there. We'd never be able to locate it, anyway."

"Oh, Father, don't you see? The Long Gallery! The Jacobite disappears there. Belinda—the maid who saw him—claimed that he seemed to walk into the portrait of his wife so the entrance must be there, somewhere near the painting!"

"And then," quoted the Rake, "we 'look'd at each other with a wild surmise—' "

Mary laughed, her eyes bright with excitement. "Oh, and we do! But that is not Shakespeare, it is from that new book of poems by Mr. Keats."

"True, but from his 'Sonnet, On First Looking into Chapman's Homer.' "

"Then I accept it! Oh, Rake, Father, let us go at once to the Long Gallery and search for the passage!"

Clarence grinned. "Have a care if you find it. Do not disturb Captain Hideless or you'll feel his rusty blade."

"Now who—?"

"The guardian of the passage! Do tell him the story, Father."

"Well, it's just that. A story." Clarence refilled his glass from the fast-emptying decanter. "The way my father told it to me, it was made up to frighten him out of exploring for the entrance. The tunnel, you see, was supposedly dug by the first earl, a man of somewhat negligible ethics. He pursued the trade of piracy on the high seas to amass the family fortune, which, by the way, you now enjoy."

He waved his glass at Harborough, who bowed an apologetic acknowledgment.

"Even in those days," Clarence continued, "it was frowned on when practiced on ships of the royal merchant force. My father said the passage once ran from the estuary at the base of the cliff up into some part of the castle so that booty could be easily transported."

He settled back in his chair. "This much is probably true, but the legend of Captain Hideless I believe to be pure imagination, an embellishment to entertain the children. However. Supposedly, the first earl fell out with the captain of his nefarious fleet over the division of some loot and murdered him in the passage, leaving his body where it lay to scare off intruders. If anyone dared enter the tunnel, the skeleton would collect his rattling bones and spring up, cutting down the trespasser with his long, curved sword."

The Rake was plainly delighted. "Do you know, I can't wait to find the brave captain's tunnel! No doubt he and the Jacobite's ghost are fast friends."

Mary opened her mouth to speak, but he suddenly held up his hand for silence. He listened for a moment, then jumped up and jerked open the door to the Great Hall. Andover walked across toward the staircase with far too much nonchalance.

"I thought he'd gone out with Rowena." Harborough frowned. "He must have seen you come in, Clarence, and was listening to make sure the ousted Rushmore didn't murder me."

Had he been listening? What had they said? Mary clutched the Rake's arm. "Andover knows there is a passage," she cried. "I heard him ask Rowena if she knew of it. Could he suspect we are on the trail of the rubies and now think he has discovered the location of the secret passage?"

"Hell and the devil confound it." The Rake

ran a hand through his hair. "If he believes we are up to something, we'll never get rid of him. He is a born Paul Pry, a scandalmonger who cannot bear not learning everyone's secrets."

"If he follows us, he will spoil everything!" Mary exclaimed, dismayed.

"We can but try to keep him out of our way while we search. I say, Clarence, are you acquainted with Andover?"

"Aye, for my sins, I am."

"Do you think you could keep him occupied for an hour or so while Mary and I try to discover the way of the Jacobite's disappearance? We cannot sound walls with him snooping after us."

"Certainly, certainly." Clarence felt his pockets. "If you can see your way to banking me, Harborough, I will engage to challenge him to a few games of piquet."

The Rake began to peel bills from a roll of soft he took from his pocket. "Will this do?"

Clarence held out his hand. "M'yes, indeed. Even though he's no pigeon for my plucking, I may manage to fleece him of a couple of quid." He accepted a thick wad of flimsies. "Don't mind saying I could use a bit of blunt. Got into a little game last night at the tavern and overreached myself a bit."

"So that's where you were, Father. I wondered."

"That reminds me, Mary, my girl, what are they paying you here? I'm a trifle short of the sheckles to cover my shot at the pub."

The Rake shoved the remainder of his roll

back into his pocket, watched by Clarence's en-
vious eyes. "Only keep Andover busy and that
will be no problem."

At this juncture, the door opened and Wesson
presented himself at his most butlerish.

"Dinner has been Ready this half hour," he
intoned. "Knowing you dined Alone, my lord, I
did not venture to sound the gong, but rather
have Awaited your Pleasure."

"Oh, by all means, put it on at once. Places
for four only, Wesson. Miss La Fleur does not
seem to be with us."

"Four, my lord?" For the first time, the butler
looked fully at Mary, mentally counting heads.

"Four," said his master firmly. "Please locate
Sir Archibald—he seems to be still at home—
and tell him we dine in ten minutes."

"I have already eaten," said Mary, sensing
Wesson's dilemma. "Only three places."

"Then you'll join us for coffee and dessert. As
I said, four settings."

Wesson's eyes, always protuberant, bulged
until threatening to pop out. Mary caught herself raising her hands to push them back.

Harborough kindly explained. "Myself, Sir
Archibald, Mr. Danforth, and his daughter.
Count 'em, four of us." The Rake grinned, as
Wesson, dumbfounded, tottered away, no doubt
agog to spread this news below stairs. "That
shook up the old boy. I hope he remembers to
order our meal laid on. You do join us, do you
not, Clarence?"

"Well, I had intended to drop in on Mrs.
Beecham in the kitchen, but no doubt the fod-

der will be the same in your dining room." He rolled his eyes heavenward. "Now there is a woman of rare talent, and mighty comely at that." He came back to earth. "Though a bit plump for my taste."

The Rake threw up his arms. "Good God, you two are totally disrupting my household! The domestic hierarchy in this castle is going all to hell! My housemaids, my footmen, and now my cook—have I only my butler still incorruptible?"

"Well, as to that"—Clarence snapped open his snuffbox—"I find he throws the ivories with uncanny skill. Took three pounds off me the other evening."

Mary frowned. "I thought you had sworn off the dice."

"Temporarily." Clarence took a pinch and waved an airy hand, scattering the snuff. "Only temporarily."

"I give up." The Rake held out his hand. "Come here, Miss Migglesworth." He reached up and pulled the mobcap from Mary's dark curls. "The apron, too." He spun her around and untied the strings. "This farce has gone far enough."

"Oh, wait—wait!" Mary snatched at her apron and rescued Holly's bag of herbs from the pocket. "I may need this if we are to disturb the ghost!"

"What the devil is that?"

"Why, a ward, of course." She waggled the little package before him, swinging it by the ribbon loops. "Holly made it for me. It keeps away all sorts of evils, not merely ghosts."

Mischief danced in his eyes. "Oh, keep it, by all means. You have great need of that."

"It doesn't seem to be very effective so far," she retorted. "However, perhaps it only works on disembodied evils."

Harborough chuckled, surveying her hopefully as she searched for a place in her gray uniform to hide the herbs. She finally tucked the cheesecloth bag into her belt.

"What, not in with the Jacobite's clues?" he teased. He held her off at arm's length. "Here, let me look at you. Yes, you'll do. Uncommonly pretty daughter you have here, Clarence."

Replacing his snuffbox, her proud father nodded complacently. "Runs in our family."

"Oh, I think not!" The Rake grinned, remembering. "Wait until you clap eyes on your Jacobite!"

Clarence's eyes flew open. "You've found him, by God!"

"His portrait, at least, in a storage room over in the old wing. We had him brought over to the Long Gallery and rehung in the place beside his Beatrix. Whale of a job! Took 'not two strong men,' but four. And that was the closest we came to finding any clues over there, so all my hopes now rest on the secret passage!"

Clarence sniffed. "Good luck to you. I'll wander up and have a look at the old boy later. Wouldn't do for me to meet his ghost and not recognize it."

"First we dine." The Rake shepherded them

across the Great Hall to the dining room and seated Mary on his right at the head of the table. Clarence, without hesitation, took the place at the foot, a good ten feet away.

As they sat down, Andover drifted into the room and came to a stop in a theatrical pose denoting surprise. "Danforth! You here?"

"Is that all anyone can say? Why should I not be?"

"No, no. No reason at all." Andover found the empty place, set at the end beside Clarence. He took in Mary, sans mobcap and apron, with narrowed eyes. "Of course. I thought once or twice you looked familiar."

"What have you done with Rowena?" the Rake inquired, mildly curious. "I thought when I heard the carriage leave that you two had gone out to dine."

"She wanted to go to the opera house for a party with some of her play-acting friends. Not my sort of thing, so I sent her off alone." Andover sat down. "She'll be all right; took one of the footmen with her."

Mary smiled. She had noted that it was James who carried in the covered dishes from which fragrant steam escaped. So Edgemont was once more on display! She first hoped Rowena wouldn't try the Rake's patience too far—and then hoped fervently that she would.

"Why didn't you go into town with her anyway?" Harborough scooped out a spoonful of an elegant chicken fricassee with a testy gesture. "You needn't have attended her party, you know. You could have gone on to one of the clubs and had a pleasant evening."

Andover shrugged an elegant shoulder. "Felt I should stay here and keep an eye on you. Confound it, can't lose you now that you're an earl. You've become a social adjunct instead of the detriment you once were."

"Merci du compliment. Are you now proposing to spend the evening standing guard over me?"

Clarence, who was doing justice to a full plate, coughed gently. "May I suggest a far more amenable pastime? What say you to a few quiet hands of piquet?"

"Count me out," the Rake said shortly. "Play with Andover. He needs company tonight, for he shan't have mine. I've other fish to fry."

Andover dropped his fork. "You're not going out!"

"No, no. But I've some business to take care of. I'll be in the library. Household accounts, you know."

Clarence turned to Andover, clapping him on the back. "Well, Archie? How about, say, a pound a point? Not enough? Then let's add a monkey a game."

Andover raised his ornate quizzing glass and surveyed Clarence carefully. "This is not like you. Money to burn, eh?"

"Well, as to that—" Clarence winked and glanced about in a surreptitious manner. "I may say I've come into some unexpected funds."

Andover tapped his quizzing glass against his chin. "And where, may I ask, did you drop into a fortune?"

"Ah, that's for me to know." Clarence glanced at the head of the table where Harborough seemingly was deep in conversation with Mary over a plate of fruit tarts. "There's many a secret about this castle," he confided in a loud stage whisper, "that none knows better than I."

His eyes suddenly arrested, Andover considered his shifty friend. Clarence imitated a clam and gazed at the ceiling, a finger beside his nose, and Andover capitulated.

"In fifteen minutes' time," he agreed. "I must go up to my room for a moment, and then you are on." He pushed away his plate almost untouched and rose. "Where do we play?"

"Meet me here, I've no intention of leaving before my port. By the by, I know of a neat little parlor near the butler's pantry where we may procure an excellent decanter of old brandy if I can catch his ear. Played there the other night with old Wesson."

Mary watched Andover leave. "Do you think you can keep him away, Father?"

"After the act Clarence put on?" The Rake flashed his teasing grin. "I'm sure Archie thinks Clarence has found those rubies, at the very least, and he'll spend all evening trying to pry out the secret."

Half an hour later, armed with a multibranched candelabrum, Harborough and Mary stood just inside the Long Gallery. Mary considered it, somewhat dismayed. It ran the length of the oldest wing of the castle, a seemingly endless hall. Over-life-size portraits of long-forgotten Rushmores stared down their aristocratic noses as though sneering at their feeble attempts to fathom the secret of their castle.

"Haughty bunch, your old ancestors." The Rake strode down the gallery, lighting some of the candelabra between the multipaned windows set into the four-foot-thick stone walls. Intricately carved wainscoting reached upward as high as a man's head, nearly halfway to the ceiling. The portraits leaped into life in the flickering flames from a dozen candles as he moved along. He paused before the newly hung Jacobite.

"There's a strong family resemblance, but I must admit Clarence is an improvement on the old boy."

Mary shivered. "Why must we always do these things at night?"

He came to her at once. "Because that's the only time you are free to play with me." A gentle arm encircled her waist and gave her a light hug. "What, afraid of our ghost, little housemaid?"

"No, I have no fear of something made of air that cannot physically touch me. I think what would really terrify me would be to discover that there *are* ghosts. Do you see what I mean? That horror I could never escape; it would haunt me all my life."

He laughed, and hugged her again. "Aye, let us keep with our fear of the unknown. It is far more comfortable."

Mary tried to disengage herself. It was far *too* comfortable pressed so close to him, held in his strong arms. "We waste time, my lord."

"Rake." He whispered the word into her hair as she moved away. "Very well, Mary Migglesworth. Where shall we start?"

"By Beatrix's portrait, of course. Oh, dear, only look at the carving! How can we sound stone walls that are covered with wood?"

Even the Rake seemed a little taken aback by the task before them, but he squared his shoulders. "Chin up, my girl. We'll find the way. It must be a trick panel, you know. One of these hundreds of carved knobby bits should turn and release a spring-loaded section of the wall. I believe that is the accepted method."

They began in the vicinity of Beatrix's portrait, since that was the rumored exit point for the Jacobite's ghost, each taking a different side. Tapping produced no results, so they tried to turn all the protrusions in the carving that they could reach, meanwhile searching for hidden cracks in the wood. For an hour or more, they worked steadily, covering an area several yards to either side of the painting. At last, Mary, her fingertips sore and her muscles aching, sat back on her heels. She stretched and sighed.

Above her, the lovely face of the Countess Beatrix smiled down as though encouraging. No powder hid her glorious dark hair, piled high upon her head to create a setting for a magnificent ruby-laden circlet with three tall fleurons.

Mary studied the painted jewels, fascinated. The gold pieces in the glass case in the library only half promised the glory of the Rushmoreland rubies. She began to count the stones in the tiara. Seven large ones in the fleurons and probably at least six smaller interspersed with pearls in the fillet from what she could see. It must have been the court crown of the Countesses of Rushmore.

A pearl-and-ruby choker around the lady's neck, tied with a black velvet riband, sported a Renaissance oval pendant with a huge table-cut ruby glowing red. The gold surround of cut-out scrolls set with multicolored gems in high collets finished with a hanging tear-shaped pearl. Nine more rubies. It must have been, an awestruck Mary decided, a gift from a very special earl to a very special lady.

The Girandole earrings each had three pearl drops swinging below the central ruby cabochons. One of Beatrix's bracelets consisted of a ring of paired golden hands, each pair holding a square-cut ruby and joined at the wrists to the next by pearl-studded cuffs. The other, a solid gold bangle, bore three oval stones.

She wore four rings, two adorning each hand, one circled with pearls, another cradled in intricate gold traceries that must be ancient indeed. A third was carved into a signet, and the last matched the drop earrings in Beatrix's dainty ears. A pointed satin slipper showed beneath the folds of her gown, and even its buckle contained rubies.

Mary wondered, curious all at once, which stones were the gift of the Jacobite to his Beatrix, and settled on one of the brooches as a possibility.

The Countess Beatrix had two, one centuries old, an oval of twisted gold vine-work with delicate leaves that wrapped about a female figure worked in blue enamel with a cabochon ruby for her skirt. Five pearls were mounted about it in the medieval manner, in transverse gallows clamps. The other, on which Mary had settled as her great-grandfather's gift, was of a far later date, a woven gold basket with four rose-cut ruby flowers set amid green enameled leaves, just the thing for the Jacobite's period.

Mary counted on her fingers: tiara, brooches, bracelets, rings, pendant, shoe buckles—there must have been forty stones at the very least! A king's ransom indeed; no wonder the rubies had been the object of intensive search for so many years—and Beatrix had held the clue, unknowing, for all that time!

The Rake stepped back, rubbing his tired hands, and looked down at her.

"Not quitting, are you, Miss Migglesworth?"

Mary smiled and shook her head. "No, just resting. And looking at Great-grandmother Beatrix's rubies. If only she could talk and tell me the way!"

As she spoke, Mary really looked at the painting as a whole for the first time, seeing not merely the depiction of the rubies, but Countess Beatrix the woman, posing for her portrait.

Garbed in sapphire blue satin, the lady stood gracefully in a queenly attitude, one hand resting on the back of an ornate gilt chair upholstered with a needlepoint scene from mythology.

Mary rose slowly to her feet. In either corner of the canvas, the artist had placed a Grecian urn. The two urns—and the throne of Jove! She tried to call to the Rake, but no sound came from her throat. She tried again and produced a thin squeak.

" 'She moves a goddess and she looks a queen'! Rake! Rake, look here, I—I think I have found my rubies!"

Chapter Thirteen

Pointing dramatically at Beatrix's portrait, Mary quoted in a voice that shook with her excitement. " 'It is not strength, but art, obtains the prize'! The Jacobite meant it literally! See, here is the art!"

"What the devil are you on about all at once?" The Rake stared at her. "We know the passage is here, that's why we—you can't mean the entrance is *in* the picture!"

"No, no, but only look at it! See, she looks a queen, and there's the gilded throne with Jove worked in needlepoint and the two urns beside it! Rake, the rubies must be here!"

"Where?" He frowned. "Those are only pictured rubies. Could he have meant the place where she was painted? Good God, that could be anywhere in this damned pile!"

"Oh, don't be stupid, for you are not! This is the entrance to the secret passage—we know that for the ghost disappears here. And the rubies will be inside!"

The Rake considered the painting thoughtfully. "I'll wager you may be right, but don't build up your hopes, little housemaid. If our ghost gets in, chances are he has found anything that may be inside."

Mary shook her head. "Oh, no. Or he would no longer walk, don't you see?"

"But how are we to get in? We've pushed every likely knob and there's not a crack in the paneling that could mark an opening." He sounded discouraged.

"The clues," Mary exclaimed. "We must study them again, keeping in mind the painting. Something may read quite differently now that we have a beginning. You had the copy last, where is it?"

"Me? I do not have it."

"You must!"

The Rake clapped a hand to his forehead. "Good God, I remember. I stuck it between the pages of one of the books when we went in to dinner. It's down in the library. Come on."

Mary was already on her way. "Do hurry, my lord. What if Andover overheard our conversation and has found our clues?"

He caught up with her and slowed her steps. "He'd not know what to make of them. Besides, Clarence has him in tow, remember? He won't have had a chance to get into the library."

"Oh, my father! Won't he be furious to be left out of this! But we cannot include him."

"No, indeed, he's quite necessary where he is." The Rake pushed open the library door. He headed for the table and began to leaf through the volumes of the *Iliad* that lay scattered about. The copy of the Jacobite's clues was not there.

"Are you sure you left it here?" Mary demanded. "Can you remember exactly?"

"No, but I'm certain—that is, I did not bring it into the dining room. Maybe Clarence picked it up."

"We cannot ask him now!"

The Rake stacked the books neatly on the table. "You know them by heart, that I do remember. We'll have to rely on you until we see him."

Mary grabbed his hand, pulling him to the door. "Oh, yes, I know them all. Only think, we may have the rubies before we see him again! Oh, won't he be cross!"

The Great Hall lay in darkness except for the night wall torch. Wesson, no doubt believing all to be out or abed, had already bolted the huge front doors while they were in the library. The Rake took a taper from a candelabrum on one of the hall tables and lit it from the torch.

"We'd best take care," Mary cautioned. "All is set for the night and Wesson has ordered James and Edgemont to stand shifts. He may already have mounted his guard on the landing again. If we start an alarm, Andover will be upon us in spite of all Father's efforts."

The Rake snuffed his candle. "By all means then, let us be quiet and go in the darkness." His arm circled her waist. "I much prefer this mode of travel."

Mary pulled away, but he managed to keep her hand while they tiptoed up the stairs. As their heads topped the third-floor landing, they came onto Wesson's guard before they themselves came wholly into view.

Moonlight from a high circular window over the stairwell disclosed not one but two figures seated on the floor, wrapped in each other's arms. Even in the pale light from the moon, Rowena's orange hair was clearly recognizable.

"You have a rival," the Rake whispered. "If I mistake not, that is your footman my light-skirt is kissing."

"He's not my footman!" Mary hissed in his ear.

"Nor is she any longer my mistress." His arm once more slid about her waist. "It would seem we are both out of our predicaments."

As they continued up the stairs, dimly lit by the moon, Rowena opened her eyes. From her position on the floor, looking over Edgemont's shoulder, it must have seemed to her that their two pale figures rose through space. With a strangled cry, she fought free of the footman's embrace, pointing at the Rake and Mary.

Edgemont turned, following her gaze, and stared, wide-eyed. His Shakespeare deserted him and he gave a wordless gurgle of terror. He scrambled to his feet, jerking Rowena after him. For a moment, both stood clinging together, white-faced and mouthing silently, before they broke and fled.

The Rake watched them go. "Now how shall I explain wandering about the halls in the dark with one of my maids?"

Mary, overcome by giggles, collapsed on the huge carved chest behind which they had hidden from Wesson and his ancient gun.

"You won't have to, my lord! They must think we are the ghosts of the Jacobite and his Beatrix! Do you know, we have probably taken ten years off their lives."

"And lost me every domestic I have!" He joined her on the chest, throwing an arm casually about her once more. "Good God, when this story gets about, every one of them will leave and I'll have only my little housemaid."

Mary removed his arm and stood up, her giggles stifled. He would not have her in the way he must mean. Oh, why must he be a rake? "Do light that candle so we can see our way," she commanded. "Have you a tinderbox?"

He rose reluctantly. "You are a very difficult housemaid, Miss Migglesworth, always ordering me about. I thought I was your master." Mary let that comment ride, merely handing him the candle he had dropped on the chest.

More affluent than Clarence, he carried in his coat pocket a modern Instantaneous Light Box filled with fabric soaked in sulfuric acid. Striking a chemically treated splint upon it, he produced a very beautiful flame and relit the candle. By its wavering light, they finished the trip into the Long Gallery, where the candelabra still burned.

Once more they stood before Beatrix's portrait while Mary silently ran over the clues in her mind.

"The second line is the one about two strong men not lifting the weight. Could that perhaps refer to the painting itself?"

The Rake considered the large canvas, fully four feet wide and nearly eight feet tall. "We certainly can't lift it. Nor could a single ghost, but yet he is said to melt into it."

"It must move aside in some way that we have not discovered." Mary considered it, her head on one side. "We have not touched the frame itself, only tried the wall beside it."

Together they pushed and shoved, but the painting refused to budge an inch.

The Rake stood back, running his hand through his hair. "It is not hung like the others. It is attached solidly to the wall. There is some secret. Quickly, Mary, what clue is next?"

" 'And seems to walk on wings and tread in air.' What can that mean?"

"It describes our ghost possibly, but is no other help."

Mary began to run her hands over the gilded frame, examining the ornate carving. It consisted of a romantic pattern of cherubs and twining grapevines—and the cherubs had wings. Mary caught her breath. One, at eye level, seemed to stand on the winged back of another.

"Rake, this one is different—it seems to walk on wings!"

With eager fingers, she pushed and poked all over the carved cherub, but nothing happened.

"No, wait!" The Rake shoved her aside. "It's pointing! See, the hand points toward the carved wall molding outside the frame!"

The ornate curlicued border on the wainscoting had an odd flower less than an inch from the frame, scarcely noticeable unless one knew where to look. He reached toward it, almost hesitantly, while Mary once more held her breath.

He touched it. It moved slightly, and turned beneath his fingers.

Slowly the huge painting of the Countess Beatrix swung away from the wall like a door, revealing a narrow black cavity in the stone wall behind it. A rush of cold air exhaled out at them and Mary found herself somehow in the Rake's arms.

A long minute went by before she eased herself free and straightened her skirts.

"I beg your pardon, my lord, it frightened me for a moment."

"Rake," he corrected softly, drawing her close again. "And no need to apologize. I'm enjoying myself immensely."

This time she jerked away in a hurry. "It was just that for a second, all I thought of was the ghost of my great-grandfather and I didn't realize it could only be trapped air from a damp tunnel."

He reached for her once more. "Perhaps the Jacobite waits inside," he offered helpfully. "We should go in and see."

Mary leaned forward, peering nervously into

the blackness. "We'll need a lantern. Have you
one?"

"Of course not. Should I wake Wesson and
send for one from the kitchens?"

Braced by his joking attitude, Mary's courage
suddenly returned. This was her secret passage!
At last! And here she stood, wavering because it
was dark! "A candle," she ordered impatiently.
"Light one and do let us go in at once. I cannot
wait!"

"Yes, ma'am." He bowed meekly. "At once,
ma'am."

He entered first, one hand shielding the candle, and Mary followed holding on to his coattails. They left the portrait of Beatrix standing
open in the gallery.

The painting hung on the inside wall of the
stonework castle and the sides of the narrow inner passage felt damp and smelled of mold. No
wonder the ancient Castle of Rushmoreland was
so dank and cold in all its rooms, Mary thought
as she pressed close behind the Rake. The foun-
dations of the oldest masonry walls probably
lay in the depths of the estuary and moisture
seeped continuously upward and hung in the
darkness. They would be kept humid by the wet
winds that swept up the river, came in through
some opening far below them, and circled in
drafts within. Their candle flickered. Mary
reached a hand sideways, feeling the moving air,
and her fingers shrank from a slime-covered
wall.

In moments, stumbling along the uneven
floor, they passed beyond the faint light in the

gallery opening. A nightmare of her childhood haunted Mary, a horror of being shut under a lowering ceiling, a terrifying sensation of being coffined alive under sodden earth. She clung tightly to the Rake's waist and a comforting hand stretched back to pat her shoulder.

Their way led downward along a passage paved with stones that had settled unevenly over the centuries. Once Mary tripped, almost fell, and the Rake drew her beside him where he could hold her in a strong, protective arm. She remained because, as she explained to herself, it was so much easier to see the path traveling up beside the candle and really, there was no room for them to walk very far apart.

The tunnel leveled suddenly and the candle-light passed across a closed and bolted door on their left. Releasing Mary for the while, the Rake slid back the bolt and pushed. It opened inward into a dark, unused linen closet, a shelf of musty forgotten bedding swinging out into the small room. Mary remained, holding the entry open while the Rake looked outside the room to see where they were.

"Now we know how our ghost vanished from the second floor." The Rake's deep voice echoed in the vacant space, practical and reassuring, driving thoughts of disembodied wraiths temporarily from Mary's mind. "We are in the old wing we followed him through."

At this point, Mary had no patience for past adventures. "This is not an end," she urged. "Let us go on!"

They left the shelf-door standing open, the

Rake remarking helpfully that it could do no harm to leave available as many exits as possible, just in case.

"In case of what?" she asked as they once more continued along the dark tunnel, but he only squeezed her to him and made no answer.

The passage turned sharply, and even with the light from their candle, they nearly fell down a flight of steep, winding stone steps, so narrow that their shoulders brushed the clammy sides. Mary shrieked as something small and furry ran across her foot.

"Only a rat," the Rake assured her.

Mary clung to him, welcoming his arm about her, as she heard more little feet scuttling away from the candlelight as they approached. The stone walls were more than damp and slimy now; slow drops of water fell on them from the ceiling. Mary shivered.

"We are 'Wrapt in the cold embraces of the tomb,'" she quoted in a sepulchral whisper, and promptly succumbed to an overwhelming attack of hysterical giggles.

"No, now, Mary Migglesworth!" the Rake scolded. "That is above what is pleasing. I'm nervous enough in here without you gibbering!"

There was indeed an eerie atmosphere in the tunnel, even without a specter, the blackness, the dankness, and the silence except for their footsteps on the slippery rock stairs. For a moment, Mary fancied she heard another set of footfalls echoing theirs and she clutched the arm that encircled her waist.

"Someone is in here with us!"

Harborough paused, listening, and the deep silence settled about them like a physical pressure.

"Nonsense," he said heartily. "You are imagining things. Not that I blame you," he added, squaring his shoulders. "This place would unnerve Achilles himself!"

Mary giggled again. "How lucky that you are not he!"

He laughed and hugged her, endangering the wavering candle. "That's my little housemaid."

Mary's imagination was far too active, she knew that well; nevertheless, she slipped her arms about him and made no objection when she felt his lips press lightly against her cheek. He held her so closely that she felt his heart pound against her and for a moment—but only a moment—she surrendered to the utter heaven of his warmth and strength.

"This—this is not finding our treasure," she said, pushing him away, but only enough so they could go on.

He chuckled, a soft, satisfied sound. "I seem to be finding mine."

She tried to ignore his meaning, but her treacherous pulses raced. And she had once thought a specter constituted the greatest danger in this black passage!

The wet slippery steps wound on, down and down, until the Rake remarked that they must be below the castle cellars when they finally reached a level area once more.

"We should be at the foot of the cliff." He

tried to look ahead. "Clarence said the tunnel ended at the estuary."

They seemed to have entered a natural cave. The space about them widened and the wall they felt their way along was rough. Their feet shuffled on sandy, uneven rock.

Ahead, a dim light glowed, and they turned toward it. A pile of loose boulders blocked the far end, a few of which had been pulled away, leaving a hole large enough for a body to crawl through. Beyond it they glimpsed moonlight shimmering on moving water. The tide was coming in and every now and then the wash from a brackish wave seeped between the lower rocks and poured into a small pool, a hollow formed in the floor of the cave. The candle flickered in the salt-scented draft blowing through the chamber.

Suddenly, Mary shrieked again as the candle shed its light on a grinning skull.

The Rake leaned down, illuminating an entire skeleton clothed in moldering rags. "I'll be damned!" he exclaimed. "It's true."

"Captain Hideless!" Mary, no longer afraid, bent to examine their find. "I didn't really believe in him! Only wait until I tell Father!"

"He hasn't gathered together his rattling bones and struck us down, however. I imagine Clarence will remind us of that."

" 'Unwept, unhonor'd, uninterr'd he lies,' " Mary intoned, her voice shaking with excitement.

The Rake caught her in his arms, spinning her

around. "By God, Mary, it is all true! Quick, what comes next?"

"Oh, I cannot think! Do let me down." She regained her feet and began to count on her fingers. "Where are we? How many have we found? The tomb, the skeleton—oh, yes, 'Without a sign, his sword the brave man draws.' Rake, Captain Hideless has a sword!"

"The sign!" he cried, as excited as she. "The sword must point the way!" It lay with the hilt beneath a pile of finger bones and the rusty blade stretched toward the boulders blocking the cave entrance. "Oh, the devil! Must we now go out into the river?"

"Oh, I cannot!"

"But is the last clue not 'plough the watery deep'?"

Mary caught his arm. "Hold still that candle! Let me see the sword. Oh, but see!"

"What?"

"Rake." Her voice was suddenly quiet. "Look close, it points not at the river but at that little pool." She was trembling now and clutched the arm she held. "Rake, could the Jacobite have hidden his rubies in there under the water? Could that be what he meant?"

Dripping some wax on a low outcropping of rock above the water-filled hollow, he implanted the candle. He struggled out of his well-fitting coat and handed it to Mary, then rolled up the sleeves of his linen shirt.

As she crouched in the dark while he fished down under the water, a disquieting sense of being watched crept over Mary. They were not alone. And not visited by a ghost—no ghost took that quick indrawn breath. She shrank back deeper into the shadows, staring around, but her eyes could not pierce the blackness from which she and the Rake had come.

Not a sound but the slosh of water as the Rake felt about beneath the undercut rock edge of the pool . . . but she knew someone or something was there. Kneeling slowly, she felt about for the end of Captain Hideless's sword and drew it into her hand. She waited in the blackest of the shadows.

Then, before she could scream a warning, a dark form leaped out at the Rake. Strangling hands seized his neck from the back, choking off his startled cry. The assailant threw his weight upon him, slamming him to the ground and forcing his face under the water in the pool.

Mary, without thinking, flung the coat away and, holding the unwieldy sword by its rusty hilt, brought the flat of the blade down broadside on the attacker's back with all her strength. The wind exploded from his lungs. His hold broke and the Rake erupted from beneath his opponent, throwing him against the rock wall and leaping on top of him.

The two men rolled out of reach of the candle's weak beam, into the shadows, a struggling indistinguishable mass. Mary hovered, holding the sword aloft, dancing about the outskirts of the battle awaiting her chance. It was impossible to see which fighter was which. She found herself shouting some of Clarence's choicer phrases and didn't care.

All at once, it appeared to her that the Rake was on the bottom and again being strangled to death. She took careful aim at the villain's head, shut her eyes tight, and flailed downward with the flat of the sword. Her feet slipped on the sandy rock and she struck merely a glancing blow.

The next instant, she screamed aloud.

It was the Rake who sprawled senseless by the pool.

Had she killed him? A cold horror seized her, turning her to stone. The dark cavern swam before her eyes. He could not be dead!

Out of the mist that clouded her vision, Mary saw a black figure rise from beside the fallen Rake and come toward her, arms reaching out.

"Now for you, my girl—" The voice was a hoarse whisper.

Mary came to life. All her terror, her rage at this murderer, her crushing grief for her lord, came to the fore. Bracing her feet and swinging her cumbersome weapon with both hands, she caught the man on the side of the jaw and he dropped like a felled ox.

The Rake sat up and groaned. He staggered upright, holding his aching head, and looked down at his erstwhile opponent.

"Thank you," he said. "I think."

Mary still clutched the heavy sword, suddenly near fainting with relief. "Are you all right? I am so sorry. I couldn't tell which one you were."

"Put that damn bludgeon down." He felt carefully over the back of his head. "It doesn't seem to be broken. Thank God, you used the flat side and the edges have rusted away or you might have split my skull—to say nothing of decapitating our friend."

Mary, so shaken that she spoke the first words to come to her tongue, choked on a tiny giggle.

"And if the head had rolled into the pool, we might—might never know who he is."

The Rake grinned, his white teeth gleaming in the pale candlelight as he bent over her victim. His expression changed. "Oh, damn! How could I have been such a confounded nod-cock as to underestimate him!"

"C—cousin Kendrick?"

"Oh, no. I feel my Uncle Jameson told me the truth. Kendrick is gone." He tapped his chin with a thoughtful finger. "Perhaps I shall send my uncle that note of apology after all."

"Who—who is it?" Mary peered down at the still figure. "Oh, dear God, is he dead?"

"No, luckily. We can't have you up for a murderess. It's Andover. Like a fool I thought him my friend, but I see now why he didn't want me killed by Kendrick. It must have been he who paved the way for me to gain the title. I imagine he knew that would give him a clear field to search the castle for the rubies. He would have known of them, for his father played here with my uncle when they were boys and they must have either found, or been told, of the entrance to the passage, but he didn't know where to look for the rubies until now."

Mary caught the hurt in his voice. "The rubies are quite a prize, my lord. And we must nearly have them."

"Oh, aye!" The Rake plunged his arm into the pool and began again to search the cracks and crannies under the water. "I don't suppose you remember exactly where that sword pointed before you displaced it?"

"Of course not."

"Naturally."

Mary looked at the prostrate Andover, uneasily. "Suppose he should wake up while you are still hunting?"

"Why, hit him again. You still have that sword."

Mary, surprised to find that she had, dropped it. "No, now! I could not!"

He grinned. "Why not? You did it before."

"That was different. I thought he would kill you."

He sat back on his heels, his arm dripping. "And you cared?"

"Of course. I cannot bear to see anything killed."

"Then you'd better tie him up before he wakes. I don't believe he will take kindly to any of our actions in the future."

Mary looked about a bit wildly. "We have no rope!"

He undid his neckcloth and handed it to her. "This will do for his arms." He grinned and went back to the pool. "For his legs you must rip a strip off your petticoat. I understand that is what females always use in emergencies."

She started a retort—and realized he'd probably hit on an excellent scheme. Sacrificing the under portions of her housemaid's uniform presented no problem. She had a feeling she no longer needed the disguise.

Tearing the stout cloth, however, presented difficulties, but she finally managed to shred a beginning hole with the blunt tip of Captain Hideless's sword. All in all, she reflected, a most useful weapon.

She had finished binding the wrists and was just tying the last knot on Andover's ankles when she heard the Rake exclaim "Hah!" on a long, slowly expelled breath.

In an instant, she knelt at his side. He passed her a flat metal box and wiped his slimy hands on his breeches.

Mary's own hands shook so that she couldn't find the catch.

"Here, please . . . you open it." She handed it back.

He tried, but his fingers were cut and bruised from the sharp rocks and his knuckles were bleeding. "Damn Andover," he muttered, rubbing his injured joints. "I must have hit him harder than I thought."

Andover!

Mary remembered suddenly. How came he to be here? Clarence was to keep him busy playing cards!

Clarence!

"Father!" she cried. "What has he done to my father?"

Rubies forgotten, Mary jumped up and raced blindly back through the dark passage.

Chapter Fourteen

"Mary, stop! You'll break your neck!" Grabbing up his coat, Harborough rolled the dripping brass box into it and ran after Mary, praying she wouldn't fall on the rough, wet stones of the dark passage.

He heard her ahead of him, sliding and crying out as she banged into a curve in the wall.

"Mary, wait!"

She reached the winding stair before he came up with her, reached it unexpectedly, and stumbled into the bottom step, falling forward and barking her shins. He caught her up, dropping his coat and gathering her into his arms.

"Mary, love, are you hurt?"

She clung to him, weeping. "My f–father—"

He tipped up her face. "Tell me," he ordered sternly. "Are you hurt?"

Already she was struggling to get free. "I'm all right, but my father—"

"Come on, then." He scooped up the coat-wrapped box. His arm still about her, he half carried her up the stairs, striving to soothe her fears. "He's a tough old bird."

"No, he's not! He's old—and—and vulnerable!" She tried to wipe the tears from her face. "Oh, Rake, we must find him quickly!"

"We'll find him." He heard the grim note in his own voice and tried again in a cheerier vein. "He's like a cat; his kind always lands on its feet."

A lighter area broke the darkness ahead and they nearly fell as they ran out of stairs and their feet dropped suddenly on level ground. They had come to the top of the spiraling stairwell. A few more steps and the shelf-door in the old linen room waited, open, and they were back inside.

The castle lay dark and silent. Mary broke away from him and ran toward the Great Hall, fairly tumbling down the wide staircase, the Rake beside her.

"He said a small parlor." She gasped for breath. "Near the butler's pantry."

"Where the hell would that be?"

"Wesson—Wesson has a room off the dining hall. That must be it." She turned toward the wing outside of which she had wandered with Clarence only a few nights before. Would they ever wander anywhere again?

"Here, hold on. We need a light." Harborough took a candelabrum from a hall table and lit the tapers from the wall torch. Mary grabbed it from him. By its light, they passed down the corridor beyond the dining room, throwing doors wide as they went. The first two rooms were dark, with no sign of Clarence; then Mary opened the third, screamed, and flew in.

In a litter of scattered cards, guttering candles, and spilled wineglasses, Clarence lay slumped across a table. Mary threw away the candelabrum she carried, dashing hot wax on the Rake's inexpressibles, and ran to her father's side.

"Oh, God, he is dead!"

Harborough, by far the calmer of the two,

reassured her. Clarence was not dead. He breathed—in fact, he was snoring.

"But what has happened to him? Did Andover strike him down? Oh, is he badly injured?"

The Rake sniffed at the glass nearest Clarence's hand. "Drugged," he diagnosed.

Mary, kneeling by her father's side, looked up with tears streaming down her cheeks. "Can we not wake him?"

The Rake grinned at her, relief relaxing his features. "I fear not, my little watering pot. He'll have to sleep it off, but I believe him to be in no danger. Let us see if we can move him over to that sofa."

He dropped his coat, with the metal box still inside it, onto the floor. Mary seemed to have forgotten its existence in her fear for her father.

"Here, love, I'll take his shoulders, see if you can manage his feet."

After a bit of a struggle, they succeeded in laying him out on the couch. The Rake crossed Clarence's arms on his chest, and thoughtfully placed a sheaf of court cards in his hands. "We do not have a lily, so I'm afraid that will have to do." Clarence gave a gentle snore.

Mary had so far recovered that she almost giggled. "Much more appropriate," she said.

"And now, my love, let us see what we found in the pool!"

"The box!" Mary exclaimed. "Where is it? Are my rubies inside? What did you do with it?"

"It seems to have completed the ruination of my coat." He unrolled that sodden garment with a grimace of distaste and took out the slimy metal box.

It would not open. Not only was it locked, but also the hinges and indeed the very edges of the lid were so corroded and encrusted as to be frozen shut.

"What we require is a chisel." The Rake shook the box, holding it to his ear. "I can't tell if there is anything inside, though it feels heavy. A chisel is definitely called for," he went on. "And a large hammer."

The door behind them opened suddenly, and with great presence of mind, the Rake sat on the table, hiding the box behind him.

An amazing figure entered: Wesson, his tremendous girth wrapped in the staggeringly colorful dressing gown Mary had seen before. He now wore it with a striped nightshirt, his official black knee breeches, and purple moroccan pom-pom-toed slippers. A tasseled nightcap topped the ensemble. He also carried his ancient fowling piece and it was aimed at the Rake's chest. He lowered it at once.

"I beg pardon, my lord!"

The Rake folded his arms austerely. "And so you should. What the devil are you doing up at this hour?"

"I heard a voice cry out, my lord. And running feet. I felt it my Duty to ascertain the Cause," he finished virtuously, casting a disapproving eye on the snoring Clarence. "Is everything all right, my lord?" He glanced meaningfully from Clarence to the Rake's soaked and filthy shirtsleeves.

"Everything is fine." About to dismiss the man, Harborough recalled the problem. "Wait, Wesson. We have need of a hammer and chisel. Procure them for me, please. At once."

"Yes, my lord." Indicating perplexity by a slight rise in his eyebrows, Wesson made his dignified retreat.

"Why did you hide the box?" Mary demanded. "What difference does it make if he sees it?"

The Rake picked it up and turned it about in his bruised hands. "Well, I feel that until we discover what we have, the fewer loose tongues who know of our find the better." He grinned, a bit shamefaced as he laughed at himself. "No, to tell the truth, I feared for a moment that Andover had escaped."

"Whatever shall we do with him? We can't leave him in the passage forever."

The Rake shrugged. "That I have not decided. I am afraid it is a matter for the Bow Street Runners." He glanced at her, and away again. "I very much fear he may have made sure of my succeeding to the ownership of Rushmoreland by removing a few of my relatives. He must have wanted those rubies very much."

"I believe Father once said he was monstrously in the wind."

"Aye, he has never a feather to fly with. He even has broken my shins upon occasion, but I do not feel I care for his method of repaying his debts. By the way, love, do not count too much on our find. This box may contain nothing of value. You must not get your hopes so high. It may be empty, or have only someone's collection of loose coins."

Mary gave him a disgusted look. "You know perfectly well it is my rubies. What else could it be?"

He grinned and brushed her cheek with a finger, leaving a dirty streak. "I don't want you disappointed, love, that is all."

A measured tread approached the door, and once more he hastily hid the box, this time shoving it under his stained and waterlogged coat on the table.

"Your tools, my lord." Wesson remained in the doorway, obviously curious and showing a tendency to linger. "May I be of help, my lord?"

"Oh, do get rid of him," Mary whispered impatiently.

The Rake nodded. "There is someone else we must get rid of. Wesson, we have captured the ghost that has haunted our halls. It seems we have a secret passage and he has used it to enter at will. You will find him in a cavern at the foot of a flight of stairs inside the walls of the old wing."

He gave explicit directions on how to locate the linen closet. "The door stands open. Take both James and Edgemont; the man is bound hand and foot, but he may yet be dangerous. Perhaps you had best bring a couple of the stable hands as well. And a lantern, for the stairs are very dark. Oh, and watch out for the skeleton in the cave at the foot."

Wesson's eyes bulged but, to Mary's admiration, he maintained his butlerian dignity. "Yes, my lord."

"Also, before you go down, have someone awaken one of the grooms and send him into London for the Runners to come and take the miscreant in charge."

"At once, my lord."

The Rake watched him leave at his usual stately tread. "There goes an excellent butler. I must give him a raise in pay."

"Never mind that now. The box."

He began to turn it this way and that, searching for the best mode of attack. Mary sat on the table edge, watching and chewing her knuckles.

"I'm glad now you sent them to the linen closet," she said. "Somehow I'd rather only we knew of Beatrix's portrait."

He smiled. "I shall have the closet boarded up, but I defy anyone to guess the Jacobite's secret without your clues. Andover must have been told of the passage by his father, who probably learned of it as a boy from my cousin's father. Let us hope that is the end of it. You'll think it a shame, I know, but I shall have to block up the lower end once more. I really feel we've had a sufficiency of uninvited guests."

"And Captain Hideless?"

"Oh, he has slept there for so many years, I could not bear to disturb him. Only think what pleasure he will give to some future generation. Damn, I cannot get a purchase on this thing. Hold it for me, love, while I set the chisel."

Before he could strike, the door opened again. Mary, who was holding the box, thrust it under

Clarence's feet. The Rake's admitting he had feared Andover's escape had planted the idea in her head, and she sprang protectively to his side. She stepped back, somewhat dashed, when Wesson appeared again. James, avidly inquisitive, peered around the butler's massive bulk.

"My lord," he began ominously, "I have been unable to Locate Edgemont, and my Suspicions have been Aroused."

"So have mine," said the Rake. "But for a different reason." He waved them away with the chisel. "Go on about your business. Our villain is bound; you and James should be able to handle him with the help of the stable men."

Wesson managed to bow formally, moving only his head. "Yes, my lord." He retreated, majestically carrying his gun before him, at the ready, and followed by James, who bore both a lantern and a dubious expression.

"Now." The Rake fitted a chair beneath the doorknob, much as Holly had done. He ran a muddy hand through his hair. "I have been doing some serious thinking. This box may be empty, you know, but just in case it isn't, Miss Migglesworth, I have something of great import to settle with you before we open it."

Mary eyed him suspiciously. "And what is that?"

"Why, the disposition of my rubies, of course."

"*My* rubies!" Mary braced herself for the inevitable battle, the confrontation she'd been blocking from her mind in her newfound happiness. "The rubies are mine!"

The Rake grinned, those devils dancing in his eyes. "Mine, I think. Or will be, when I wed."

Mary turned on him, pale with disbelief. "Never! You shall never have them!"

"Never?" he asked softly, catching her hands and pulling her into his arms. "Not when they shall come to me through my wife?"

"Your—your wife?"

He wound a hand in her dark curls, turning her face up so he could see her eyes. "Mary, will you have me?"

Staring into his glowing gaze, she tried to collect her scattered wits. Would she have him? She recalled her sensations in the tunnel when she saw him lying as though dead at her feet, and a remembered chill gripped her, freezing her heart —only to be followed by a rush of warmth and wonder such as she had never imagined. Oh, yes, she would! He lived, and so did she, and life could hold no greater marvel than their love fulfilled.

She smiled tremulously, and nodded. "I knew —I knew when I hit you with the sword—when I saw you lying there—"

"Yes." His lips touched her forehead. "My head still aches. I pray you won't feel the need to protect me anymore."

She opened her mouth for an indignant reply, but he closed it with a gentle kiss.

" 'It were all one,' " he quoted, " 'that I should love a bright particular star, and think to wed it.' "

The particular star to whom he spoke felt herself flush brightly indeed. "One—one would think you a footman, spouting the Bard as you do!"

"If I must be a footman to marry my housemaid, so be it. Mary, the title—the rubies—Rushmoreland—all mean nothing to me if I cannot thus return them to you."

"Seems an ideal solution," remarked a croaking voice from the sofa. Clarence sat up, holding his swimming head. "Oh, my God," he added.

Under the spell of the moment, they had forgotten his presence. He regarded the box on the table with one bloodshot eye. "Do not tell me you have found them!"

"Father!" Mary rushed to his side. "What happened to you?"

He opened the other eye and looked at her solemnly. "Never," he pronounced, "play at cards with Andover. At my age! To be so duped! Piqued, repiqued, and capoted!" He clasped his head and groaned.

"Father, what did he do to you?"

"Made an April-gowk of me! He must have had something in his valise, for he insisted on going up to his room before we played. And the wine we opened was so vile, I never suspected it was drugged. That cousin of yours," he added to Harborough, "must have been a nip-farthing skinflint. Never have I seen a poorer cellar," he complained, forgetting the excellent Dijon.

"I'll restock it at once," the Rake promised, regaining his hold on Mary.

Clarence took a good look at them for the first time. "Good God, what have you two been doing? Having a roll in a fish pond?"

"Father!"

"Hush, love." The Rake laid a finger on her lips. "Sir, may I have your permission to pay my formal addresses to your daughter?"

Clarence flapped a feeble hand. "Good heavens, yes. A bit late for that anyway. Well, your great-aunt Emily will be pleased. When are you going to stop mooning about and open that box?"

Mary retrieved the box, and, seeing a copy of the *Morning Post* lying on the floor by the sofa, she spread it out to protect the table with true housemaid instinct.

The Rake went to work with the hammer and chisel while she held the box steady. The lock proved to be hopeless, corroded solid, but after several tries one of the hinges broke loose. Another assault with the hammer took care of the second. The box split open, and he tipped it up.

A stream of greenish water, muddy sand, and slime-covered pebbles poured out onto the newspaper. The flickering light from their candle caught gleams of pigeon-blood red as the stones slid out.

Mary gripped the edge of the table as her knees gave way. The Rushmoreland rubies . . . She stared at the heap of muddy gems, awestruck, unable to believe that her search could be over. She had inhabited a dreamworld since arriving at Rushmoreland, and only now did she realize that she, like Clarence, had never actually believed in the existence of the jewels—that they could have survived all these years.

She caught up her bedraggled skirt and wiped

the dirty water from a few of the stones with shaking fingers. "My rubies!" she whispered. "At last."

Clarence staggered to his feet and maneuvered carefully over to the table, where he poked a finger into the wet and slimy pile of stones. "Where the devil did you turn them up?"

The Rake and Mary, speaking both at once, gave him a garbled account of their evening, and he nodded sagely. "I could have told you not to trust Andover. I wonder if they are all here. I've no idea how many there should be."

"Forty," said Mary, having studied Beatrix's portrait well. She spread them on the newspaper and began to count them off.

"An excellent dowry, my girl."

The Rake lent a hand. "It is no wonder Andover went to such pains to secure the title for me so that he would have free run of the castle."

"Andover's hand there, too, eh? After tonight, I wouldn't put it past him." Clarence groaned and held his head. "I think I'll go lie down somewhere quiet. I don't seem to be in very plump currant. Is there a bedroom I can use?"

The Rake glanced up. "Take Andover's, next to mine. He'll not be needing it."

"Taking up residence in Newgate, eh? I thought as much." Clarence tottered toward the door and removed the chair from under the knob.

"First door on the right," the Rake called after him. "Second-floor landing." He turned back to Mary and for a while time stood still.

They sprang apart as the door opened once more. Edgemont, his face a pale green, entered, followed by an equally shattered Rowena.

"Wesson informed me of your whereabouts, my lord, and I ventured to seek you out."

The Rake backed up and sat on the pile of rubies, but Edgemont had not seen them. He had a subject of greater moment on his mind.

"My lord, I have come to give my notice."

"Aren't you happy here?" Harborough sounded faintly irritated, and with reason: his breeches were getting wet.

Edgemont struck a theatrical pose. " 'O I have passed a miserable night. So full of ugly sights, of ghastly dreams. That, as I am a Christian faithful man, I would not spend another such a night. Though 'twere to buy a world of happy days!' "

The Rake's eyebrows raised in mild interest. "What's that from?"

Edgemont stepped off his stage. *"King Richard III,* Act One, Scene Four. My lord, I cannot serve in a house that is haunted."

"No, now! There is no ghost, man! That was Andover, playing the Jacobite to scare us all."

Edgemont shook his head, adamant. "I observed a female, my lord. The Countess Beatrix has come to join the Jacobite. I know what I saw and Rowena will bear me out."

Rowena, who thus far had remained silent, casting nervous peeks at the Rake, stepped out from behind the footman.

"Harborough," she began bravely. "I'm leaving you and going with Edgemont. It's not that I don't love you too, my lord, but I'll not stay here to be murdered in me bed by the Jacobite—to say nothing of his lady who thinks I'm to rob her of her jewels." She sighed wistfully for the lost rubies. "I'm marrying Edgemont and going back on the boards. We're joining me uncle's touring company in the north where they're doing *Romeo and Juliet* next season." She batted her eyelashes at Edgemont, who actually blushed.

Well, Mary thought, that settles it for poor Holly. How lucky there is to be a new footman!

The Rake astounded both defectors by shaking their hands heartily and wishing them the best of luck. He shepherded them out of the room, pressing a wad of bills into Edgemont's hand with many adjurations to lose no time in starting his new career.

He came back to Mary, heaving a deep breath of relief. "That has saved me a most painful scene! It's a good thing they are leaving. In no way could Rowena remain as the wife of the second footman in the castle where she once reigned as mistress."

"Oh!" Mary suddenly remembered the dining room chairs. "You must call off her decorators before they desecrate Rushmoreland!"

"Never fear, I did that already, immediately they came to me with their lists of charges."

Mary, however, felt overcome by guilt over their scaring Rowena from her newfound glory. "She did so want to be a fine lady and wear the rubies just once."

The Rake grinned. "Well, she can't have them; I have other plans." He laughed suddenly.

"Could you not see her, gowned in that mulberry satin, her emerald green shawl looped over her elbows, and rubies—rubies, yet—adorning that orange hair?"

Mary started to giggle, but all at once a dawning awe transformed her face.

"Rake—oh, Rake, I have it! For a wedding present you must have her portrait painted by Sir Thomas Lawrence or someone equally famous. She must be standing by a gilded chair, wearing her mulberry satin and emerald shawl —and all the Rushmoreland rubies! She shall hang it in her drawing room above her mantelpiece for all her friends to gaze at and die of envy! Oh, Rake, it will give her a lifetime of indescribable triumph!"

The Rake gave a joyous shout of laughter and gathered her into his arms. "And she will have posters made of it to advertise her plays. Mary Migglesworth"—he nuzzled his nose into the soft hair by her ear—"you can have no notion how much I love you!"

Mary buried her face in his wet and grimy shirtfront and sighed with pure ecstasy.

" 'All's well,' " she murmured to herself, " 'that ends well.' "

The End?

The end of a book is never really *the end* for a person who reads. He or she can always open another. And another.

Every page holds possibilities.

But millions of kids don't see them. Don't know they're there. Millions of kids can't read, or won't.

That's why there's RIF. Reading is Fundamental (RIF) is a national nonprofit program that works with thousands of community organizations to help young people discover the fun—and the importance—of reading.

RIF motivates kids so that they *want* to read. And RIF works directly with parents to help them encourage their children's reading. RIF gets books to children and children into books, so they grow up reading and become adults who can read. Adults like you.

For more information on how to start a RIF program in your neighborhood, or help your own child grow up reading, write to:

RIF
Dept. BK-1
Box 23444
Washington, D.C.
20026

Founded in 1966, RIF is a national non-profit organization with local projects run by volunteers in every state of the union.

GOLDEN HEART AWARD
from the
Romance Writers of America

Joan Overfield

The Prodigal Spinster

Sara Belding has her life all figured out and that's
exactly why she *doesn't* need her pompous older
cousin, who wants to see her properly wed! But with
the same determination he used to defeat the French,
Lord Mallingham sets about the matchmaking as if
it were a military campaign he's bound and determined to win—even if he has to marry the girl himself!

ISBN: 0-517-00092-X   Price: $2.50

ON SALE NOW!

A HISTORICAL ROMANCE TO CAPTURE YOUR HEART!

KAT MARTIN
MAGNIFICENT PASSAGE

Mandy Ashton is fleeing her stifling existence at Fort Laramie and is heading toward California. Travis Langley, a white man raised by the Cheyenne, is hired to escort her, although he mistakenly believes she is the rebellious daughter of the governor. This dangerous deception becomes even more perilous when the two discover they've become captives of a passion as untamed as the wilderness of the American West! Will they be able to overcome their contest of wills and let true love reign?

ISBN: 0-517-00620-0   Price: $3.95

AVAILABLE AT BOOKSTORES NOW!

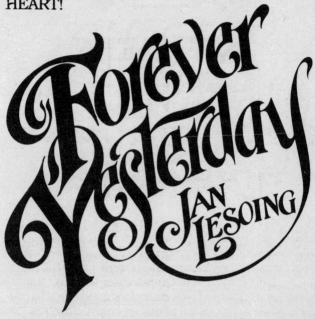